T.S. Weaver

Published by Under the Moon, LLC Pelican Rapids, MN

This book is a work of fiction. Any resemblance to actual events, locales or persons, living or dead, is completely coincidental.

Hell's Children.
System Wars Book 2

ISBN: 978-1-938339-46-2

Editor in Chief: Terri Pray

Hell's Children

By

T.S. Weaver

A System Wars Book 2

Author's Note.

Each System Wars book will be marked with the suggested reading order. Most of the books will either be part of a trilogy (with or without novella and short story extras), a duology, or a standalone. For example, the Hell's collection all tie in with each other, and are part of the Frontier Wars setting – stories set away from Earth and anything in her immediate orbit.

System Wars Reading Order

System Wars – Over Arching Series
Hell's Own: Frontier Wars Book 1/System Wars Book 1
Jones: A Hell's Own Novella: Frontier Wars Book 1.5/System Wars 1.5
Hell's Children: Frontier Wars Book 2/System Wars Book 2
Helen: A Hell's Children Novella: Frontier Wars Book 2.5/System Wars 2.5 coming September 30th 2019

Frontier Wars – Stories set in our Solar System and beyond
Hell's Own: Frontier Wars Book 1
Jones: A Hell's Own Novella: Frontier Wars Book 1.5
Hell's Children: Frontier Wars Book 2: Frontier Wars 2.5

Home Guard – Stories set on Earth

Prologue

Fragments of the two destroyed United Terran Government Naval ships hung in groups and thin lines above Pluto. A handful remained trapped by the tug of the gravity, others still in denial of their ultimate fate. Larger pieces spun in lazy circles, slapping smaller pieces out of their way as the dance continued, unseen by human eyes.

Treizaek rolled his shoulders and stretched out his wings, his gaze following the display of twisted and warped materials. His people had gathered small treasures from the hulks before they had been reduced to rubble. Now the pieces waited for his inspection, either in the cells or laboratories. He'd deal with them when the moment suited him, but for now, he continued to watch the pieces of debris. "I had expected more of a fight from these humans. They are not like the ones we have known before. They are armed, ready to fight, but they lack the challenge I had hoped for. I ache for a battle, a true one which will test my skills and those of my warriors."

Nyanaek, his would be mate and second in command, traced one slender claw over Treizaek's left wing ridge, following the line of veins and taut muscle before she reached the start of his scales. He fought back the desire to lean into her touch, then take the female beneath him. There would be time for such things when Pluto belonged to them, and the last of their new prey brought to heel. "We only had the word of those in the servant colony. Memories passed down by the untamed ones. They did not understand our language, nor we theirs for many years, so we do not know what details are lost to time."

True enough, but the lack of a real fight above the planet's surface sat ill with him. "Perhaps the inner worlds will offer more of a challenge. These things did little more than scream and run inside their dome. Did they truly believe it would protect them?"

"We can hope things will improve because if it doesn't, we will be left with discontent building within the bellies of our people. The warriors crave a battle of worth, but these beings ran from the sight of our bravest. Only a handful offered any fight, not enough to satisfy the weakest of our kind."

He turned to wrap his mate within the confines of his wings, holding her close. Few might see his actions as a weakness, but he knew better. He cupped the back of her head with one claw, tracing patterns across her skull. "What do you crave?"

She tipped her head to one side. "The expansion of our territories so our young may remain ever safe from the dangers this race might present to us. New servants to train, their offspring bound to our will as happened with those now on the servant's colony. And the formal announcement of our union."

He cupped her chin, tracing the lines of her jaw with his claws. "Nothing else?" She had overstepped the line by bringing up their potential union, but she was a female in need of a mate -- the drive to form a nest a vital part of the female in front of him.

She lowered her inner lids. "Perhaps."

He laughed. "Ah, my bloodthirsty beloved. I know what you desire, what many of the females desire. A chance to bath in the life fluid of our enemies before we bring them to heel. You have nothing to be ashamed of." Shame was the last thing he expected to see in her eyes, and a quick scan of her features confirmed she showed no hint of the weak emotion.

"It is the way of our people. Only a warrior deserves to bring new life into the world. Should I not prove to be worthy of the title, you are then free to seek a new potential mate to sire your line upon." She gave a slight shrug of her wings. "That you will take other females, betas, to soothe your needs, is understood. I may do the same thing with beta males, but any young will be of your line and no others."

"It will never happen. You and you alone will be the mother

of my young. Once we have taken this system as our own, we will settle and choose the time to breed." His female, his strong, dangerous beauty. "I fought for you, and claimed you." A small matter, but one they both enjoyed. Who, after all, wanted a beta, or worse, an omega, at their side? "I'd be a fool to cast you aside when I have the perfect second, a warrior, brave and bold, able to keep the other fighters in line."

"Commander Treizaek, there is word from the advanced parties," said Grantham.

"Speak, and be quick about it," said Nyanaek, her tone cold.

"Be at ease, my one." He gestured to Grantham to continue. His mind wandered as he waited, as did his gaze. He didn't move, didn't have to to see the others on the bridge. Male, female, neuters. Alphas and betas. Only the omegas were missing.

As they ever would be on his ship. Omega's had no place among his warriors. Dangerous creatures who answered only to their Great Mother.

"Thank you, Commander." Grantham's wings shifted, opening a fraction before closing one more.

His communications officer was nervous? Strange, the male was experienced, accomplished, and had been in his service for half a lifetime.

"The humans, a small group of them, have fought back. I fear there have been losses on our side, and I have yet to hear of the numbers." Grantham offered a datapad. "The details are here, Commander. I don't know exactly how many escaped, but they deployed explosives, which brought down part of a cavern on our honorable warriors, instead of meeting them in fair combat. Injured warriors have given reports to those who stand above them, and the search for these cowardly creatures has begun."

Nyanaek hissed, her wings snapping out to her sides, fingers curled in claws. "Foolish. They will be punished for their cowardice. Commander, I wish to join our forces on the ground. This insult to our people must not go unanswered. I would personally seek vengeance for the wrongs done to our people."

"There is more, Commander. I fear I must share the rest with you." Grantham didn't meet his eyes as Treizaek read through the information on the datapad. "A small group of humans was discovered in the tunnels. Several of the scouts were injured or killed, but they left one of their people behind. It is a male, alive, and afraid, but offers trade. I do not believe it is wise enough to understand what has happened to it, but there may be a chance it has access to useful information."

The scouts, the small, but a highly intelligent race of flyers knew how to avoid larger prey. The news some of them had been hurt, even killed, didn't make sense. "Explain to me how these things found the means to harm our scouts?" It wasn't possible. Their people were well trained, skilled fighters, the smallest of their combined forces, the scouts, were able to fight with far more fury than any of the humans he'd come across.

"With their energy weapons, Commander."

"But the scouts move erratically, with skill and speed. They should have been able to avoid any attempts to kill or injure them." Had there been a problem with the training of the scouts? His gaze shifted to his female, then away. Nyanaek held responsibility for their training. The knowledge sat ill with him for a heartbeat, but he recovered with a small shrug. If Nyanaek had shown weakness, it didn't matter. He would find another to build his nest with. As Commander, he could do nothing else.

Weakness could not be tolerated in a mate. Not by an alpha.

"I know, Commander, yet it happened. One of these bipeds appears to have greater skills than those we have dealt with before. He killed several of the scouts and others were injured during the same encounter. Before the hunters were able to join the scouts, this group made their escape."

"All but one?" Nyanaek took her place at Treizaek's side.

"Yes, and there is a strangeness in this detail. The human was bound, its primary limbs behind its back, and unarmed. Cast out from the rest of the survivors."

"Banished. I see. The human obviously isn't to be trusted. Place the male with the other prisoners. He, like the rest of the adults, will be trained or slaughtered and added to the food supplies as their actions dictate." Why waste the meat? It wasn't as if the creatures had many uses save as servants or herd beasts.

"As you order, so shall it be." Grantham inclined his head before withdrawing to his station.

"I wonder if these things will taste any different to the ones raised on the servant's colony," mused Nyanaek. "It will be interesting to discover."

"But not until we have this planet under control, we have plenty of supplies shipboard. The dead humans have been gathered along with those still living. There will be a time when we can relax and enjoy the spoils of the mission once the last remnants of resistance have been dealt with."

Chapter One

She couldn't move. Heavy bands held her in place as Leigh Winter blinked against the sweat dripping into her eyes. Cotton wool clouded her mind, pins and needles attacked her limbs, and she bit back a groan. Muscles complained a deep ache seeped into her body as she closed her eyes again. Sleep, rest, she needed a chance to bring her body back under control. Not as if there was anything she needed to do. No officer or senior NCO yelling at her to get out of bed, she could afford a few extra minutes of sleep.

Something nudged her left thigh, a hard, insistent push.

"Few more minutes," she mumbled. Who else was in her room? "Tired." No restraints in my chamber, except in the acceleration chair. She struggled to break free from the persistent grasp of sleep, heavy eyes, and a fog-filled mind.

The nudge came again, harder than before. A weight pressed her thigh, shoving at her before it dropped away.

Her ears rang, and vision blurred as she forced her eyes open. "Let me sleep." What was so important she had to get up now? She wouldn't have drunk herself into a stupor if she'd been scheduled for duty this early.

A sharp bark cut through the air, the sound bringing reality back in a crash she couldn't ignore. "Mags."

Magnus Stalker, her canine companion for the past ten years, nudged her hand until she lifted it enough to allow his head to sneak under her fingers and blinked. His headpiece, hers, where were they? Where was the ship? Her crewmates, fellow Marines?

With a groan, she eased back against the padded covering of the built-in seat and reached for the harness. An attack. Another vessel had opened up on them, but who and why were pieces of the puzzle she didn't have access to. The restraints clicked open. Had there been anyone else in the pod with her? Her head throbbed, refusing to release information without a painful price.

Leigh forced herself to take in her surroundings. Her vision now hazy, and with a pounding in the back of her head, it became difficult to think straight. But despite the problems, her eyes still worked well enough to confirm she was alone, with Mags. A pair of mismatched eyes stared up at her with love and concern, a gentle nuzzle against her leg before Mags stepped back enough to allow his human to stand without being in the way.

"Just you and me then, for now at least." The words more a groan than anything else as she stood. Every muscle and bone in her body complained, confirming the hard landing. If it hadn't been for the chair and padding, she'd feel worse.

Mags? Had he been hurt? She turned, searching the pod, heart racing until she spotted the thickly padded carrier lying against the curved inner wall. "Got yourself out did you when I was busy sleeping. Smart boy."

A long pink tongue poked out of the side of Mags' mouth as he panted, a canine grin firmly in place.

"Can't say I blame you, I wouldn't want to be locked in here for any length of time." She rubbed the back of her neck and rolled out her shoulders. "Damn it; I should be able to pick up any other pods in the area." Leigh continued the conversation, a habit she'd picked up when Mags had first come into her life.

Canine companions, among other species, had been one of the plus sides of the changes Earth and her people had been through. Without the corporations trying to make money from everything they could touch, many of the issues with purebred dogs had been dealt with by bringing in mixed breeds, taking the strengths from one to help fix another. Genetic advances also extended the lifespan of the dogs, as a result, despite the fact Mags was already ten years old, he had anywhere between twenty-five and thirty years of active life ahead of him.

"Hey buddy, we need to find out what's going on here, see if we can pick up signals, search for other survivors." There had to be others, didn't there? She made her way over to the controls and pulled up the sensors. Her vision swam but settled again.

Static flickered across the screen as Mags sat down next to her right foot. He leaned against her leg for a second, silently offering love and support, before he sat upright, eyes bright as he peered up at the screen.

"Not supposed to be like this, is it?" She murmured and tried to bring up the information. Any information. But the white and black static continued to glare back at her. Five minutes later, it continued to offer her nothing but electronic noise. "Damn, it doesn't look hopeful. It's green across the board, it shouldn't be giving us problems, but no denying what's going on, is there Mags? We've lost the ability to run full scans or use the comm."

Her canine companion nudged her leg before adding a familiar woo-woo, one of the sounds she'd come to associate with his husky bloodline. Husky, German Shepard, and Grey Wolf, perhaps a touch of the other older breeds. At least, that's what she'd been told, not that the background breeds mattered. Only his temperament and ability to learn. At least until she'd come to know Mags and the companionship he offered her. His silver-gray fur and miss-matched eyes, combined with the love and loyalty Mags offered her, were all she'd ever needed in a canine companion. But his skills as a working dog had allowed her entry into the Marines as a canine handler.

The first handler to be sent to Pluto and its colony.

"We haven't made it to the colony yet, have we Mags?"

He snuffled his agreement.

She settled in to try other scans, but nothing came up. After another ten minutes, she growled and slapped the screen. "Dumb tech. You'd think they'd have decent equipment in the pods, you know, in case we had to use the blasted things." She sighed and ran one hand through her short white-blonde hair. "I'm putting off the inevitable, aren't I? And it's not going to do us any good in the long run. Time we got our combined asses in gear."

"Woof." The tip of Mags' tail wagged back and forth.

"Best get you into your suit," she glanced down at him. "Can't go out there without protection. No air, not like Earth."

Mags glared at her, then turned his head away, nose held high, a barely audible whine punctuating his distaste.

"I know, buddy. I don't like to wear these things either, but it's for your protection. Not as if you'd let me go out there on my own, is it?" The suits for canines were supposed to be comfortable, but going by Mags' reaction to wearing one, the designers didn't know what they were talking about. "You wear it and come with me, or don't and stay here until I can get you out of here in another way. It's not as if we have other options." She opened the cover on the small porthole. The thick carbon polymer window enough to allow her the ability to do a visual check of the area. "Not unless you have a few tricks hidden under your collar I don't know about? No, well then, time we get moving."

Mags grumped as he shifted down on his belly and rested his head on his front paws.

Leaving Mags behind wasn't an option, and they both knew it. No matter what she said to her companion, they understood their duty, and Mags would never suffer being left behind in the pod. Not even if it was his own well being.

She ruffled his head. "Let's get you ready; then we'll see what's out there." No sign of the colony. Not even a distant glimmer from the lights of the dome. How far they were from the settlement was anyone's guess, but the lack of communication continued to be a problem. "We'll figure it out. If nothing else we can use the old fashioned way of using the stars and a map to guide us. Not as if they didn't train us for this." She paused, glancing at the controls which had refused to provide much-needed information. "We'd better check the datapad, see if the information we need is there. No point waiting until we're a klick or more away from the pod." If the pad was damaged, they were hosed.

Alright, not hosed, but it'll be harder than it was before.

Mags let out a soft woof, enough to pull her out of her thoughts.

"Yeah, I know, the longer I put it off, the harder it will be." She smiled and shifted down onto her knees as she pulled Mags close. Like the rest of the Marines, Mags wore his suit on a belt, or in his case, a harness. She hugged the dog, ruffling his fur before she activated the suit, and helped to smooth it into place, sealing it to the boots Mags loathed but had come to accept as part of his official dress.

The hood was the hardest part, but after bugging the quartermaster, she'd been able to snag one with a two-way comm system, tied into her private frequency. He'd grumbled the entire way but eventually had given her the suit she wanted for Mags. There were other ways of communicating if they needed to, but they had side effects, as such, she used them only in dire need. Nor had she told anyone how she managed to convey orders to Mags when comm lines were compromised and doubted they'd believe her even if she did share her secret.

Mags ducked his head under her hand.

"I know, I'm lingering. Don't like the idea of going out there alone. It's not my idea of fun, any more than it's yours."

A grumble vibrated through the comm.

"Fine, I won't be alone, I have you. But you know what I mean. I don't know if anyone else survived. Who attacked us. What happened up there. I don't like the fact we're walking into whatever this is blind." She rose and smoothed her suit into place, sealing it in place as it connected to her boots and gloves. The suits were better than the ones she'd used in training Sims; they had to be to allow people a chance to become used to working in them.

She lingered for ten minutes, gathering the supplies needed, checking her datapad still worked and avoiding the door.

"Come on. No point standing here all day." Right, get out there. Easy to say, harder to do. She wasted another few minutes double-checking both suits, though she knew there was nothing wrong with how she'd sealed the suits, and she'd already confirmed the suits were intact.

Mags nudged her thigh. Hard.

"Alright, alright, I get the message. I'm ready." Physically sure, emotionally was another matter. "First damn mission and the ship gets blown out from under us. Of course, this leaves us stranded in the middle of nowhere. Not the best start in life, but we'll deal." She punched in the code to open the hatch, took a deep breath, and stepped out onto the surface of Pluto.

"Fuck!" No gravity. Still swearing, relieved there was no one else around to see her mistake, she slapped the controls and glared at Mags. The dog had already turned his on and flashed a cocky dog grin her way.

"Yeah, yeah, I know. Dumb mistake. Don't get too confident, not as if you've never made a mistake. Remember the first time in the suit during training when you tried to scratch your neck?"

Mags lifted his left front paw and rested it over his nose, head bowed.

"Right, you didn't see me making fun of you, did you?"

He lay down, both front paws over his nose.

"Oh, come on, it's the first time I've brought it up." Sure, she'd had to fight not to laugh at the time, but she hadn't teased him. She glanced back at the pod. "Can't leave it open either. No idea who else might be around and get into the pod if we leave it unlocked." Would the miners or other colonists try and strip the pod bare? Muttering under her breath, she closed the hatch, then turned to glance at Mags before she checked the stars against the information on her pad.

Mags rose and moved to her side, leaning against her leg before they set off. Silence settled in as they walked if the readings were correct, they had several klicks of walking ahead of them before they'd be able to see the lights of the dome. But the map on the datapad suggested there were several small settlements closer than the dome.

One foot in front of the other,t hat's all she had to do, keep putting one foot in front of the other, and focus on finding a source of food, shelter, and assistance.

Four hours later, her body demanded a rest. At least with the lower gravity, she'd been able to go longer without taking a break. Between the aches from the hard landing and the tug of the gravity boots, her body now complained about each step. Mags kept pace with her, but she didn't need to ask him how things were going to know he needed to rest. A normal dog, one who hadn't had the additional genetic changes, would have been ready for a break an hour, or more earlier. Not Mags, though he was weary, he'd keep going for as long as she needed him to.

She settled on the top of a ridge made up of ice and rock, grateful for the warmth her suit offered. Without it, if she hadn't died from lack of air, she'd have frozen to death by now. Not a pleasant way to go, from what she understood, but it wasn't a fate she wanted to experience.

Mags rested against her leg, panting, or so she assumed from the way his body reacted. "You okay, boy?"

He sat up, proud with his feet planted in front of him. It didn't matter what he wore on his feet; she could still imagine the way his paws sat, the way he'd tilt his head and his tongue hanging out of the side of his mouth.

"You don't have to fake it for me."

He dropped down onto his belly and rested his head on the ground with an inaudible sigh.

"Yeah, I know, we've still got a long way to go." Leigh shifted her head enough to take a sip of water from the tube in her helmet. All aspects of life support were dealt with by the suit, waste, food, water, air, but despite this, she couldn't spend more than a few days wearing it before the resources ran out. Less if she continued this pace. "Drink, Mags. You know how it works."

He grumbled, the vibration playing through the connection at her calf as he leaned in.

Leigh sighed. By now she should be able to see at least the distant glow of the dome. With a more prominent ridge ahead, she'd have to wait before she tried to assess what lay in front of her.

"Come on then, let's get to the top of the next ridge and see what's waiting for her."

They didn't talk as they continued to walk. Not in the manner of a human or a dog. The more they talked, the more oxygen they'd use up, and the stress of walking, climbing ridges, pulling themselves over a dangerous and unstable edge, ate up enough supplies, to begin with.

Mags slipped but regained his footing before she had a chance to turn and help him. Fear tore through her until she caught sight of his canine smile, and he rejoined her as they climbed up to the top. She waited to be sure her footing was safe before shielding her eyes with one hand and peered out into the darkness.

There, in the distance, a flickering of lights caught her attention. She frowned. There weren't enough signs of illumination to be the dome, yet they were spread out enough to suggest it was the main colony. "Not sure what we're seeing, Mags. Looks right, the spacing I mean, but there's something wrong." She pulled up her controls and adjusted her view, zooming in on the lights.

"Oh..." her heart dropped into the pit of her stomach.

Mags leaned against her, panting within the confines of his suit.

"I think we're in trouble." The colony, or the remains of it, beckoned them with a twinkling of lights. But the dome, the protective shield which kept the colony safe from the environment, no longer stood in one piece. A large crack ran in jagged lines across the remains of the clear shield, and a fifth of the upper part of the dome was gone.

Not damaged.

Destroyed.

"Well, shit."

#

Zac stumbled back, landing on his ass with a thump. How he avoided smacking his head in the process, he neither knew nor cared. Being free from the tight confines of the clear cage, and tossed back into the larger one, was a relief, despite the fact a collar remained locked in place around his throat.

Not only his, but his companions wore the same thing, as did the man on the other side of the partition separating him from the three prisoners.

"See, my friends, things will become easier once you accept your place in life. I bid you sit and rest. I will return when it is time for the next lesson. For now, you will be fed, given fluids, and sleeping mats will be provided for you." Edward smiled, his voice gentle, eyes bright and eager. "This is a wonderful thing, and you will soon come to realize the blessings which have been bestowed on you."

"Blessing? Are you nuts?" Matthew snapped. "We're prisoners of war. Taken against our will."

"The will of a servant means nothing; in complete obedience, do we find joy. Should we serve well, and please those who protect us, then we are rewarded. In time you will come to not only understand this but embrace your new life." Edward continued, the gentle tone never changing. "Please, be at peace. I will return when time permits. I have other duties I must attend to."

The three men inside the clear cage didn't reply, didn't speak at all until Edward and the winged alien had left.

"What. The. Fuck." Charles slumped against a wall; knees pulled close to his chest. "He was serious, wasn't he?"

"Deadly," said Matthew.

Zac's mind raced. Servants. Slaves. A servant's colony. The information mashed together in a thousand ways and still, he couldn't make sense of the matter. Why any man would claim to be happy as a slave, was beyond him.

A hiss from the back wall drew his attention. Through a narrow opening, three sleeping mats appeared, followed by pouches of food and water before the small gap closed, vanishing as if it had never been.

"Least he honest about supplies." Matthew grabbed the mats, distributing them to the other men before doing the same with the pouches. "Bit like the pouches they used to use for space travel. Or on the older stations. You know, before they perfected gravity for off-world locations."

Zac tore open the water pouch, adjusted the built-in straw, and sipped. Slowly. It didn't matter that his body demanded he drain the water in one long gulp, he knew better. Nor did he have to look at his companions to know they were doing the same thing.

In silence, the small group ate and drank.

"Iris." Matthew murmured.

"We'll find a way to get her back, we have to," said Charles.

"How? Not as if they're going to give us free rein around here. I don't see a way out," protested Zac. "Shit, we're hosed. We're unarmed, outnumbered, and corralled here like cattle."

"Don't know about you, but I've seen cattle, and they at least are free to feed, get water, take care of business. They get access to real grass, the sun, and--"

"Alright, Charles. You made your point." Zac set the pouch aside, still half full. God alone knew when they would get their next meal or drink. "Sorry, I know, we'll do what we can to help Iris, and anyone else they have stored with her. I'm not hopeful about getting out of here. Not unless a miracle happens." Miracles. Right. When had those last been a part of history?

"I understand." Charles opened his food pouch. "If we're lucky, they haven't added anything else to the food."

"Like what? Shit, you mean drugs, right?" Zac glared at the food pouch.

"Exactly. Be smart; eat only a little at a time. Same with the water. No more than you need. If it's drugged, you'll feel it but not get the full dose." Matthew set his sleeping mat down in the middle of the chamber. "And unless you want to make it easy for them to grab you when you're asleep, I'd stay far away from the walls."

Chapter Two

Mason Stone sat down on a makeshift chair, a rock covered with his trench coat, and groaned. Every muscle in his body ached. His joints complained. His feet yelled at him in the way only abused feet could manage, and he ignored the temptation to pull his boots off and rub his feet. Wouldn't work either, not with the way they needed the seals kept in place to ration their oxygen and heat loss.

It didn't prevent him from imagining what it would feel like if he worked the ache out. A shower. Hot, with a decent force behind the water. He grinned at the idea. A real shower with enough pressure behind the water to massage his back and chest. Yeah, he could go with the concept. The sensation of a hundred tiny fingers playing over his skin, washing both grime and exhaustion from his body. What more could a man want?

Better than sex.

If given the choice of sex or a shower, he'd be hard-pressed to choose anything but ten minutes in a shower, eyes closed, where he could ignore all they'd been through in the last day.

God, had it been that short a time? In a single standard day, the twenty-four hours those of Earth were used to, everything had changed. The dome cracked. Navy ships destroyed or chased off. Men, women, and children killed, captured and carried off, and who knew what the critters did with the bodies. Messing with the dead was the last thing he wanted to think about, yet the question rolled through his mind whenever it pleased.

On top of that, he'd sided with a group of blasted Marines. A walked nightmare if he'd ever seen one.

He shook his head, not wanting to sink into the thoughts going over what had happened would conjure. When things were calm once more, he'd take the situation apart piece by piece, search for the options he should have taken instead of the ones he'd been forced into.

In his saner moments, he was willing to bet there'd been no other choices available to him, not if he wanted to stay alive.

Walker moaned as he shifted his weight on the padded stretcher. The set up was nothing more than blankets and coats slung between two temporary supports created from rifles, and a broken walking stick. Where it had come from he neither knew, nor cared. The civilian survivors had built the stretcher, and it was neatly done considering what they'd had to work with. No doubt Harvard had assisted them or at least offered a few pointers. A short conversation with the man earlier on had confirmed Harvard could see possibilities where others didn't. Still, he wasn't about to seek out the Navy Pilot for another conversation.

He had no use for officers. Not unless they were buying from him. Too damned full of themselves, especially those who served in the Navy.

He glanced over the small gathering before his gaze fixed on a duo. The youngest child among the survivors now slept in her mother's lap, he assumed the woman was the mother, but it wasn't a given with the losses the group had faced before the Marines had found them. How many other children would find themselves raised or comforted by strangers? It wasn't a comfortable feeling.

"How are you feeling?" One of the civilian women asked, but kept her distance from Stone.

"Like someone took a red-hot staff and beat me with it," he said and flashed a grin. "I'll heal. More bruising and a cut here and there, than anything else."

"Have the wounds been washed?" A gentle tremor carried her words.

"Not yet. Besides, Walker over there needs more help than me. The sooner we get him to a doctor, or field medic, the better it will be for the Marine." Yes, he hurt, but he wasn't going to make a fuss, not when he knew the injury wasn't too bad. He rolled his shoulders and winced. Sure, it would slow him down if they had to run, but it wasn't the plan. He could still fight, keep up with the rest of the group, and he'd proved it during their journey through the tunnels.

"I have a few skills when it comes to patching people up," the woman lowered her gaze, a flush coating her cheeks.

Was she flirting with him? He coughed and sat up. "Nurse? Doctor?"

"Not as such, I worked as an aid for the school. Patched up more than a few cuts and scrapes." A small shrug. "I'm trained in first aid, nothing more. But I might be able to make him more comfortable."

"I wish that all Walker was dealing with were a few cuts and scrapes." He rummaged in his trench coat pocket, grateful he hadn't abandoned it when they'd found the military-grade suits in storage. Fine, he'd appeared foolish with it worn on top of the tight suit, but he wasn't about to leave it behind. Not when it had been a part of his life for the last five years.

You didn't abandon decent leather when you had no idea where you'd be able to replace it, and you knew the answer wasn't on the rock you found yourself on. Be honest; I'd repair it, not replace it. His lucky charm.

His fingers closed on the scanner. "See for yourself." He handed the instrument over. "Mason Stone."

"Nyssa Barker." She flushed again, taking the scanner in her smaller hands. "Bit like the ones they use in school. I should be able to figure it out."

A school ma'am. Well, not exactly, but close enough to recall school uniforms stretched over an adult's body. He shook off the image. Even if she was flirting with him, it wasn't the time or place. Besides, she'd expect things from him. Promises of more than a roll in the sack. A ring. Marriage. All those things he did his best to avoid whenever possible. "I managed it, and it should be easy enough for you to use."

Her gaze, a pale, gentle green, lifted to his, then away as she tucked one loose strand of honey blonde hair behind her left ear. "Yes, I think so." She activated it and moved to Walker's side. Her lips set in a tight line, a small quiver running through her body as the color washed out of her cheeks. "Oh, I see." She sighed and turned off the scanner, returning it to Stone. "He's going to need a lot of help. More than I can give. But I might be able to help with the pain." Her eyes narrowed, bottom lip caught between her teeth.

"You'll want to check with Lawbook before you do anything. He's one of her people, might get a bit annoyed if you try to help without her agreement."

"Yes, of course." Nyssa glanced in the direction of the rest of the Marines. "I'll be right back."

Yeah, it was a given. The woman wanted to be useful, show she wasn't dead weight and flirting was a part of worming her way into the hearts of the strongest members of the group. Cold, man. Damn cold. Didn't make it any less accurate, and like it or not Nyssa reminded him of the women he'd dealt with in the past, always taking care of themselves, seeking the strongest man to protect them.

He rolled out his shoulders and bit back a groan. A small trickle of blood seeped from the wound and traced a path down his back, but it was nothing. He'd dealt with worse. Still, maybe letting Nyssa tend the torn wound would keep her from getting into Lawbook's path. She was pretty enough, and as long as he was careful, he might have a chance to enjoy a little feminine company.

What could he say, he was, after all, a man. And he enjoyed willing companionship, whenever he had the chance to enjoy them. Delicate feminine flesh. The feel of bare skin beneath his fingers. A moment of pleasure to chase away the darkness. He tried to imagine what the woman would look like in his bed, face flushed, gaze lowered, her smooth, naked skin bared for his touch.

His body should have reacted, welcomed the idea of spending time with one like Nyssa but instead of a rush of lust he had... nothing.

He tried ripping the clothes off the mental image of the woman, but it didn't help. His body refused to react to the idea of the woman. Any woman. Again his body refused to respond no matter how tempting he made the images.

It didn't make sense. He was a vigorous, healthy man who hadn't been laid in several weeks. By now, the idea of any woman willing to share time with him should have triggered a physical response. Except he'd been injured and running hard since the first shakes had struck the bar.

Pain. Had to do with the stress and injury. Lack of real sleep. Yeah, nothing else made sense. He was too young to have those types of problems. Certainly hadn't experienced it before. Situational. When they were no longer in danger, things would return to normal.

Wouldn't they?

Interlude One

Earth: Alpha Comms

Sheila Cavanor focused on the screen, watching the new wave of data scroll past. "Nothing doesn't matter how much I boost the signal there's still no answer from Pluto." She switched to another set of data. Neptune, Uranus, both areas were reporting in, but with difficulty. She adjusted the signals, boosted them, tried everything she'd learned both during training and since.

It didn't work.

She growled and tried again, bringing up the limited information she'd been able to gather. A message pod had alerted the colony on Triton to the alien presence, but they had nothing else to go on. Three ships, a handful of reports from sensor sweeps, plus information that both ships had launched escape pods.

Aliens.

Military she might be, but she'd never been in the field of combat. Never expected to deal with -- well, whatever they were.

What had they done with the colonists? Had any survived?

She punched up another set of screens, letting the information scroll until there was nothing else for it but to admit defeat. Until more data reached her and the others, there was nothing she could do.

Men and women worked at a feverish pace at their stations, but she doubted they'd have better news than she had been able to uncover. Eventually, they'd reach the same point she had, unless one of them possessed skills she lacked. Sheila lifted her hands, checking them. Her nails remained short, but the cuticles -- she'd chewed them. She winced. Once her shift was over, she'd get cream on them, reduce the chances of her biting them again.

Admiral Stirling paused in his walk of the chamber and rested one hand on the back of her chair. "We'll have ships there soon enough, once we have people who can give a full report, we'll understand the situation. We will find a way of fighting back. Our people on Triton will be gathering information, and once we have the pieces we need, we'll take care of these invaders."

She bit back a response. At least he listened to her, unlike Grant. Damn man, if she'd been allowed to do a full sweep earlier and nudge this up the chain of command, then they'd already have ships heading out from Triton, instead of forming a protective patrol around the colony. "I understand, sir. It's just... I don't like how this looks. We're outgunned if the report from the message pod is anything to go by."

"None of us like how this appears, but we aren't going to abandon our people, no matter what the council might believe." His voice hardened.

People like Grant. If there were one's like him on the council, then she understood a few of the problems Stirling faced. "Yes, sir." If he was bringing the council up, it had to mean he'd already spoken to them.

"Have trust, if not in the council, then in me." He patted one friendly hand on her shoulder and continued his walk-through Alpha Comms.

She had to act, be involved as more than a watcher, observing the reports, waiting for the next and left on the sidelines. But this is what she signed up for. To work where the UTG thought she was best suited. Her skin itched, nudging at her to find a means of defending her home. Sheila glared at the console. The longer she stared at the information, or lack thereof, the stronger the need to act became.

"With respect, sir. You can't expect us to sit here and do nothing."

"And what do you believe you should be doing instead, Sergeant?"

She struggled not to make it obvious she was watching,

listening into the conversation. It didn't matter; everyone else in the room did the same thing.

"Sir. I'm a Marine. If there's a fight, it's my duty to be out there, with the others risking their lives." The response calm, despite the combination of situation and words.

"We need people on the ground, Sergeant. Not only out there, but here. If those things make their way to Earth, we'll need men like you fighting to protect the civilian population." The Admiral raised his voice, ensuring it would carry through the room. "This applies to all of you. I understand your need to get up and do something, anything to change what's happening out on Pluto. You're not the only ones. I doubt there is more than a handful of people, out of those who are aware of the situation, who would prefer to be left behind while good men and women face the unknown."

She stood, aware others were doing the same to see the Admiral as he spoke.

"But you must keep one thing in the forefront of your mind. You signed the line, and no one forced you into the military. You walked into the recruiting office and volunteered. You didn't expect a situation like this, none of us did, but unless you want to put in your papers, and see if you can be processed out, you're still expected to knuckle down and obey orders." His sharp gaze moved around the room. "Is that understood?"

"Sir, yes Sir." A dozen voices responded.

"Is that all you have? I'll ask again, is that understood?"

"Sir, yes Sir." The answer rang out.

"Now, get back to work. We've got aliens to deal with."

Chairs squeaked, butts hit the seat, and conversation ceased to exist.

No, walking away wasn't an option, not unless she wanted to be listed as AWOL or worse, a deserter. She didn't like what the Admiral had said, but every word had been accurate. She had signed the contract, sworn the oath and would follow through,

and would continue to work no matter how useless she felt.
What other choice did she have?

Chapter Three

Leigh swore. She ran through every swear word she knew, made up a few more and began again as she stared at the remains of the damaged dome. Mags leaned against her leg, offering silent support until she ran out of curses to throw at the fates, the dome, the Navy and anyone else who might be involved in the situation. She sat down and pulled her knees to her chest.

Anger wouldn't help. Nor would cursing, though it had let off steam enough to allow her a chance to think. "Now what? It's not as if the colony is in one piece."

Mags planted his butt down.

"Yeah, alright, I know. We need to find a safe place. Would be different if we could reach anyone on the comm." She checked her readings. "But everything except close channels is blocked. We might be able to pick up signals if we got close enough, but this type of damage means the inside of the dome is exposed, and whatever was responsible for our ship being attacked was likely responsible for the damage to the dome."

Mags remained silent.

Smugglers? It didn't feel right. No matter what she'd read about those who lived on the edge, and bent the laws to suit themselves, they'd never taken on anything as substantial as a full colony. If they had the ability to take on an outpost of this size, they wouldn't have destroyed two Navy vessels, and risk bringing down the wrath of the entire UTG. She closed her eyes and tried to make sense of the situation, without the ability to talk on comm she couldn't check with other survivors from the ship. But there is another way.

She pulled up her datapad and scrolled through the information, jabbing a finger at the screen until the information she was hunting for, appeared. "Alright, it's not ideal, but we can check on these three pods. If they didn't meet a problem on the way down, they should be within a klick or two." The first one at least. Once she found the first pod, she'd be able to make her way to the others.

A soft woof carried through the personal comm.

Without thinking, she reached out to ruffle Mags head and laughed when she realized the suit prevented direct contact. She'd spent enough time with Mags to know he was a part of her, always by her side, working, listening, ready to take whatever action was needed.

"Sitting here isn't helping." At least with the limited gravity, her feet weren't taking a pounding the way they did when she had been through basic training. Then again, who didn't complain about aching feet during basic?

Believed the damn recruiter, that was my first mistake. Second mistake, same as the first.

Not unheard-of. Some joined up with stars in their eyes, thanks to the tales told by recruitment officers. Others knew what they were joining up for, beyond better pay, food, and status once their service was over. Out here, away from Earth, things weren't as easy. The farther away from Earth you traveled, the greater the differences. Not only lack of gravity, or change in it, but days changed, years held different meanings, and your best friend, if the drill instructor was to be believed, was the weapon you slept with.

Sitting here wasn't going to do her any good. If there were other survivors in walking distance, finding them and reporting in was her best bet. At least she wouldn't be on her own.

Mags nudged her. Hard.

"Fine, fine, I'm not on my own. Jeeze, you know what I meant." She glanced at the cracked dome. "If the ones responsible for this mess are still around, we've landed ourselves in a whole heap of trouble." Mags stepped away to give her enough room to stand without problems. Under other circumstances, she would have teased Mags into helping her up, but the time for joking, playing, and relaxing was back on Earth.

Her mind roamed as she walked, time had no meaning, and she refused to check her pad for local time again. Instead, she allowed herself to check it only once or twice to be sure she was going in the right direction. Between the stars above, and the map on her pad, she only had to make one small correction.

Water and food. She'd need both when she reached the pod, but she could take a chance to relax when she found the others. Mags had access to water and food in his suit, like her own the food was nothing more than a high concentrate paste taken in via a tube, and if you didn't swallow water with it, the damn lump would stick in your throat until you coughed and half choked the mush down.

Not the best of designs, and if she ever found the one responsible for the foul-tasting gunk, she'd tip him into a vat of the stuff and make him eat the lot.

I'd have help.

She chuckled as she climbed the ridge then made her way down the other side.

Lots of help. Entire squad. Maybe most of the Marines and Navy out there. As far as she knew, every recruit had to go through time in a suit, using it to survive, including eating the paste. It wouldn't have been as bad if there'd been no taste, but no matter what the official flavor might be, it always tasted of over-spiced, over peppered gritty oatmeal, with small splinters of protein.

Fine, they weren't actual splinters, but they felt like it if you tried to swallow without extra fluid in the mix.

Her gaze narrowed, focusing on a shape in the distance before Leigh realized what she was staring at. She picked up the pace, breaking into a job, Mags at her side.

Mags whined but kept the pace. Despite everything the genetic teams had done to improve dogs, they still became tired, same as humans did. And after many hours on her feet, walking, searching, she hurt, and no doubt Mags was feeling the strain at the same time.

"We found them Mags."

He woofed.

"Yeah, okay, we've still got to get there, but we're getting closer." With the low gravity, she had the option of turning off her grav boots and taking advantage of the situation, but she didn't feel confident enough to attempt it. Mags was better at zero or low gravity movement than she was, but she hadn't told the dog how she believed. Bad enough he'd seen her mistake earlier.

Not as if he knows how to communicate with anyone else.

The bond between them was rare, beautiful, and she'd learned not to take it for granted.

The pod lay, half-buried in the surface of Pluto, ice and rock spilled to either side of it, but the closer she came to the pod, the better it appeared. At first glance, it seemed to be intact, but she didn't attempt to run a scan until she was close enough to see the ports on the pod, but the door faced away from her.

Cold fingers of fear traced down her back and across her ribs.

The door was open. Not had been opened, then closed, as she'd done with her pod. No point in wasting resources, and it wouldn't take long for the interior of the escape pod to ice over. The small amount of moisture in the air would cling to the inside and turn to frost, then ice within a matter of minutes. One minute tops.

Mags edged in front of her, and she bit back the instinct to order him back. This was one of the things he'd been trained to do. Inspect a situation and let her know if it was clear to proceed or not. It didn't matter that Mags wouldn't be able to pick up on scents because of the suit unless she activated the built-in secondary chamber beneath his nose. The device created to allow canine companions the ability to use their sense of smell in limited oxygen conditions. In this case, it wasn't needed as dogs had a strong sense of intuition, and she'd learned to trust his instincts.

Mags disappeared into the pod, and she forced herself to wait. Her heart raced, and she forced herself to take long, slow breaths, bringing her pulse down until her nerves settled, and she was able to watch and wait for her companion.

He reappeared head high, tail wagging.

All clear.

"What the hell happened here?" She rested one hand on the edge of the opening and peered inside. Wires, circuit boards, damaged seats. Not from the landing, you didn't get long slashes across the interior of a ship, or pod, from a landing. She eased inside and traced one of the marks.

Deep.

Claws?

Humans didn't have claws. This had to be from a weapon. A blade? It was possible, but one which created cuts similar to the claw marks of a bear or a large cat seemed unlikely. She peered at the damage, taking note of the power behind the slices. Not from an animal she knew despite the surface resemblance.

"What the hell happened here?" She followed the marks, tracing them before she forced herself to turn away and check for supplies. Oxygen, they both needed to top up, and the pod offered them three hours each from the supplies. As she filled one set of storage, she emptied another, ridding both suits of the waste produced. The first time she'd had to do this, she'd been embarrassed. However, everyone around her had done the same thing, and she'd learned to view it as a normal part of life. No one was looking at her, claiming her shit was worse than other peoples or making fun of her for needing to use the built-in unit to empty her bladder or bowels when wearing the suit.

She checked the readings and took a recording of the interior of the craft, downloaded what she could in the way of information and glanced at Mags.

"We can't stay here much longer, no point, we've picked up anything useful."

Mags woofed.

"Next pod location?"

He jerked his head up and down.

"Then let's get on it. Faster we move, the faster we'll find our people." The short rest, not enough to recharge her for a full day of walking, would have to keep her going for the time being. Mags had done the wise thing and curled up as the suits had been flushed of waste and refilled with air and water. Neither of them had used enough of the food paste to need to top it up.

"Drill sergeant would have my head for not topping up the food, but he's not here and doesn't have to eat this crap."

Mags tipped his head, and she could easily imagine the way his ears perked up.

"Let's get going. Longer we stand here, the harder it's going to be to leave."

Mags pushed to his feet, stretched out his front paws and arched into a stretch before he shook himself out and led the way to the opening.

It was time to get moving.

#

Walker groaned in pain. Cora glanced down at the man, taking in his pale features with sweat beading across his features as the stretcher jolted and bounced. His knuckles white as he grabbed the poles, jaw set, but it didn't matter how hard he tried, he couldn't hide the pain from the all too observant eyes around him.

"Rest stop," Cora ordered as she moved to the side of the stretcher. "Set him down, I'll keep an eye on him." She smiled at the two civilians. Virgil sent the other man away and leaned against the tunnel. "You don't have to stay. I'll be fine here."

"I figured you'd want privacy for this, but I've worked with amber before, know what to look for if there's a reaction." Virgil's calm voice belayed the dangers of the drug. "Surprised you waited this long, but I understand why as well. He needs help, but amber isn't the best choice."

Cora inclined her head. It was the most she'd heard the man say in one sitting. "Thanks, but I don't believe we have another option, not unless he's willing to be muddle-headed." She dug the vial out and worked the stopper free. She paused long enough to meet and hold the wounded Marines gaze. "Walker, you don't have to take this."

"Sergeant?" His voice shook. "What you got for me? Anything good?"

Was he so far out of it he hadn't been aware of Virgil speaking? Possible. "It will help with the pain, but I'm not going to lie, there are risks in using this." She held the vial close to his face. "It's Amber Dreams."

"Not like you to deal in illicit drugs." Tears slipping from the corner of his eyes. "I'll take it; you wouldn't offer it unless you believed there was no other choice."

"Oh, there is, but not if you want to be able to think straight."

He closed his eyes. "I need to be myself."

"I understand." It was one of the reasons drugs like this were popular. Didn't matter about the risks, traditional medications knocked you for six. You were pulled into a deep sleep, one where you couldn't feel what was going on, but neither could you respond to things around you. "One drop, don't need more. It's going to hit you hard, and you'll crave more."

"I can handle it."

"We'll try one drop, see what happens." It might be enough if nothing else it would put a thin wall between himself and the pain.

"Yes, sergeant."

She tipped the vial, watching the liquid closely before a single drop formed at the lip. One small drop, it's all she'd agreed to give him, and when it spilled into Walker's mouth, she tipped the vial back to prevent more from falling on his lips.

He closed his eyes and sighed.

It had to work. One dose of Amber Dreams had to be enough

this time around. If she had to give him more, then there would be a problem. If he wanted a second dose, it would need to be discussed, but the way he'd reacted, she doubted he'd demand more.

Please let me be right.

The pain eased from his face, the stress vanishing, only to return but less than before. At least to her eyes. She smoothed one hand over his brow. The sweat glistened across his skin, and he shuddered.

"How do you feel, private?"

"Better, I think." He sighed and opened his eyes. "Doesn't hurt as much."

Clear. Nothing close to the pressure and pain she'd seen before. As she watched, the lines around his eyes vanishing a little at a time. She continued to watch, taking in the small changes, his breathing smooth, no longer rattling in his chest, or followed by a touch of pain, a hiss, or shudder. "I'll keep a close eye on you."

"Won't be the only one," Virgil added. "I've been around Amber Dreams users before, know what to watch for. Don't try to getÂ off the stretcher, no matter how you think you feel. It›ll tell you that you›re fine, no longer in pain, or injured. Don›t listen to the lies.»

"I won't."

Virgil glanced at Cora. The look said it all. Walker wouldn't be able to ignore the desire to move, the lack of pain, and the belief he could move again without pain, without damaging his body. "I'll watch him, Sergeant."

"I won't need watching. I'll be fine."

The tone of voice changed, lacking the weariness of before. It wouldn't be long before Walker fell prey to the lies, and he'd try to move unless someone stayed with him, and kept him focused on reality.

"Two minutes, and we move out."

"You heard the sergeant, get your gear together." Lackey

walked through survivors. "If anyone has a problem, speak now or forever hold your peace."

Cora hid a grin as she took hold of the poles behind Walker's head, Virgil taking the ones at his feet. Fifteen to twenty minutes, and they'd be at the ground cars. They'd make it out of here, in one piece, for the most part, then the real work would begin.

#

"Ian?" The middle-aged woman moved through the room above his head. "Ian? You down there?"

He didn't need to see her to know his mother was standing at the top stairs leading down into the sleeping quarters. Her voice changed depending on where she was when she called for him. Why she didn't use the house comms was beyond him, but he'd learned to accept the small quirks his mother embraced. "Give me a minute, Mom."

"Alright, but no longer. Need you up here." She walked away from the stairs, plastiboards creaking beneath her feet.

She always needed him.

He rolled out of bed and yawned. How long had she let him sleep this time? A glance at the propped up datapad confirmed he'd grabbed an entire six hours. Enough to function, not enough to prevent him from bemoaning an early wake-up call. He groaned and grabbed five seconds of water from the fresher, washed his face, and pulled on pants. It didn't matter she'd seen him naked more often than he wanted to know about, he was a grown man now, and the last thing he was willing to do was parade around in front of his mom either naked or in his skivvies.

Pants in place, feet in thick-soled slippers, he made his way up into the family room, not bothering to hide the fact he was yawning. "What's wrong, Mom?"

"Can't get the main comm to work. I've tried everything you and Helen showed me, but it's not helping." She glanced back at him, her hair touched with silver, face lined from the hard work which came with running a household on the edge of nowhere.

"All I'm getting is static, and I can't reach your dad or your sister. I don't like this. Can you take a look, see what I've missed?"

"Where's Helen?"

"With your dad, didn't I say that?"

"No, not really." She'd implied it. Now he had a chance to recall her words. "Sorry, I'm still waking up."

"I wouldn't have called for you if it wasn't important. I can't reach anyone on the comm, not even Hawthorne, and he was due to check in an hour ago. If I can't get hold of him, then I'll have to take the ground car and check on him. We both know what your father would think of the idea."

Ian paused, brow furrowed. "I understand."

Hawthorne might be the best example of a grumpy old miner, but the one thing he didn't do was miss the check-in. Not after it had taken ten years for his mother to badger the old-timer into agreeing to contact her at least once a week. Only the threat of his mother turning up on Hawthorne's doorstep had persuaded the man to agree to her demands.

"I won't hear the end of it." His mother scowled. "You'd think I was a child, but if I go out there without him, or at least you, then he'll decide I can't be trusted with the car, and he'll hide the keys."

"You did crash it the last time you were out on your own."

"Ridiculous. I scratched the door. A small scratch. He's making a fuss over nothing."

"Weird, the comm I mean." He nudged the conversation back on track. "Have you checked all the circuits?" He settled on the stool next to the comm.

"Your sister keeps this in running order. I don't know how she does it, but the girl is a wizard when it comes to these things." Elena Hunter gathered her long, gray marked hair into a tail and wrapped a tie in place. "There are green lights across the board. Mom, according to this, there's nothing wrong with the comm. Still, all I'm getting is static."

"Storm?" Ian opened the side of the comm set up and peered

in. Where was his sister when he needed the brat?

"Nothing predicted."

"Huh," he checked the interior, searching for a sign of what was going on. Everything appeared to be in place. "I can't see anything wrong." Not that he knew more than the basics. Helen had a way with machines, one he wasn't able to replicate, but he wasn't above making fun of his little sister. "When will she be back?"

"An hour, maybe two."

Ian made a show of checking the connections, he didn't need to, not with what he'd seen so far, but it would calm his mother down. "Then we'll have to wait until she comes back. I've checked what I can but--"

"You should have Helen walk you through repairs, and we can't always rely on her being around."

"I know how to handle the basics, Mom." Rolling his eyes wouldn't help, but damn if he didn't want to. "It's the more advanced tricks Helen performs, remain out of my league. Besides, as long as I'm still here, I don't have to worry about keeping the equipment running."

As soon as he said it, he wanted to take the words back.

"Rebecca is of marriageable age."

"Mom, please." He sighed and closed up the comm system.

"Well, she is. She'd make a good wife."

"We'd kill each other within a week."

"You could try," she pleaded.

"It's not going to happen. Besides, she's got her eye on another man, over in the colony. The last thing Rebecca wants is to end up as a miner's wife." It took a special type man or woman to want to be stuck out in a claim. Especially here. "Drop it, mom. Please. I'll find the right one eventually." He sighed and glanced around the family room, gaze settling on the coffee station. It wasn't real coffee, but it tasted semi drinkable. You got used to it, or you found something else to drink. "Want a cup?"

"Sure, but it's not going to stop me from trying to find you the right woman. You should have been out on your own claim last year."

What would happen here? His father wasn't getting any younger, nor was his mom, but bringing the point up would lead to an argument he didn't want to repeat today. "It'll all work out." There. Noncommittal. If luck were with him, she'd allow it to pass and drop the subject for the time being.

Coffee in hand, he handed over the mug to his mother and vanished back into the small kitchen. How she made the meals she did in the tiny space was beyond him, but his mother was a miracle worker. A few minutes of rummaging around, and he had oatmeal and dried fruit heating through, then poured into a bowl.

"Will need to add fruit to the supplies list, next time we hit the colony. I'm down to half a can."

"Uh-huh," he dug into the breakfast, making the right noises at the correct gaps in the conversation. At times, he dreamed about setting up a pillow with his face printed on it for his mother to talk to when there was no one else around. Add a tape with the right comments here and there, and she'd be set.

She'd kill me if I suggested it.

And he'd deserve it.

Chapter Four

Leigh focused on the next location as she walked. Her body complained, making her all aware of the ache deep in her muscles and the need to rest. No matter what happened at the next pod, she needed a break. They both would. She glanced down at Mags, the canine continued to keep pace with her, though he lacked the bounce in his step she'd grown used to over the years. Neither of them was in the position to keep going for another five klicks, or however far it would be to the pod after this one.

The second pod appeared to be half-buried beneath the ice and rock, but from what she could see, it was in one piece. Not that she could be certain before she reached it.

Her steps slowed before she realized what she was doing, and she forced herself to pick up the pace. No matter what happened, she had to keep moving toward the pod. This pod would have the answers. Perhaps there'd be a crew member inside or a fellow Marine. Someone she knew or at least recognized enough to put a name to. Right now, she'd take any form of human life as long as it was breathing. Wouldn't matter if the survivor was Pontier, a man universally despised, and with good cause. She'd take any man or woman, as long as they were human and alive.

One step. Two. She counted to a hundred and began again. Automatic pilot wasn't wise, more likely to trip, slip, fall, damaging herself and the suit both. No, she had to run, walk, climb until she reached the pod.

Her eyes threatened to close, the half-mast warning she wanted to ignore but couldn't. She growled and took the water tube in her mouth and forced herself to drink. The water helped, rest would be better. A bed. She'd take a jump seat over nothing at all. All she had to do was put one foot in front of the other.

Her mind zoned out. She didn't react to the change, her eyes no longer seeing where she walked, the need to find the pod, reach it, crawl inside and close the door behind, the only thing keeping her going.

Mags barked.

She jolted into awareness, stumbling before she caught herself and struggled to remain on her feet. Shit. How long had she been walking in a daze? Leigh shook her head and paused to take in where she was as she sipped from the water tube.

An odd shape beckoned her attention, and it took a minute before her exhaustion hazed mind realized what she'd focused on.

The pod. The entrance to it above the ice and rocks, but the rest piled over it, keeping it from sight unless you knew what to look for.

"Alright Mags, we need to get inside. Maybe we'll find answers this time." If they didn't, they would at least be in a position to rest. She could close the pod, curl up in a jump seat, and catch a couple of hours before taking the next step out into the wastes of Pluto.

Mags leaned into her leg before they half shuffled, half walked to the entrance of the pod, door open, lights off. She frowned and peered inside. Nothing. No sign of life when she activated the lights. No slashes though, not like the first one.

Wrong.

One set of wounds, there was no other word for it, to the interior of the pod drew her attention once she climbed inside, let Mags follow her, then pulled the door closed behind them. They needed the rest. A time to regain her strength.

Mags. She had to take care of Mags.

The jump seats were in one piece, a small luxury she would enjoy. Ice-covered the equipment inside, the cold obvious but there was nothing she could do about it. Once again the occupants had broken protocol by leaving the pod open. The first one could be a mistake, the second a pattern. Marks like this indicated a danger she had to be prepared for. If she could stay awake long enough to make sense of them.

The deep slashes drew her attention, and she moved toward them, tracing with one finger. Same as the previous marks. Not human. Claws. She chewed on the inside of her lip. Didn't make sense, if they weren't human, what could they be? Pluto didn't have any indigenous lifeforms, not any which remained alive to call Pluto home. What scientists believed had once lived here had left nothing behind but the occasional fossil miles below the surface.

Nothing like this.

She turned away and brushed the ice away from the control panel. Life support. Did she need it? Or was it best to stay in the suits?

Suits. They'll keep both woman and dog warmer. If they were lucky, she'd find a stash of survival blankets. Unless it had been raided by the same people responsible for the damage she'd now seen in two pods.

"Sorry, boy. But if we use the suits, we have a better chance. I'm not certain I could turn the life support on enough to warm us up, and I don't think wasting whatever juice this thing has would be the best idea." She reached out and ruffled across Mags head. "I know it would be nice to be out of these things, but staying alive is better for all concerned."

He stretched out, circled three times, then settled down to sleep, nose covered by his tail, or rather his suit covered rear.

"Yeah, you have the right idea. I need to rest. We both do." She yawned and picked out a jump seat, strapping herself in so when she fell asleep, she wouldn't slide from the confines of the chair. An hour, maybe two of sleep, and they'd be ready to move again, to find the third pod then -- well, she'd make plans once she knew the state of the third escape pod and hopefully its occupants.

#

Cora didn't complain though taking half the weight of the stretcher wasn't easy work, and made her miss the power armor

Marines often used when they boarded unfriendly vessels. The last few times she'd worn one it had been during practice runs. Only once had she faced a fight in the armor, but damned if she wouldn't give her left arm for a suit now.

Not her right arm, she'd needed it to shoot, but her left, she could always get a replacement and wouldn't be the first Marine to have adaptations due to injury or illness. One of the joys of being military, you were at the top of the list for the newest prosthetics if you needed one. And, as long as you were cleared by medical, you could continue in service, be it on active duty, or as a reserve back on Earth or one of the older colonies.

"We're here." A voice, one she knew.

Salla?

"Virgil, let's get Walker to the head of the group, no point in leaving him back here." She kept her voice calm, never allowing it to show her weariness. Once she no longer had to help with the stretcher, it would be easier. Her body would have a chance to recover and, then she'd no longer have to fake being ready to take on the world, or at least the invaders.

"On it."

Walker groaned and reached back to touch her hand. "I can walk. Sergeant. You know I can. All I need is another drop of Dreams. I'll be good then. One more drop, Sergeant. It'll help. I know it will. Please, Sergeant."

"Not going to happen Walker. We're here, at the ground cars. You won't need anything more."

"Sergeant, I can't do this without another drop. Please, it hurts."

"Not happening, told you before. No more. You've had two drops." The second one had been a mistake. He was acting like an addict, but he was on the edge of it. She'd seen it before and wasn't about to watch one of her people be locked in the grip of Amber Dreams. "You've got to ride this out, alright? It won't be hard, not after only two drops, but with every extra drop it's going to be harder to shake."

"You think I'm addicted?" He growled and tightened his grip on her hand. "I'm not, Sergeant. I'm fine. I swear, I just need another drop to keep me going."

"You listen to the Sergeant. She's not doing this to cause you pain," said Virgil.

"She is, she's holding out on me. Can't you see what she's doing to me." Sweat beaded his face. "I need it."

"Walker. Are you disobeying orders?" She snapped.

"No, Sergeant." He blanched.

"Then suck it up, Walker. Don't make me think you're not fit to be a Marine." Harsh words, cruel words, but they offered a mercy she hoped Walker would accept.

"Yes, Sergeant." He released his grip on her hand and closed his eyes, trembling, locked in the grip of the drug.

Damn Amber Dreams. There were other, safer pain meds, but either she had none at hand, or they would wipe out his ability to think, speak, be anything but a slumbering log.

She set the stretcher down and rolled out her shoulders. A dozen ground cars lined the cavern, each one capable of carrying at least four people. More if you didn't mind being cramped together. Enough to get them all out of here, and out to the first of the mining claims. Forty klicks would get them to a decent-sized settlement and fifty to half a dozen smaller claims. A dozen single man or couple claims lay twenty to twenty-five klicks out from the dome to the north.

North had closer settlements.

Southwest offered more options.

South West it was.

"Alright, ladies and gentlemen, Marines and whatever you are, Stone, we're heading to the southwest, toward the larger settlements. Four to a car is standard, but we'll need to put five in most, or we won't have enough cars to get us all out of here." She looked around, spotting the men and women she knew would answer her call first. Some were little more than kids, older teens or early twenties, but they'd pulled their weight and survived the initial attacks, more than many had done.

"Sergeant, there are other settlements to the north," Jakob informed her.

"I know, but the ones to the South East are bigger and more likely to have the people we'll need."

"Need for what?"

To fight back. Put up a decent resistance. She paused, not wanting to blurt the words out. Marine or not, she was still human, they all were, except for the invaders who had stolen their home out from under them. "We need to find people willing to work with us. We have to find answers, or we'll remain outnumbered. We're facing bad odds, and we have to be careful. Those things are out there. They've taken the dome, either the Navy has been destroyed out there, or they've been chased away. Doesn't matter which, we're on our own for now."

Alone, with mostly civilians around her, and a handful of Marines. Not the best odds, but it was all she had, and she wasn't about to let them down.

"Miners like to keep to themselves," Jakob scrubbed a hand over his face. "But there are a couple of families I know from before, might be able to get them to help us, or at least find others who want to fight back."

"It's the only option we have, for now." And damned if she wasn't going to grab it with both hands. Her people would survive. If she had to put weapons in the hands of kids, she'd do it, better that than to die or be captured without a fight.

#

Stone watched from the side of the enlarged cavern as the Marine gave her orders. Most of the group obeyed without pausing to think, but two adults and one older teen lingered away from the rest of the group. He frowned, but didn't speak, didn't move away from the shadows which offered him a chance to observe without being obvious. It wasn't ideal, but then again rushing in to obey any order Lawbook snapped out, wasn't his idea of a good time. Sure, the woman and her team had got them out of trouble earlier, and she appeared to know what she was doing, but she was still military.

"Think hanging out back here won't get you noticed, Stone?" Harvard's cultured voice reached out from behind him.

Stone tensed but didn't turn, didn't react to the voice. Not externally. *Shit, he moves quietly.* "Something you wanted, flyboy? Or do you like sneaking up on people?"

The pilot chuckled and stepped around Stone. "No, just watching what's going on, same as you. Appears as if we're both stuck following the orders of a jarhead." The man nodded in the direction of the Marine and her people. "Not that I mind, she's not out for guts and glory. She wants to keep as many of the civilians as safe as possible."

"For now."

"Yeah, well nothing stays the same, and if she wants to run missions on those things back there, I'm all for it. Ruined one of my rare nights ground side and forced me to waste a nearly full mug of Jones' best beer. Those things are going to pay, for the beer I mean," said Harvard, his eyes bright for a split-second, then the humor vanished, leaving a cold, dangerous man in its place. "You planning on running out on us?"

"Not recently."

"Ah," the single sound filled with knowledge. "She'll be watching for you to leave."

"She has every right to. I wouldn't trust me if I were in her position." Stone didn't move and kept a half-eye on the trio. "You'd think those three would be happy to get into the ground cars, but I don't see them moving, do you?"

"No."

"Which means there's a reason they haven't grabbed a car. A curious man might want to know what's going on with them.

A man who'd like to stay alive." He pushed away from the wall. If Harvard wanted to follow him, he wouldn't stop the man. No point. He had enough to do, and the trio intrigued him far more than the pilot did.

Harvard shadowed him as Stone made his way across the cavern. Others were busy choosing the group they wanted to be with for the journey through the tunnels. And the blonde, Nyssa? He blanked on the name, lingered near the stretcher and the increasingly agitated Walker. Amber Dreams. Strong stuff, and useful as long as you were honest with yourself about it. Few were, which led to situations like this.

"Sergeant. Please." Walker sat up on the stretcher. "Don't let me suffer."

Bloodlaw turned, eyes narrowed. "We'll get you into a car soon. Have two cars which might work with the stretcher."

"Pain's coming back, Sergeant. I need more."

Nyssa stepped back from the stretcher, gaze frantically searching for something she could use to help Walker. What did she expect? That Lawbook would give another drop or two to Walker?

"Can't you get her to see he needs help?" Nyssa asked as she reached out to grab his arm, forcing Stone to pause. "She's cruel, letting him suffer like this when there's another option."

"He's had two drops; she's making certain he doesn't give in to the drug." Stone paused and glanced down at the small hand holding him. "Anymore, and he'll tip headlong into addiction, which you'd know if you have anything to do with the damned stuff. He needs to wait at least four hours before he uses more. Even then, there's a risk he will go through full-blown withdrawal. Do you want an injured man to go through the pains of withdrawal? Want to see him writhe until he breaks bones and tears muscles?"

She shifted her weight, full bottom lip caught between her teeth.

She's the dealer. The realization hit full force, but he kept it from showing on his face. "You did the right thing bringing the Dreams to Lawbook. She knows the risk and is willing to be the mean ol' Sergeant to prevent Walker from becoming addicted. Shows she cares for her people, wouldn't you think?" What else did she deal in? Not the time or place to discuss it. And it now made sense why she'd tried to hit on him. He didn't hide the fact he was a smuggler, and it wouldn't be the first time people believed he dealt in illicit drugs.

A little smoke wasn't terrible. Few still had the addiction to tobacco, but he'd smuggled in cigars from time to time. Along with hard to find liquor both for Jones and other private establishments or personal. The hard stuff? Hell no. Between the sentences for being caught with it and his personal dislike of anything addictive, he stayed away from jobs which would include items like Amber Dreams.

"He's hurting though."

"Mild withdrawal. He'll pull through it."

Her lips flattened. "I don't like seeing him in pain."

Maybe it was true, she might be one of those rare dealers with a heart. Nope. Not this one. He didn't know what it was about the woman, but there was something off with her. "Talk to Lawbook, she's in charge, and Walker is one of her people." He gave a pointed look at the hand on his arm. "I have things to do."

"Oh," she said, releasing his arm. Pink touched her cheeks, eyes half shuttered by long lashes. "I'm sorry. It's just I thought you'd be able to help. You seem to have a connection with the Sergeant."

No use of Lawbook's name. A means of keeping her distance from the Marine? Maybe. And the lowered lashes, half shy smile, oh he knew those weapons all too well. She was smart, but nowhere near good enough to entrap him into helping her. "True enough, but I've got a couple of things to do, and Lawbook is easy enough to approach. Go and talk with her, if you're anxious about

Walker. She'll want what's best for him." Not a lie in words, but more than one in the intent. He patted her shoulder, pasted on a smile, and gave her a half shove in the direction of the Sergeant. "Go on, no point in wasting time."

"Nicely done." Harvard matched pace with him. "Don't trust her."

"The blonde?"

"Yes. Not only the drugs either. She's dangerous." Harvard's gaze followed Nyssa.

"Maybe you don't like her choice in men?" He grinned, then nodded in the direction of his targets. The three civilians lingered close to the tunnels.

"Have at," Harvard gestured. "I'm here for the entertainment."

"Sure, you are." *Whatever you're up to, flyboy, I'm on to you.* He might not know the details, but he didn't need to keep an eye on Harvard. *Shit, he watched everyone, it was second nature.* "Hey, have a problem? You're going to run out of cars if you don't make a move." He slapped one hand on the shoulder of the oldest man in the group.

"No, erm, we're fine. Had a bit we needed to talk about." The man, touches of gray at his temples and a bald spot he'd taken care to half hide with the way he'd combed his hair, paled beneath Stone's gaze. "We'll be going in a minute."

"You mean now, don't you?" He used the grip on the man's shoulder to turn him in the direction of the ground cars. "She needs to get us all moving and quickly. We don't know how long it will be before those creatures find a way past the cave in. You wouldn't want to be standing here, still talking things over when those bastards show up, would you?"

"Hey, watch the language, there are kids around here." The younger adult, one he'd assumed was a man at first glance, but close up, he could see more feminine features. The voice was halfway between male and female. *Trans? Possibly, not that it mattered. Human was human, and he'd never seen a point in* objecting to how a person chose to live their lives.

"My swearing is the least of the problems this lot will have to deal with if we don't get moving."

"Markus, he's right." The younger adult sighed and rested one hand on the teenage girl. "We've got to keep Olivia safe, even if we didn't want to go with them, what other choice do we have? We all saw those things before we got into the tunnels. I'm not armed. You're not, and frankly, Olivia shoots better than either of us."

Of course, a family unit. Stone didn't speak but allowed the group to come to their own decision. If they made the wrong choice, then he'd handle it one way or another.

"We're pacifists, of course, she can shoot better than we can, Annabel. But that's the problem, if we go with these people, we'll be forced to fight. We won't have a choice. If we approach these newcomers, try to talk with them, we could prevent any more bloodshed."

Annabel shook her head. "You're wrong, love. I don't like it, but you're wrong. They aren't willing to listen. They didn't reach out to start a dialog. If they had, it would be another matter entirely. But they're dangerous. We don't know how many have died out there. How many more will if we don't pull together as a team. And we have to protect Olivia. She'll be safer with them than she will be on her own with us."

"Dad, please, we need to stay with the Marines. They'll help us. And we don't know what happened up there. Why the Navy didn't protect us. If they're all dead. For all we know, this group is all that's left of the colony." Olivia's gentle voice pleaded. "I want you to be safe. Without the Marines, I'd be the only one with a gun, if they allowed us to take it with us and not pass it to the others."

"Alright, alright, we'll do it."

Stone nodded to the family. "See you at the next stop."

"Have to admit, I was ready to punch Markus."

He shrugged. "I could see his point, he lacked a rounded viewpoint, and it wasn't down to me to get him to change his mind, only nudge him in the right direction. Information from his family was one thing when an outsider says the same thing it can force a man, or woman, to rethink the situation." And I'll take family manipulation for one hundred, thanks. "You picked out your car group?"

"I'll squeeze in where ever there's space."

"Yeah, I get the feeling we'll both be told where Lawbook wants us."

Chapter Five

Leigh groaned as her head jerked up. Her neck complained as she reached back and rubbed at the offending muscle hidden beneath the suit. Why had she forgotten to adjust the jumpseat so there'd be support for her neck? Because I was too tired to think straight? Good enough excuse and it was honest. At least she didn't have to explain herself to her Sergeant, or anyone else.

Mags grumbled at her feet.

"Fine. I was dumb."

The dog gave a low woof.

"Tired, I was tired, alright?" She rolled out her shoulders before unhooking from the straps which had held her in place. How long had she slept? She pulled up the readings on the suit. Two hours. Not enough to get a full recharge, but the third pod was closer than the other two had initially been, it wouldn't hurt to take a look at the third pod. If she found nothing and the pod wasn't in decent condition, she could make it back here and settle for an extended rest, search for what information she could, and plan for the following day.

Her muscles added their protests as she stood and tried to get the stiffness out of her body. She glanced at the closed door, then at Mags. "This isn't getting me out of here, is it?"

He woofed.

Great, even her dog wanted her to get moving.

"Another minute or two. I'm still waking up. Won't help either of us if I'm so tired I trip and crack a bone, or tear my suit."

She checked the suit, readings covering food, water, and air. She'd be able to top up again at the next pod. Everything showed her she had at least seventy-five percent oxygen, eighty percent water, and ninety-five percent food. The waste packets didn't need to be cleaned out after her shot nap, which removed one less excuse to linger.

Mags growled, half bowed, nose to the floor, tail up and wagging.

"Yeah, I know." She sighed and opened the hatch before she stepped out into the unforgiving landscape of Pluto, only moving when she'd secured the hatch behind her. She hadn't turned on life support, but at least it wouldn't lose more heat. Foolish, without life support, it will grow colder in there. She wanted to kick herself for the assumption but didn't waste time, or energy in beating herself up again.

"Let's get this last one checked, hey buddy? Might finally get an answer to what's going on here." Couldn't be in a worse position than she already was, and even if the pod was empty, perhaps there'd be more information in the pod's log. Enough to put the pieces together and give her a better idea of what was going on. "Come on, let's get this over and done with."

#

"Garlyn Claim, come in please," Lawbook thumbed the comm a third time. "Please respond. This is Sergeant Bloodlaw, if you can hear me, it's urgent you reply."

"They're not going to answer you, Sergeant," Jakob explained as he leaned forward to rest one hand on the back of the Marine's seat. "Garlyn is a stubborn old goat, never lets anyone in unless he knows them first hand. Sometimes not even then." He racked his memory for anything else which would help Lawbook. Odd, if he'd tried calling a Marine by their nickname only two days ago, he'd have received a slap across the back of his head from the nearest adult. Maybe two. One for disrespecting the Marine. The second for interrupting a Marine in the middle of her duty.

"How well do you know him?" Lawbook glanced back over her shoulder, then returned her attention to the comm.

"Enough to know if we turn up there he'll answer with a weapon in hand, a growl in his voice and ready to pick a fight." Jakob paused going over the rare times he'd spoken with the man. His father had known how to deal with Garlyn, but he wasn't his dad, nor was the Sergeant. "I wouldn't stop there, but there's a bigger settlement not far away, considering the distances out here. The Hunter family has an extended claim, with family members, close friends, all working various mines in the area. Mrs. Hunter is a good person, and she's always been nice to me." He smiled, remembering the last time he'd run into her. She always had a smile and was ready to visit with people when she came to the colony. No matter what happened, the woman kept her temper and had a calm word in the middle of a dangerous situation. From what he could recall, he seldom had a harsh word unless you threatened her family.

"Give me a minute," Lawbook frowned and pulled up the information. "That's the one forty klicks out. It was on my list to try."

Jakob leaned back.

Salla nudged him, her voice kept low-pitched. "Good work there. I've dealt with old man Garlyn plenty enough for one lifetime. I pity the aliens if they turn up on his doorstep. He'll have only one answer for him."

He grinned, knowing what Salla meant. "You know the Hunters?"

"Had the occasional dealing with them. Their son is a year or two older than me. Ian, quiet enough, hard-working, like his parents. There's a daughter too, young, maybe thirteen."

Thirteen was young? He shifted uneasily. Maybe it was to Salla, and he'd had enough dealings with tweens and early teens to agree, but what was he? A kid in her eyes, or a man? Please let her see me as a man, not a child. "Cool, be a better option for all of us. More space, and if she's the type I think she is, Mrs. Hunter will have the low down on the surrounding claims, which of the miners could be reached out to, might help us, or take in the younger kids until matters are settled."

Salla patted his thigh. "My thoughts, as well. She's decent people. And we're all tired and hungry now. She'll have at least blankets and a spot on the floor for the majority of us. Maybe not in the main house, but in the outer buildings."

His skin tightened beneath the cloth, tingling at her touch. Heat flushed his cheeks as he glanced away. Don't react, don't let her see what her touch does to me. Easier said than done, but if she said anything, maybe he'd be able to laugh it off. "Brilliant idea." They could do this, get out to the mines, the settlements, and find help. It was possible their communications weren't as scrambled. "Helen, isn't that the name of the daughter?"

"Yes, I met her once or twice. Tech nerd, deep into it. More so than my dad. I swear, she'd give him a run for his money when she'd a few years older," agreed Salla, her voice filled with pain.

"He might be alive, Salla. Remember, they've been taking prisoners. You don't know he's dead. If there's a man who could keep himself alive through this, and take a few of those things out at the same time, it's your dad." His arms ached with the need to wrap Salla in a tight hug. They'd all lost people, but Salla only had her dad. The man had been her world. "We'll find him."

"Don't make promises you might not be able to keep." She scuffed one hand across her cheeks. "Shit, it must be dusty here."

There was nothing wrong with crying, but Salla wasn't in the right head space to hear it. "Yeah, must be. Don't know when these things were last cleaned." No one wore the helmets in here, better communication within the ground cars, and allowed them to feel more at ease. A small blessing but one he wasn't going to turn his nose up at.

She closed her eyes, going silent.

Do I say something? He glanced at Salla. No, better to give her time.

Lawbook reached for the comm and opened up the short-range communication between the cars. With the blanket jamming, they'd been left unable to communicate most of the time. Not all channels had been affected, but anything designed to reach beyond the colony, if you were inside the dome, or more than a couple of hundred meters of gaps between the ground cars, resulted in broken communication, or static.

He frowned as he let the information sit. How were they blocking the high power communication beams but missing a few of the lower ones? "They can't hear the personal comms, not now."

"Worked that out a while back," said Lawbook.

"No, I mean they can't hear them. It's a frequency they either don't know about, or they really can't hear at all. Out of their natural range of audio signals. They blocked us by accident, it's the only thing which makes sense."

Salla sat up and reached for his arm, fingers tight. "Damn, you might be onto something there."

"No might about it," said Lawbook. "We might be missing a small piece of the puzzle, but it makes sense. Nicely done, Jakob. Don't hold back on any other ideas, both of you. We're all in this together. If one of us comes up with an idea, the rest of us might be able to build on it. So, neither of you hold back."

#

"Hey long legs," said Helen a heartbeat before a pair of arms wrapped around his waist. "What are you doing up this early? Didn't you have a long night?"

"Mom woke me. Comm isn't working, sprout." Ian turned and pulled Helen into a tight hug, grateful she was able to allow his touch. "Might be best if you take a look at it before she appears."

"This one is out as well? Odd." Helen frowned and glanced over at the comm. "I was having problems with the one in the ground car, took a while to get it to work enough to keep in contact with Dad. It shouldn't have happened. Not like this. I keep these things in top condition." Her focus on the electronics.

Ian followed her gaze, tightened the hug, then let go. "Weird." It hadn't been many years since she couldn't stand being touched unless it was on her terms every inch of the way.

"Totally," she glanced up at him with a mock vapid gaze. "It's like it doesn't want to work." She flipped her hair back from her eyes.

"Cut it out, you know we don't buy the empty-headed teen routine. I've been around you too long and know all your tricks." He laughed and pushed her in the direction of the comm. If anyone could get it to work, it was Helen.

"If I'm going back to work, you need to get me a cup of caff." She wrinkled her nose. "With honey. I know Mom's got at least one jar back there."

"She hides it for a reason. You use it faster than she can barter for it." Bees. He'd never thought he'd see bees on Pluto. But in the hydroponics sectors, they kept small beehives. Between the honey, wax, royal jelly, and the pollination the small insects took care of, they were worth the extra attention to bring them out to Pluto in the first place. "If I use it, and she yells at me, it's on your head."

"I'm worth it." She didn't meet his eyes but allowed her gaze to slide in his general direction before she returned to the comms. "Nothing smells wrong. Not a short."

And mom will blame me regardless. He sighed and opened the cupboard, pushing aside the handful of cans and jars. Dry goods, rare supplies of fruit in juice, and other small luxuries, all sat in front of the lone jar of honey. "This is a new jar, which means it's her last. I'm not going to give you much, okay. I like my head where it is."

"You love me."

"Yeah, which is the only reason I'm doing this."

"Nope, you don't want Mom shouting at you about the comm, it's why you're doing this." Her words muffled as she set a panel aside and peered into the comm. "It has to be the same problem with the signals we were getting out there. Not sure what's blocking the signal." She wriggled deeper into the comm. "Nothing appears out of place at first glance. Connections are tight. Same situation as the ground car comm." She edged out and peeked over at him. "Ian, caff. If I'm going to work on this, I'll need the caff before I turn old, gray, you know, like you."

"Hah, keep that up, and I'll give you tea instead. One of Mom's herb and fruit things." Not real tea, but his mother like them, and with the hydroponics, it was easier to get those types of tea than the real stuff. As with coffee, real tea wasn't a priority when it came to shipping things to Pluto, and only the rich indulged in the real thing.

"You wouldn't dare." Her voice half-muffled by the confines of the comms outer shell.

"Try me." He grinned and set the mug down, filled with caff. He added, as she watched, a spoonful of honey, closed the jar and returned it to its hiding place.

"You have to sleep sometime," Helen grumbled as she wandered over to the counter. "I'll take another look in a bit, but honestly, if it's the same problem we had out there, I can do a workaround. Once we have a partially working comm, then I'll explore other solutions. Might need to check in with the surrounding settlements. If we're having problems, odds are they will be." She shoved a loose strand of hair behind her ear. "Sucks. Big time. We've not had problems of this level for at least a couple of years. Long before I took over fixing things around here."

He didn't respond. Helen had been tinkering with electronics for years. What had she been, five? If that? The image flashed through his mind, a toddler with pigtails, kneeling in her nightdress next to Dad, pointing out what piece he needed to reach for next.

She'd been non-vocal at five. A pretty young girl with wide eyes, unable to meet anyone's gaze, but happy when she worked with anything electronic.

"We all appreciate the work you do."

"Only because it means you don't have to see to the repairs yourself." She flashed a grin and took a sip from her caff. Her eyes half-closed, a low moan of pleasure escaping. "One day, I'll get the chance to try the real thing."

"You keep inventing things, being able to fix pieces others have given up on, and it will happen."

"Yeah, yeah, and I'll build my own ship, then I won't have to rely on anyone else."

If there was a man or woman on Pluto capable of pulling off whatever miracle would be needed to get things working again, it was his sister. Helen Hunter.

Interlude Two

Treizaek walked around the bridge, checking in with each crew member before he settled into the command chair. The remains of the human vessels no longer offered a threat even to their smallest ships. "Anything from their homeworld? I would know if these creatures have the gall to strike back." He paused, waiting for an answer.

"There have been several attempts to reach out to this colony using their primitive communications." A female stationed at the scanner controls replied. "Our system has blocked their attempts at communication. They will continue to try if our reports about these creatures are to be believed."

"They will not wish to lose what they believe is theirs." He inclined his head, and opened comms. "Science."

"Yes Commander," a male voice, one he knew, but he seldom used the names of those beneath him. They were lower status, and the use of their name would be a way of praising the crew member in question.

"Report."

"These humans are different from our own, Honored One." A pause, the tapping of claws against screens. "I have completed the first stages of biological exploration, and there are several major differences. Their males and some females are aggressive, willing to fight, save for a handful we have met. Differences in diet, gravity, socialization, these all combine to--"

"Put it in the report. Anything we need to know for combat and survival?" His wings ruffled, then settled back into place against his back.

A pause, a small clearing of the male's throat. "There are differences with their muscle build. Stronger, and their warriors appear to be twice as stubborn. Ready to fight to the death. Nothing we have seen before from the servant's colony. However, their warriors are fewer in number than the other types, and there are young who have been collected, we will be studying them. Like the servants, these creatures have only two biological genders. Both number in their warriors, a few are better trained than others."

A fact he could admire. "Good, it will make this assignment easier to deal with. Our people have lacked in true challenges."

"Yes, Honored One." Another pause. "Perhaps it would be best to increase the level of testing. If you would permit one or two of our warriors to report to me, I'd be delighted to see how these humans stand up to them. The testing might reveal other differences we have yet to discover."

"Not at this time, our warriors must be prepared to face the next stage of the invasion. Bridge Out." He closed the comm and leaned back in his chair. Yes, a real combat situation. His people had been long without the ability to stretch their wings. They needed a chance to rend their claws into the enemy and bite the flesh from human bodies.

A small movement behind him drew his attention, the scent of the female known to him. "Yes, Nyanaek?"

"There is a report from the planet." A gentle tremor in her voice drew his focus.

"The ones who attacked our people?"

"Yes," Nyanaek replied. "They have vanished. The tunnels collapsed behind them, and we're having problems finding where they fled to. No doubt it's somewhere beneath the colony, but there are so many of these tunnels we're running into difficulties."

He frowned, turning the chair to watch her. "Are you telling me your scouts have failed you?"

"Yes, Commander." She bowed her head. "Should I report for retraining and correction?"

"No, this may be an aberration, it will be followed up on. However, you will report to Commander Ploitier, and accompany him down to the planet. There you will take personal control of your troops. But have no doubt, I will not tolerate a second failure."

Her gaze lowered even as she raised her head. "Then I fear I must disappoint you before I have a chance to regain your pleasure."

Heat built within his chest, a knot he didn't want to acknowledge. "Speak. Now."

"The scouts found another group in the tunnels, close to the colony. They captured one human male, but the rest escaped, and the scouts have been unable to locate them." She lifted her head. "I am displeased with them, but I know I must answer to you for their failure."

Two failures. Did his female not understand how this made him appear? He took a moment to look around the bridge. They were listened to. Their conversation always observed, noted, and filed away for another time. Should he be found lacking by the great council, he would answer with his life. As would she. "We will discuss this matter once you return to your post here. I will not tolerate weakness, Nyanaek. Is that understood?"

"Yes, Honored One." Her voice calm and steady to anyone who didn't know her.

"Dismissed." He gestured for the female to leave his presence.

She took three steps back, gave a formal sharp jerk of her head up and down, turned and exited the bridge without another word.

He didn't watch her leave. She would either fix the mistakes she'd made in training her scouts, or would pay the price either with her wings, or her life. There was no room for weakness among their kind. His mate or not, she was replaceable. They all were. Including himself if the council decided he had failed them.

There was no room for failure. Not when you served the whole. Weakness wasn't tolerated among the warriors, the fighters, those strong enough to be deemed capable of breeding the next generation. If he had to replace his mate, he would do so and only grieve in private. But others would seek his attention, warriors and civilians both. Those who served their empire in other ways, as healers, scientist, builders, and others.

Do not fail me, Nyanaek. I will cut off your wings myself if you do, then offer your head to your replacement as a courting gift.

He smiled. Yes, there were other females he could form a union with. Not all would be strong enough to breed with. However, some might be enough to warm his nest at night, and for now, it was all that mattered.

Chapter Six

Mags ranged out in front of her. The final walk to the downed pod wouldn't take long, and once there she'd be able to put together a better plan of action than wandering the wastelands of Pluto in the hopes of finding other survivors. She didn't need to check how long she'd been walking to know she moved slower, her steps heavier than they had been. Whatever was going on here, it wasn't good news. Pods didn't get torn up inside by accident, and the marks -- she'd been around animals enough to recognize claws had been used.

Fake? She'd mulled over the idea several times. There was a possibility artificial claws had been produced, but why? Things like this didn't happen without reason, and that was the missing piece of the puzzle.

Pirates?

Sure, it was possible. Pluto, like the other colonies, had the occasional problem with pirates. Not as much in the last ten years, but they still existed, and she couldn't dismiss the option without proof.

Not pirates. Those were real claw marks.

She didn't know they were real, she assumed. Without the ability to run full scans, searching organic markers, Leigh understood she was guessing.

"What I wouldn't give for access to the UTG database."

Mags ran back to her side, blocking her path. Silent. He didn't bark, whine, or make any other audible sound. She crouched down and rested one hand on his suit covered head. What had he seen? Mags didn't move, his body trembling beneath her touch. If he wasn't verbal, then it told her she needed to remain quiet, not use the personal comm link between them. It wasn't easy to hack into those links, but he'd been trained not to take chances.

Leigh glanced in the direction he'd come from. Ripples in the landscape, not full ridges, but enough to block her line of sight. Her body ached, the need to curl up on a real bed, hammered at her. Foolish. She hadn't had access to one since leaving Earth. Jumpchairs in the place of beds. Small cubicles with no room for personal items or visitors. Still, it was better than the options she currently had access to.

She gestured forward, giving the hand signal to indicate she'd take it slow.

Mags relaxed but didn't move.

She gave the same signal again. This time Mags stepped took a dozen paces, but kept close enough to block her path still should the need arise. Smart dog. Most were. But the bond she had with Mags was unique.

Her companion continued in front of her but dropped to the ground and belly crawled to the deepest ripple. She frowned but copied him, knowing he wouldn't crawl unless needed. If she made a sound as she approached him, one which could have carried in the barely existent atmosphere of Pluto, she neither knew nor spared the time to find out. Anyone out there would be in a suit, and if the survivors from this pod had been captured, odds said it would be by settlers who had a problem with strangers or pirates, perhaps smugglers, trying to keep their work quiet.

Except killing or capturing a member of the Unified Terran Government was an invitation to bring the wrath of Captains like Hermes Longfellow, Jade McCann, or RodenKilmare down on them. Captain's whose names were used to frighten would-be pirates into surrendering. No, pirates and smugglers did their best to keep a low profile. A smart pirate attacked people who lived on the edge of the law, smugglers or made it appear as if it had been an accident, rather than a pirate attack.

Movement caught her eye as she reached the top of the ripple. Shapes moved around the opened pod. Three humanoid shapes knelt, hands behind their heads, watched over by a taller, bulky figure with--

Wings?

She blinked and ducked down behind the ripple. She was seeing things. Right? Wings weren't possible. A costume design one of the more flamboyant pirates had adopted? Leigh took a second peek, then hid again. No, not a costume. Two arms, two legs, and a pair of freaking wings.

Aliens. They have to be aliens.

If so, why had they captured members of her crew? What was going on here? Aliens wouldn't have come all this way to attack and kill them. It didn't make sense.

Mags leaned against her, offering his weight in support. She slung one arm over his back, holding him close. No, she this wasn't real. She was back in the pod, or her own jumpseat come bed, dreaming. Aliens. Everyone knew they existed, but the first contact should have been peaceful. Not like this. And if these were aliens, then the break in the dome made sense.

Her heart sank.

What about the civilians. Those who called the dome their home? Had they been able to pull on suits before the dome had failed?

What the hell am I supposed to do now?

#

Cora indicated for the convoy of ground cars to halt, and thumbed the comm. If the kids were right, she should be able to reach the Hunter settlement. "Hunter Claim, this is Sergeant Bloodlaw of the UTG Marines, please respond."

Static.

Was she too far away? Possible, or there was no one manning the comm on their end. Unless Salla was wrong, and Helen couldn't fix it, so the comm unit was able to reach past the jamming field.

"Repeat, this is Sergeant Bloodlaw, please respond." She kept her voice calm despite the uncertainty clawing a path through her stomach. Lack of sleep, real food, rest for more than fifteen minutes, threatened to crash in on her. A stim would help, but she hated the damn things. Once they were safe, away from the dome, and able to relax, she'd grab sleep.

"Hunter Claim, please resp--"

"This is Hunter Claim," an older, male voice replied. "Tim Hunter here, what can I do for you, Sergeant?"

"I have a convoy of ground cars, we've been traveling through the tunnels, and need a place to rest. News we need to share with you, not suitable for open comm channels." The information pushed at her, begging to be shared.

"How many?"

"Cars? Nine." Three remained in the cavern. One small family had argued with her about leaving the extra cars, but she wasn't going to cut off transport for anyone who followed them. The aliens wouldn't use the vehicles, they had no means of knowing how they worked. At least, she assumed they didn't, but people like Jones would be able to use them, read the message left behind, and she wasn't going to steal the last means of transport from those who followed through the tunnels.

If there were any other survivors. She swore beneath her breath. If there weren't anymore, then they were FUBAR'd in the worst possible way.

"People?"

"Thirty-plus." Numbers, she knew the amount of people with her, but couldn't find the information stored away in her sleep-deprived mind.

"Why should we let thirty or more Marines eat up our supplies, Sergeant." Tim's voice was cold and disinterested.

"Because the majority of this group are civilians, Mr. Hunter. And there's a hell of a lot of children in the mix."

"Tim, we can't leave kids out there, it's not right." A woman's voice. His wife? Sister? Daughter?

"We don't know if she's telling the truth or not. You know what these military types are like. Steal the shirt from your back and repay you with a token no one accepts."

"Mr. Hunter, it's Jakob and Salla, from the dome." Jakob leaned forward. "Sergeant Bloodlaw is telling the truth. There are only a handful of Marines in the group, sir. Lots of kids. Most are frightened, tired, and don't have their families with."

"Tim, please, we know those two. They're good kids. They wouldn't lie to us."

"Fine, fine. Alright, Sergeant, have Jakob give you the approach, don't deviate, you'll end up in the middle of a dig, or worse." Tim Hunter grumbled. "We'll talk with you when you arrive, Hunter Claim out." The link closed.

"Cautious type." She murmured, "alright, you have the approach we need to use?"

"I can punch it in from back here, it'll be easier than trying to do it over your shoulder." Jakob pulled up the built in controls, waited for the green light to indicate Lawbook had given him access, then typed in the details. "This should be it. It's a couple of months since I've been out here."

Salla shifted closer to him and peered at the screen. "Yeah, it's fine. The same one I used last month. Be about a year before he has to change it again." She settled back into her chair. "Once you send it to the rest of the cars, you'll need to keep your speed down, no more than ten kpm, faster and it'll trigger the defense system."

"What type of claim needs an automated defense system?" Lawbook sent the information to the rest of the group, with a few notations of her own. "It's a claim, not a prison."

"Helen, the youngest kid, has a way with machines. Likes tinkering. After Mr. Hunter came back after a visit to the dome with stories of pirates, he gave her free rein to build one. More to keep her out of trouble if you ask me, but the damn thing works. I wouldn't want to mess with it, or her."

Cora closed her eyes for a count of five, pushing back the pressed building behind her eyes. Sleep, she'd have to crash not long after they arrived. Thank God for Mrs. Hunter, if the woman hadn't been present, then what? Would they all have been turned away? Not a question she wanted to answer, yet it continued to roll through her mind.

"Anything else we need to know about?" At least her two younger passengers were trustworthy. Harvard had filled her in on how everything had worked out when they'd sent the civilians ahead of them. Marines in the making, not as if Duncan would approve if he were around.

Too many people lost.

More to follow if her instincts were right.

"Mrs. Hunter is a fantastic cook, kind, you get the feeling she likes having lots of children around. She has three. Ian, Lloyd, and Helen. Lloyd is off planet, went back to Earth for a series of courses he wanted to complete. Being honest, he didn't like the idea of spending his life on Pluto." Salla paused, the next words uncertain. "Helen is... odd. Yeah, I mean, she's got the magic touch when it comes to tech. All sorts of tech. But she's kinda standoffish. Doesn't take to new people easily."

"She's on the spectrum. And she's great once you accept this is how she is. You'll get to see her with family, that's where you see the difference. Around them, she's more like you'd expect a teenager to be around them."

"Spectrum?" Cora frowned. Had she heard the term before?

"What they called autistic back before the first crash."

Wasn't there a cure for it now? She kept the question to herself, or was she misremembering? If one had been discovered, some rare families didn't go for medical improvements for their kids from birth. They left the choice down to the children when they were old enough to make an informed decision. "Alright, never dealt with someone on the spectrum before."

"Odds are you have and didn't know it if they were on meds.

Or had gone for the full treatment. But Helen's is amazing. Just don't be surprised if she doesn't meet your eyes, or looks to one side when she's talking with you. She's bright. I mean she hits the insanely intelligent level without trying. Her speech occasionally falters, but she told me it happens when she gets pulled into her own thoughts and colors."

Colors? She didn't know enough about this. "How do I treat her?"

"Like a person."

Cora didn't need to see the eye roll, not when it came across in Salla's words.

"It's simple, Sergeant. Polite, don't stare and be open to the fact that not everyone is the same way. It's what my dad told me years back when I first met Helen. She's about thirteen now, can fix anything she comes across, and extremely protective of her family. As long as you don't hurt them, she'll be fine. If she gets frustrated and walks away, let her. She's taking herself to her room to get the ideas in order."

"Thanks, Jakob, Salla. Here's hoping I don't screw it up." She glanced at the readouts. "Everyone's ready, we'll be there in the next twenty minutes." Unless the world blew up beneath them. After the events of the last twenty-four hours, anything was possible.

#

Ian leaned against the counter as his parents talked. Visitors. From the colony. But why would the Marines be bringing a bunch of kids out here? Sure, there were families in the dome, and a school, but dome colonists belonged beneath the protective cover offered by the transparent dome, not out here in the badlands among the claims, working and abandoned mines. He'd seen what could happen when a handful of dome dwellers tried to make a living out on the edge.

It didn't work.

Nor was it pretty to watch as the family unit typically broke down.

"They're kids, Tim. If they're coming without parents, there has to be a reason. And they'll be frightened." His mother explained, one hand touching his father's arm. "I couldn't leave them out there."

"I know love, I know. I didn't expect you to put up with the idea of leaving a bunch of children out in the wilds, but for all we know the Sergeant thinks I'm pussy-whipped."

She sighed, a weary smile touching her lips, gaze gentle. "You're not, you're a good husband who listens to his wife's pleas. You know how upset I'd be if those kids were left out there. They have to be hungry, thirsty, exhausted, no matter what's happened."

"Ian, Helen, anything you two want to add?"

"I like kids, not often I get to spend time with ones my age, or younger." Helen bounced from foot to foot. I've got toys -- oh, they might break them. Or put them in their mouths." She spun on her heel and darted to her room.

"Ian?"

He rubbed his chin, stubble catching at his fingers. He was overdue a shave. "Salla has a good head on her shoulders and knows the right words to say to alert us to a problem. If Salla and Jakob are with them, then we'll be able to find out what's happened." Repeated attempts to raise comm control in the dome had been met with static, though Helen had made it possible to raise the locals, static met them when they tried anything more.

"Then we meet them as friends, but keep an eye out for anything hinky." His father announced. "Might want to get a pot of oatmeal started, and I'll dig out the emergency blankets, protein bars, and water. They'll all need help."

Ian stretched, yawning. "Once they're settled, and we know more, I'll hit the sack. Still need to catch a few more hours." He'd have time, once things were calm. Not as if the world was ending around them, or the mines were in danger.

"Go get washed and dressed. I don't want visitors seeing you wandering around in threadbare PJs," his mother flushed and waved a hand in his general direction. "Off with you, I've got this. If I need help, I have your dad."

Sure, you could eat his cooking if there was no choice and you'd been without food for a couple of days, but enjoying it was a whole different matter. He glanced down at the faded sleep pants and shrugged. Arguing with his mom wasn't the best use of his time, and maybe he'd be better off grabbing a shower.

After all, Salla wasn't dating anyone, and if there were a woman he'd met to date, who might work as a miner's wife if was Salla. As long as her father didn't catch wind of the idea before he'd laid out a baited hook.

Fishing.

He missed being able to dangle a line, but the last time he'd enjoyed fishing with his uncle, he'd been what, five? Six? No fishing on Pluto and you either accepted what you had, or risk being driven crazy.

"They'll be here soon, no hanging around, or I'll take a scrubbing brush to you myself." His mother threatened.

"On it, mom." With a grin, he hurried down the steps into the sleeping quarters. A shoulder, brush through his hair, no cologne -- not that he had any, and his dad would notice if he dipped into his father's scant supply. Besides, Salla wasn't the elegant dresses and perfume type. She was like him, willing to get her hands dirty, and not afraid of hard work.

Didn't hurt she was easy on the eyes either.

Chapter Seven

Stone glared at the message, then scowled at the other occupants of the ground car. Nyssa had opted to travel with him, instead of with Walker in Lawbook's car. Not that he could blame the woman. Staying away from the Marines was her best bet now she'd tried to persuade them Walker needed more of the Amber Dreams.

Drugs.

Sure there were a few which had been useful in the old days, and the ones generally used by medics were safe -- under supervision. But there would always be those people searching for the next edge, the high, a sweet, undisturbed sleep, something they believed they would be unable to get through legal methods.

Nyssa would be a problem. The blonde didn't react well to being told no. She used her appearance, the seductive smile, a fake shyness, to get her own way. It hadn't worked this time, and by the way she sat, her back straight, jaw tight, she wasn't happy with the situation.

Understatement.

"Coming up on the settlement," he announced as he tapped the controls and the ground car slowed down. "They're waiting for us, and we'll have to see wait and see to find out what Lawbook has in mind." The settlement offered opportunities.

"I don't know why we came here, not when there were better settlements elsewhere," Nyssa grumbled, but didn't pay any attention to the others in the car. "We could have been there ages ago instead of heading out into the wastelands. It doesn't make sense."

"Ever thought being near the colony would make it easier for the aliens to attack us?" Stone kept his voice calm and steady. Damn woman. He'd been right to keep an eye on her.

"Humph," the sound filled with irritation. "As if. They attacked the colony and have enough to deal with beneath the remains of the dome. The rest of us will be ignored for the time being."

"And you know this for certain?"

"No, but it makes sense." She folded her arms. "I mean, what do you think they will do? It's nothing like the mess back in the colony. Think about it, they wouldn't have the time to head out beyond the dome yet. I doubt they've found this take over as easy as they originally planned."

He took a deep breath. "If it were true then they'd have left us all alone in the tunnels, not chased us." What was so difficult to understand here? He didn't want to be involved in this mess, but he was alive, and there were damned aliens out there. He might not know what they believed, but he could extrapolate from the current situations. "They aren't going to give up."

"They might. But no, you have to follow Sergeant whatever her name is." She rolled her eyes, making no attempt to hide her pout. Without the mask in place, the head of the suit pulled back, he could see emotions flashing across her features.

Under other circumstances, he might have enjoyed playing with Nyssa, pushing her to the point where everyone else was able to see the type of person she truly was. But this wasn't a game, but survival and if she continued, she'd go from an annoyance to a liability. If Nyssa and the other survivors didn't accept the reality of the situation, they'd end up dead. Like the Gunnery sergeant. "Lawbook knows what she's doing. It's her actions and the command of her people, which allowed you and the others to escape."

She frowned, her brow creased before she turned to look at him, a gentle smile touching her lips. She ran the tip of her tongue across her bottom lip, leaving a glistening trail in its wake. "You were there, how do we know it wasn't your actions which saved us?" Her voice now a teasing, sexual purr.

"I'd love to take credit for it, but Lawbook ran the operation. No point denying it." A shrug. He didn't have to turn to see her to know what the woman was up to. Thank God for peripheral vision.

"I like to think you had a strong hand in the situation." She reached out and rested one hand on his arm. "I know how skilled you are. You're a smuggler, means you have to think on your feet." She edged closer, but the design of the ground car prevented her from achieving her goal. If she wanted to get to him, she'd have to climb into his lap.

She'd do it if she believed it worth the risk.

"Think what you like, it doesn't make it true." He checked the readings and closed the gap between his car and Lawbook's. "Almost there. Should be able to be out of the cars in ten minutes. If you have any personal items, gather them together, don't want to waste time. I'll give a two-minute warning to seal suits."

The others in the car acknowledged his words, and he didn't look at Nyssa. If she wanted to talk, it was up to her, but he wasn't about to invite her to start a conversation.

This was why he didn't form permanent relationships. They always wanted to change him or saw him as something other than a smuggler. He didn't care what they desired, he wasn't going to change his career, his path, or whatever else she wanted to call it.

Nyssa mumbled, but he didn't catch the words and refused to respond.

Silence settled into the car as the others shifted, rearranging their suits, collecting small items. Nyssa shot him a glance or three, but he didn't respond. There was no need to say anything to the woman as they approached the settlement.

"Two-minute warning." He fixed his suit with one hand as they drew closer to the first of the buildings. If there were security devices out here, they were hidden, but Helen had done a decent job in protecting the mining claim. "Seal and check your suits."

"What a dump," said Nyssa, voice muffled by the suit. She hadn't activated the built-in comm, but he still caught her words. "They can't expect us to stay here. It doesn't make sense. It's ridiculous."

No, he wasn't getting into the middle of this. Nyssa would adapt, or she wouldn't, there was nothing in between.

"Give the car a minute, I'll let you know when it's safe to exit without venting the interior atmosphere." He punched a fast sequence of buttons, listening as the vents pulled the oxygen back into the storage tanks built into the car. "We're clear." He didn't wait for Nyssa to speak, or the others in the car, as he opened his door.

He joined Lawbook, Salla, and Jakob. Walker remained in Lawbook's car, sitting in the front passenger chair, face pale and drawn beneath the suit.

"We leaving Walker behind?" He asked Lawbook.

"No, but I need to make sure we're welcome here before I put any more stress on his body." Lawbook's weary smile spoke volumes. They were all feeling the strain. He'd tried to bury it but knew there would come a time when his exhaustion would catch up with him, and he'd be forced to rest.

Or collapse.

"Makes sense." He glanced back at the ground car. "How's he holding up?"

"He's coping. Amber Dreams is burning through his system, but he hasn't asked for another dose." Lawbook paused in front of the closed airlock and tapped the built-in comm. "Sergeant Bloodlaw here, please respond."

The comm crackled, then Mr. Hunter replied. "Five at a time. Any moreÂ and the airlock won›t cope with it.»

"We have a badly injured man with us."

"Bring him in with the first group. Then the kids, they need to be out of this mess." Mrs. Hunter took over the conversation. "Please, I don't want them left out there."

Stone grinned. A mother figure. He could handle dealing with one of them. They knew what to do with kids, especially frightened ones.

What did he know about kids and how they behaved? Not as

if he had any. No plans on changing it either. Children were other people's problem.

"Understood, I'll send the Jakob and Salla in with my injured Marine."

Wasn't she coming going in first? He frowned but kept the comment to himself.

"Stone, if you'd enter with the first group, I'd appreciate it." She turned away from the entrance, walking back to the car. He followed, wanting to know what she was doing.

"You should be the first one inside."

"Not happening. I'll get the rest in first. I want you in with the first group in case anything goes wrong. I don't hear any unwanted stress in their voices, but doesn't pay to assume all is well until you see it first hand." She stoppedat the passenger door. "You alright with this?"

No, he wasn't. "I'll be fine."

"Yeah, you will. I hear Mrs. Hunter is a decent cook."

Anything was better than the thick paste used as emergency food in the suit. No one liked the damn stuff, but it beat dying of starvation. "Useful to know. Let me help you with Walker."

"Figured that was why you'd decided to follow me." She inclined her head. "Stretcher is in the back." She tapped on the door, alerting Walker to her presence.

The man jerked out of the light sleep he'd fallen into, checked his suit, then opened the door. "Yes, Sergeant?"

"Time to get you inside. Stone's grabbing the stretcher, then we'll get you in with the first group. Remember, you're a Marine. Don't let us down in there."

"Yes, Sergeant." The words strained.

With the injured man on the stretcher, they returned to the airlock, Jakob taking Lawbook's place with the stretcher. A moment later, the airlock opened, letting the first group in. Including Stone.

This is going to be interesting.

Had he dealt with the Hunters before? He couldn't recall. They were a small family, decent sized claim, but out away from the main colony, not by hundreds of klicks, but enough to make the journey to the dome a matter of planning instead of a quick run in and out.

The airlock opened on the other side, allowing the group the chance to enter. The door closed behind them with a hiss of atmosphere as it was vented back into the main structure. A simple enough setup and one he'd come across plenty of times before.

A man, with gray at his temples, and a worried glimmer to his eyes, approached him. "What's wrong with that one?"

"Damaged shoulder, took a blast to it. Honestly, it's a mess in here." Stone explained.

"Hurts," Walker murmured.

"Oh dear, yes, of course, he's going to need help. I don't know if we'll be able to help patch him up, but we can at least make him comfortable." Mrs. Hunter gestured for the tall boy -- no, a man not a child -- to help with the stretcher. "Ian, get him into the family room. We'll need to set up a room for him, depending on how many people are in the group."

Stone relinquished his hold on the stretcher as the noise behind him informed him the second group would be joining them shortly. "Thank you for this, we've been through a lot." How much was he supposed to tell the family? "Sergeant Bloodlaw will be able to fill you in, but she's decided to be in the last group, wants to make certain all her people, civilian and Marine alike, are taken care of."

"Sounds like a decent woman." Mr. Hunter admitted.

"She is, and a damn fine sergeant from what I've seen." Who'd have thought he'd be a cheerleader for the woman? How things changed.

"We'll wait and see."

Calm, but not willing to take things at first glance. Smart. He'd already pegged Mrs. Hunter as a mother figure, which left the two kids. Except the oldest wasn't a kid. In his early twenties, perhaps a little older. The girl was another matter. She didn't look directly at him, or the others, but responded when Salla waved at her.

What had they said? Autistic? Everyone was different, and he'd long since accepted the fact he had to work and make deals with various types. Helen was simply nothing more than a person who handled things in a manner he wasn't used to.

"Thank you for letting us in. We need the break, and I know there's a lot of information the Sergeant will want to share with you." Leave the explanations to Lawbook, he wanted nothing to do with destroying the Hunter's world with a few carefully placed words.

#

Cora watched as the third group entered the airlock, and forced herself not to pace. Whatever was happening, Walker hadn't given the emergency signal, and she'd heard nothing from Stone. Sending the kids in first, was a priority she had no problem with. With a mix of older kids and younger, it didn't take long to get the rest of them through into the main building.

Stress and pain flickered behind her eyes. If she didn't crash soon, she'd have no choice but to use a stim. Her jaw clenched at the idea. Wasn't going to happen, and she could push through no matter what she faced. Cora turned her head enough to sip water from the built-in tube. It helped, not enough to keep her going for hours to come, but she'd stay upright until everyone was safe.

"I should have gone in with Walker," said Nyssa. She glanced at Cora, then away. "I'd have been able to keep him from hurting. I don't know why you wouldn't let me give him more of the Amber. He wouldn't be in this condition if he had a grip on his pain levels."

"No, he was perfectly safe with Stone and the kids." Kids. Hah, she had to stop thinking of them as children. Salla and Jakob had proved their worth, more so than some of the adults in the mix. "I trust them, and they know the Hunter's."

Nyssa grunted but didn't step away. "I would be able to keep his pain under control. You're cruel, do you know that? He doesn't have to suffer."

"Drop it. He's not going to take another drop of Amber Dreams. Any more would cause a problem long term. He's fighting the addiction as it is." Her right hand clenched, and she forced it to relax.

"You don't know what you're talking about."

"I don't? Funny how a woman I don't know appears to understand what I've learned through the years. I'll give you one last piece of advice, and I suggest you take it." She paused long enough to meet and hold Nyssa's gaze. "Don't push me on this. As far as I'm concerned, you're a dealer, and I hate dealers. Got it?"

Nyssa smiled through the mask, her eyes wide and innocent. "A dealer, me? Nothing of the sort. You have me all wrong, Sergeant. The dreams fell into my keeping during this mess, and I kept it in case it could be used. I wouldn't have kept my position before the attack if I was a dealer, surely a military woman like yourself can see the truth when it's in front of her."

I will not kill her. Not yet. "You don't fool me. Remember. I'll be watching you." She regretted the cliched words the moment she uttered them. "You'll go in with me in the last group."

"What for?"

"Don't argue with me."

She huffed and turned away from Cora.

Nyssa didn't say another word until it was time for the last group to enter the airlock. Cora gestured to the other woman to approach the airlock, along with Ready, Lackey, and Virgil. Surrounded by the men who'd fought alongside her, put Nyssa in a position where she'd be an idiot to try anything, but it didn't prevent the woman from assessing each man as if they were a piece of real meat, cooked to perfection.

The door closed behind them, and she waited for the airlock to run its cycle. Her eyes threatened to close on her, and she took another sip of water. She was running out of steam, but a small meal would help. Anything which didn't include her eating the damned paste in the suit. She shuddered at the idea.

The airlock opened, and she stepped out with the others, opening her suit to make it easier to communicate and not eat into the suits reserves.

The taste of the air hit her. Not stale the way the oxygen in her suit became, or the salty taste in the air beneath the colony. But oatmeal, spices, sugar, a hint of something bitter? Caff? Could be, and if there was caff, she'd be able to keep moving for a time.

"Sergeant Bloodlaw?" A man with gray at his temples stepped forward and offered his hand. "Nice to meet you."

She took the hand, exchanging a firm grip. "Thank you for letting my people in here. They've been through a lot."

"Stone was saying, but he's given us no details."

She sighed, of course, he hadn't. Perhaps it was just as well. "I'll be happy to share what I know, but I need to check with Walker, the injured man, first. And if you've got any caff on hand, I'd be grateful. How we're all standing up is beyond me." Stale. Fresh. It didn't matter. Either would work.

"You're dead on your feet. Yes, of course, I'll bring you a mug. Ian, will you escort the Sergeant to her man?"

Her man. She smiled. In other circumstances, she might have taken offense to the words. But Mr. Hunter didn't mean any harm, and she wasn't going to verbally slap him for a figure of speech. "Thank you, it's appreciated."

Ian flashed a grin, his dark hair cut short but ragged. A self-cut? She shook off the idea and followed the young man through to the family room.

"We're setting up a room for him, downstairs, but it might take a bit. Need to figure out who else to put in the room with him."

"Not Nyssa. The blond who came in with me. Anyone else should be good. Stone, myself, Ready, Lackey, Virgil, any of those work. But honestly, as long as she's kept out of the room, it'll be fine."

"Oh, right." Ian glanced in Nyssa's direction, then back to Cora. "Got it."

Walker opened his eyes when Cora sat down next to him. "How you holding up?"

"Okay, I guess. Still want more of the other stuff, but yeah, I know you're not going to allow it. Part of me is grateful, but the rest..."

"It's the drug talking to you, trying to take over." She kept her voice gentle. "It'll pass in the next couple of hours." At least, she hoped it would. With the way Walker reacted, the chills and shakes he fought off, only to be assaulted by them again. "Water might help, but until we can strap your shoulder, get it so you can't move it, I don't want you to have anything in case you throw up."

"Understood, Sergeant." He paled and turned away. "Don't like being helpless."

"No one does, Walker. You'll be back on your feet once we have you patched up. It's not going to be a quick fix unless they're hiding a doctor out here, but we can keep it from getting any worse." As long as he didn't try to strain it. Marines were a stubborn lot at the best of times. "Walker is going to want to get up and fight if the need arises, and he can't. Not with the damage to his shoulder." How much should she tell Ian? She'd have to tell the older Hunters, explain what had happened back at the colony. Not a task she was looking forward to.

"Sergeant, you don't have to sit with me. I know there're things you need to do." His eyes closed as he spoke, a shudder claiming his body. "Need to focus on what's going on. Get the reactions under control." A pain-filled smile claimed his features, stress lines deepening around his eyes, across his brow and at the corners of his mouth. An unhealthy sheen of sweat glistened across his skin, his jaw tight, skin pale.

She refrained from patting his arm or shoulder. Any extra touch would only add to the discomfort he already endured. "I'll check in on you later."

Cora schooled her thoughts into order and turned to face the other members of the family. "There's a lot to tell you," she smiled at Helen as the teen brought her a steaming mug of caff. "But no point in holding off any longer. We've been invaded."

#

Aliens. They'd been invaded by freaking aliens. How the hell had this happened? Ian rubbed his temples and fought to make sense of the situation. Sure, there would be other life forms out there, but an invasion?

He struggled to make sense of the information. He didn't want to believe the words, but what else would it be? Not as if the Marines had a reason to lie. Besides, smugglers and pirates didn't have the manpower to take out a colony, but the attack had come from nowhere.

Now what?

"How do we deal with an unknown force, Sergeant?" asked his dad. "Are they confined to the dome, or have they spread out? Will they be coming for us?"

"I don't have an answer for you. I'll need to check in with the other settlements, see who's still able to reply, and gather information. I wish there were more to it, but we don't have enough people to retake the colony. Not with the skills needed." Lawbook spoke, her voice calm, and she made no attempt to keep her words from carrying to the others. "I'm not dismissing the men and women out here, or saying they don't know how to fight. That said, I've met these creatures, seen what they're capable of, and they beat us on numbers alone. The fact we escaped is a bloody miracle."

Ian tried to pull his thoughts into order. "Why are they here? I mean, if we haven't run into them before, what would bring them to Pluto? Is this their only target? Are they heading for Earth?"

Questions flashed into life fast and furious.

"Honestly, I don't know. We haven't been able to communicate with them." Lawbook explained. "They're like nothing we've ever dealt with before, and I don't know how it's going to work out. I only know this is what we're facing and how much work is ahead of us. The first thing, however, has to be reestablishing communication."

"I can help," Helen spoke up.

Ian grinned before he realized how out of place his reaction might be. "If anyone can get the comms up and running, it's Helen."

"If you can, we'd welcome the assistance, Helen." Lawbook turned to meet Helen's gaze but didn't object when Helen turned away. "I've heard from Salla and Jakob how talented you are." Her tone warm, and welcoming, lacking the condescension many adults showed when talking with his sister.

Helen tugged on their father's arm.

"Go on then, see what you can do."

"Salla and Jakob had an idea about the comms, would it be alright if they explained it to you, Helen?"

Helen shifted her weight, every piece of the confident sister he knew when there was only family around, hidden beneath the layer of uncertainty. He couldn't blame Helen, she'd dealt with more than a few who made fun of her over the years.

Lawbook didn't push for an answer but patiently waited for when Helen felt confident or safe enough to answer. "I know them. They're decent people."

"I'll be there in a few, alright?" Ian grinned, not wanting to be left out of the group. Helen would be happier if he joined them, and he'd get a decent chance to speak with Salla. Had she found a boyfriend in the past few months? She appeared to be pretty cozy with Jakob, but it didn't mean they had a relationship. Besides, Jakob was still in school, and he was a grown man.

He had a chance with Salla.

Hitting on a woman in the middle of an alien invasion. Not cool.

Yeah, but when else was he going to get the chance?

"Good idea, son. We'll need your help down the line. And if Helen can fix the comms, it will be a huge step forward."

"On it," he nodded in his father's direction before he joined the rest of the group. "Salla, what was it like, back in the colony?"

"Hard. They took my dad. Don't know if he's alive or dead." Salla's jaw clenched.

He swore under his breath. "Sorry I didn't know. Figured he was off-planet when this happened." Her father was dead? No, she'd said he'd been taken, not killed. "You think he's alive?"

"Lawbook saw survivors being held as prisoners. Could be they've kept all the survivors they've come across. Not sure what they'd be doing with them, frankly I don't want to think about the possibilities." Salla's voice trembled before she took a deep breath. "He's alive, and I'm going to find him. No matter what anyone thinks, I know he's alive and I won't give up on him."

"Most of us have lost family members in the attack or friends. And those things back there, I've never seen anything like them. We've seen maybe four different types of aliens now. Including a smaller one, looks like a bat."

"Alien space bat," said Salla, picking up where Jakob finished. "Weird thing, but it had claws and fangs. With something dripping from its mouth. Ugly thing. Then there were big ones, with wings. And a giant creature pulling the cages with survivors in them. The bat and the big one didn't have extra weapons but the winged one and another which walked on four limbs, but had six, both had handheld weapons."

His mind raced. Four different types of aliens. How many others would there be? "Damn."

"Yeah, that about sums it up." Salla rubbed one hand through her hair. "But we're not going to give up on our home. Pluto is ours, these things aren't welcome, and we didn't invite them to the party.

Helen nudged Ian. "Need my kit." Her voice barely audible.

"Be right back." He wrapped one arm around Helen in a quick hug. "You know Jakob and Salla, it's all going to be fine."

"I know," she replied, her gaze flicking to the main group and back again before she opened the panel on the comm. "What was the idea, Salla?"

Ian slipped away, knowing the other two wouldn't say anything to deliberately upset his sister. The difference between how she was with close family, and the walls which went up when she was around anyone else, was night and day. She'll be alright. Need to let her sink into the work, and she'll relax, become more like herself.

Or would as long as no one triggered a meltdown.

Interlude Three

Sheila rolled out her shoulders and stepped away from her station, one hand covered her mouth in a vain attempt to stifle a yawn. This many hours on duty was enough to drain the strongest of men, and she was all too ready to call it a night.

"Cavanor?"

"Yes, Admiral?" She turned toward the older man, bringing her body to a vague copy of standing to attention.

"End of shift?"

"Yes, Admiral."

"Understood. I'm afraid to tell you that you'll be taking your break on base. No returning to private quarters. Until we have a handle on the situation, we don't want to risk loose talk reaching the civilian population." The Admiral's voice softened. "I'm sorry, I know you and the others must be looking forward to collapsing in your own bed, but this is a dangerous situation. We need to have a grip on what information is shared and when."

She swallowed the response she wanted to throw at the man. His quarters were decent. With a proper bed, no doubt. But he'd relegated her, and the others, to the barracks. Thin mattresses, scratchy blankets, coarse sheets, all the delights she'd left behind after basic training.

What other choice did she have?

"Understood, Admiral."

"Dismissed."

She turned, sharply, before marching to the exit, her mind racing. What was she supposed to do about her dog? She'd never been in a full lockdown situation before, but there had to be a protocol to allow her to get her home checked, locked up, and Popcorn taken care of. The name still brought a smile to life, damn dog bounced around like corn in the air popper. The name suited the two-year-old, but it didn't stop her from worrying. He was used to her arriving home at a set time, to place freshwater and food in his bowl. She wasn't worried about accidents, the dog door prevented those, but she'd never seen the need for an automatic feeder, or water bowl.

The large dog dish of water had always been enough to see him through, combined with the backup bowl outside. Food, however, was an entirely different situation and now she cursed the lack of forethought.

"Jake?" She called out and hurried toward the now waiting man. "Thanks. Hey, you know about the lockdown, right?"

"Yup, yeah, we get to stay in the barracks." Jake rolled his eyes dramatically. "I had a date arranged, but nothing we can do about it now except deal with the situation and hope they see sense and make a formal announcement in the next couple of hours."

"Not fussed about staying in the barracks," alright, she was, but Popcorn came first. "Is there a way we can let people know our homes need to be checked?"

"Your dog, right?"

"Yes, I don't have an automatic feeder." Heat flushed her cheeks at the admission. A shortcut, one she'd rectify as soon as she could. "If I did, he'd rarely left alone for more than two shifts, if this continues any longer I'm worried what will happen to him."

"Ask the desk, see if either the MP's or the Shields can stop by and pick him up."

"Thanks, good idea." She hurried away. "Catch you in the dining hall."

"I'll be there!"

A simple call. Why hadn't she thought of the idea before? Alright, she wouldn't be able to make the call herself, but the desk sergeant would have the clearance needed to contact the right people. Men or women who could take care of Popcorn and make certain he wanted for nothing.

Except for her human.

Chapter Eight

Aliens. Damned aliens. What was she supposed to do now? If they continued to hunt down survivors, Leigh knew she'd be picked up eventually. *Only if I keep moving in the direction of the other pods.* They're following the downed ones, and circling back to the colony.

Water, food, air, and rest, she needed all three if she was to have a chance of making it to the settlements. There was a chance those mining claims had already been hit. Which put her back at square one.

Mags pressed against her, then turned to pointedly stare in the direction of the pod they'd come from.

She nodded and gestured to begin the journey, her mind racing. She didn't use the same slow, but steady pace which had brought her to the ripples, but kept a brisk half walk, half run. The sooner she was back undercover, the better it would be. If these things had drones, which she'd seen no sign of to date, they'd be scouring the surface of Pluto to find other survivors.

At least they didn't execute the crew.

Mags raced in front of her only to turn and run back to Leigh. He repeated the move twice more.

Yeah, I know, you're worried.

He sat down, head tipped to the left.

Leigh sighed and ruffled his head, missing the contact with his fur. Hide, regroup, figure out what was going on. She closed her eyes, ready to fall asleep where she stood. Her eyes drifted closed. They'd find a place to hold up, grab sleep, and make plans. Staying out here wasn't a viable option.

Mags nudged her, and she wobbled, finding her balance. She stared at the dog. When had he moved again?

He waited until she was watching him, then shoved her to the left. Once. Twice. Three times, until she frowned and stared at him. This wasn't the way to the pod. She stared at him, trying to understand as he nudged her again, pushing at her to move, but not toward the pod.

"Better know what you're doing, dog," she muttered beneath her breath. Her chest ached, lungs burned, but she didn't pause, not wanting to lose track of him. He paused often enough to allow her a chance to catch up, gave her a short break of walking before he picked up the pace again.

Did she have enough air to keep this up long term?

Fatigue lay a trembling path through her legs, and she stumbled before Mags ran back to her and permitted them both ten minutes of slow walking. Never risking a stop, and she understood why. With the way she felt if they stopped altogether, she'd never want to move again. In fact, curling up in a ball and closing her eyes sounded ideal to Leigh.

An hour later, he stopped, stared at her, andvanished around a ripple in the landscape.

She scowled and stalked toward the small ridge, clambering over it, not wanting to waste time by going the long way, and stopped.

Mags had vanished.

No, not happening. She turned, searching for any sign of her dog. Mags. God, Mags, where are you? Panic carried the words through her mind.

A small mental tug, something she'd only experienced once or twice before now, focused her attention on a patch of ice and rock. She edged toward it, bringing up the scanner built into the forearm of the suit. Static.

The tug came again, urging her toward the same patch.

A small glimmer beneath the two inches of ice called to her. She dropped to her knees and brushed the surface ice away. Her scanner blinked into life, rapid communication between her suit and the glimmering control panel before the patch of ice dropped down ten inches and slid to the left, beneath the rock.

There, staring up at her from the entrance hatch with his tail wagging, eyes bright, tongue lolling from the corner of his mouth, was Mags.

#

Jakob settled on a stool as Helen got to work, answering the occasional question but mostly there to hand tools or repeat readings from the screen. How she knew what to do whenever a piece of equipment broke down, was beyond him. He barely understood half of the readings, and he'd lived with the comm system all his life. Yet Helen chatted away, more to the comm than to Jakob, telling it stories, explaining what she needed it to do, and occasionally a mix of nonsensical words he didn't attempt to make sense of.

"If anyone can get the comms to work, it's Helen," Ian explained and clapped one hand on Jakob's shoulder. "I've seen her produce major miracles with equipment I thought was destined for the scrap heap."

"Salla told me about her skills, but it's nothing compared to watching her work," he admitted.

"I can understand. If I hadn't seen her grow into working with machines, I wouldn't believe it myself." Pride echoed through Ian's words.

Helen stuck her head out. "Machines like me. I speak to them, they speak to me, makes it easy to know what's going on, and what will work."

Was it really that simple? "Wish I could talk to machines."

She grinned and stuck out a tongue. "You're too old to learn their language." She vanished back into the comm.

"Did she just insult me?"

"She's teasing. Does it with me all the time. I've been too old to understand machines the way she does since she first began helping Pops with the comms. Then, when she was allowed access to everything else, I realized she was right. She can talk with them in a way I'll never be able to understand." Ian pressed a mug of caff into Jakob's hands. "I don't argue with her and let her take control of whatever the situation is. Faster, saves arguments, and I don't screw things up she'd find an easy fix."

Jakob yawned, then looked at the caff. "I don't think this is going to help me stay awake."

"I'll take it if you don't want it." Salla reached around and grabbed the mug. "You need to get some sleep."

"How are you still awake?" He blinked, weariness ready to pull him into a deep sleep the first chance it had.

"Stims. Took one before we arrived. I figured one of us needed to remain awake."

Stims. He shuddered at the idea. "Nasty things, and taste foul."

"You get used to them." A small shrug. "Dad made me train with them, few years ago. Wanted me to know the safe amount and when to let my body crash. I've only taken the one dose. I'm golden."

Jakob bit back a response. The idea of taking stims sickened him, but he could understand why people in dangerous situations might use them to stay awake.

"You don't use them?"

"Not unless medically ordered. I wasn't trained the way you were." Who would be unless they'd spent a lot of time with Duncan? It wasn't as if many civilians had a reason to use them.

"No, I guess you wouldn't have gone through it." She caught his gaze and smiled.

Jakob flushed, uncertain how to respond. Salla was older than he was by several years, but the past day had allowed him a chance to see her through more than curves and hormones. "I -- erm -- should get a rest."

"I'll crash in a bit, once the stim wears off."

Was he supposed to say anything else?

"Come on, I'll show you to a cot." Ian volunteered. "Helen, I'll be back in a few."

"Uh, huh," said Helen.

He followed Ian through to the stairs, pausing once to glance back at Salla.

"She's one hell of a woman, Salla I mean," said Ian.

"Yeah, I guess she is."

"Is there anything going on between you two I should know about?"

Heat flushed in a rush of flame across his cheeks. "No, she's a friend. We're not, I mean, she's older than me. If she was going to date, I couldn't imagine her wanting to start someone like me." Except in his dreams.

"Ah, yeah, makes sense," replied Ian.

Jakob tried to smother a yawn, but it didn't work. His body ached, muscles weary as he followed Ian to the rooms set aside for them.

"It's not much, but you'll be able to get some rest." Ian opened the door to a small room with three cots, plus a single bed. Two were already in use, and the bed claimed by a woman with a toddler in her arms. "I'll catch up with you later," he pitched his voice low.

Jakob nodded, not wanting to say anything in case it woke the others in the room. He half walked, half stumbled into the room, kicking off his shoes before he crawled on the cot. Another day he might have found it uncomfortable, but now he settled without complaint, welcoming the thin pillow and soft blanket. His eyes closed before he realized it, and if anything happened in the room before he fell asleep, he wasn't aware of it.

#

Stone waited until Lawbook called it a night, only then seeking out a cot, or space on the floor to use. It didn't take long to locate the room Walker had been given, and the other sleeping areas set up made it clear he didn't have to search any longer. He toed off his boots, slipped out of the suit and settled down on the cot.

Been pushing things too long.

They all had, but there hadn't been another choice. Not if they'd wanted to stay alive. Now his body screamed for sleep, a time when he could ignore what was going on around him. A chance to rest, and he wasn't about to force himself into staying awake any longer than necessary.

A small sound drew his attention. He settled on the cot, twisting enough to see who else was in the room.

Lawbook lay on her side, back to the wall, on the cot closest to the sleeping Walker. He grinned but didn't say anything, she needed the sleep. They all did. They'd pushed farther than they should have done but given the circumstances they hadn't had a choice. A few of the civilians might have used stims, but Lawbook hadn't. Small lines of strain marked around the corners of her eyes and mouth. Shadows colored the skin beneath her eyes, lips cracked from the dry air of the suits. She shifted enough to cause the cot to creak, allowing him to see the rifle she cradled close to her body.

Had she put the safety on?

Dumb question, of course, she has.

It didn't stop him from doing a visual check. He craned his neck, finding the right part of the weapon. Safety on and locked. It wouldn't take much to unlock the rifle, and it would be faster than reaching for an unsecured gun stashed beneath the cot, or elsewhere in the room. The lock made more sense with the number of children around the place. Nor was he going to wake her and ask her reasoning behind the guns positioning, or the way she slept.

Safety. The ability to defend her people. Close to Walker if he needed help.

He gave Walker the visual once over. He was gray, washed out, deep purple shadows beneath his eyes showed the strain the Marine was under. His shoulder had been strapped up, and he shuddered at the memory of Walker's screams of pain. It wasn't an experience he wanted to go through himself, and with luck, Walker would be on the mend soon enough.

With a hundred questions rolling through his mind, he relaxed and closed his eyes. A pounding built between his eyes, across his temple and down into his neck. They wouldn't get weeks of quiet, time to gather people and train before the invaders struck out at the mining settlements.

If he couldn't get to his ship, he was stuck here, unable to do anything if the aliens found them. But, if he could get to his ship, there was no guarantee he'd survivor breaking free from Pluto's orbit. They had vessels out there, had to, or the Navy ships would have sent help. They were, until the UTG got off their collective asses, on their own.

Chapter Nine

Leigh climbed down into the tunnel, watching as the hatch closed over her head. She'd never have found the place if it hadn't been for Mags. She jumped the last two steps, landing close enough to the patience dog to be rewarded with an enthusiastic wag of his tail.

"Good find, Mags. Don't know what I'd do without you." She allowed herself the luxury of speaking directly to her companion. Down here, there should be less of a chance for the invaders to pick up her communication. It didn't reduce her concerns about their supplies. One problem at a time, and better to deal with it when the aliens weren't searching for her.

A detail which would change if they discovered her escape pod.

A low woof reached back through the comm.

There'd been details in the notes about. A mention of tunnels beneath the surface of Pluto, but she hadn't taken much notice in the briefing. Why would she have needed to know about the tunnels when she'd only be in the colony during her downtime, or for a rare training session with the colony security.

Mags leaned against her leg, the weight a comfort. Leigh activated on the flashlights on her suit and peered into the darkness. The tunnel was large enough to accommodate a ground car, or four, maybe five people walking side by side without being squashed. She reached out to brush her glove covered fingers over the side of the tunnel. Rough in places, but mostly smooth. Man-made, but there would be the occasional cavern or tunnel which had been a natural part of the planet's make-up.

"Alright, now where?"

Mags sat down and rolled his eyes before he pawed her leg.

"I don't know how far these go. If I wander off in the wrong direction, we could both end up dead. Not my idea of a fun time, what about you?" She activated her datapad. "Might as well try to get a basic idea of where we are."

Woof.

"Yeah, alright, maybe I should have done it first, is that what you're telling me."

Woof.

A tail thumped against the ground, more seen than heard or felt. "Give me a break here, I'm exhausted, we both are." She bit back a yawn. If she didn't find a place to rest soon, she'd be ready to fall asleep in the first possible location which offered a hint of welcome for a weary soul.

Mags turned and started down the tunnel at a casual pace, tail still wagging.

"Fine, don't give me time to figure things out then." She grumbled but followed her companion. Who was supposed to be the one in charge here? Obviously not her as far as Mags was concerned. "Hope you know what you're doing."

Mags didn't stop, didn't turn toward her, didn't even offer a cocky bark.

She glanced at the datapad and frowned. Lifeforms? No, why would there be anyone down here? Her frown deepened, heart rate increased as she tried to make sense of the readings. She hadn't risked using the scanner to check out the aliens; if there were a difference between alien lifeform readings and human, she wouldn't know until it was either too late, or she had the chance to scan the invaders from a safe distance.

Twenty minutes of walking drew her closer to the life signs, and she slowed down. What if the readings weren't human? It wasn't as if she could check without reaching the origin of the readings. She blinked, vision blurring for a moment. She rested one hand against the interior of the tunnel, giving her body a moment to reset itself.

Weariness? Reduced oxygen? Either or both could be the cause. They offered the same danger of collapsing and being lost to the darkness.

A concerned bark filtered through the comm.

"I'm tired. Give me a bit, alright?" Her legs wobbled. A stim shot would help, but the crash from the stim would be worse than how she now felt. And if she were on her own, and went into stim shock, she'd be hosed.

Mags shoved his head under her free hand.

"Thanks. Damn, first time away from Earth and I end up worn out, crash landing on Pluto, see aliens, and now have exhaustion shakes trying to get me to sit down. Not my idea of fun." She ruffled his head. "Be glad to feel your fur again, boy. These suits are ideal for keeping us alive, but patting you through the suit isn't the same as giving you real attention."

He woofed through the comm, the sound welcoming, but it wasn't going to wake her back up.

"Best get moving, right?"

Mags stepped away, ready to continue leading her through the tunnels. "Figure if they're aliens, I'll be captured and at least be able to rest. Win-win either way? Alright, not so much if we're prisoners." She rambled as they continued to walk.

The life signs increased as they made their way through the passageways, and her ability to make sense as she talked to Mags, ceased to exist. She gave up trying to talk, the conversation more for her benefit than Mags.

She checked the datapad. They were close. Did they know she was down here? If they had working comms, they'd use a private channel, unless they hadn't thought this through, to keep the aliens from finding them. Or at least reduce the chances of being overheard.

Her heart raced as she watched the screen.

Mags glanced up at her, gave her the biggest canine grin she had ever seen, and disappeared around the corner.

She reached for him, but it was too late. Mags was out of reach. Cursing under her breath, she hurried after him, uncertain what she would find. But no matter what she wasn't going to leave Mags to face whoever was there, on his own. One hand on her sidearm, the only weapon she had with her, she rounded the corner, almost barreling into the waiting dog.

Leigh took a step back, her gaze taking in the group standing in front of her.

Men. Women. Weapons. Suits.

Her mind logged the four points before she forced it to slow down. Two of the men held rifles, now pressed against their shoulders, aiming in her general direction.

"What the fuck is a dog doing down here in a military suit?" One man demanded through the comm. "Better have an answer for me real fast before I decide to find out for myself."

Her mouth dried, throat threatening to close. She swallowed, twice, trying to force her voice to work. "Marine. We're both attached to the Marines--"

"Like hell, I would have known if a dog handler was part of the team. Not a single damn dog on this planet. Start talking." He took a step toward her.

Military. Her eyes narrowed on the uniform beneath his suit. "Came in via transport five days ago, but hadn't made it down from orbit. Was up on December Rain, then we bailed when the ship was attacked. I don't know how many others made it, but I found three other pods, and saw -- god, this is going to sound insane, but I saw aliens taking a few of the crew prisoner."

Would they believe her?

"We know about the aliens." The Marine, she recognized the uniform now her brain was no longer in full panic mode. "Dog handler, huh? Couldn't have picked the worst time to arrive on Pluto." He lowered the rifle. "Jackson."

"Winter," replied Leigh. "And I didn't pick the station, this is my first rotation out from Earth."

"First off-world assignment. Shit, you got hosed." Jackson shook his head, then gestured to the rest of the group. "Civilians.

The Gunny sent me with them."

"Gunny?" Someone with enough sense to know what was going on. "Are you meeting up with him?"

"Not that I know of. Messages came down from Lawbook about the alien invasion. Not safe up there. We ran into one group of the damn things. Small, but there are others which are a lot bigger, picked them up on scanners. The ones we ran into looked like bats. Alien space bats, if you can believe it." He chuckled and shook his head.

"Jones," one of the men offered a hand.

She took the offered hand, her gaze flicking over the rest of the survivors. "How bad is it back there?"

"The whole colony has been taken. Couldn't tell you where Lawbook and the others are, only they were heading out, getting free of the colony. Not something they'd do unless there were any other choices." Jackson explained.

What had she got herself into? "And you're heading to a safe place?"

"That's the idea." Jackson nodded back at the group. "Might as well come with us. Unless you had other plans."

She took a deep breath, giving her a chance to think. Whatever she did, she would still have to deal with the exhaustion plaguing her system. "Better if I stick with you, I think. Not as if I know what's going on here beyond seeing those things moving around out there. Just, fair warning, I'm on my last legs here. Been on the move, but for about two hours, since the pod landed. Running low on oxygen."

"We're all in the same boat with lack of sleep. A few cat naps here and there, but running on empty. But, if I'm right, we won't be doing much more walking. Ground cars are waiting for us, about two klicks away, once we find them we can rest before we head out again." He glanced at her suit. "We've plenty of oxygen supplies, and can top you up if needed."

Ground cars. No more walking. Her body screamed in need for

a rest, but she could stay upright for two more klicks. "Sounds like a plan. I'll try not to fall over on you, but no promises."

"We'll catch you if it happens."

Despite the way Jackson had met her with the business end of a rifle, she had no reason to doubt her fellow Marine. "I'll hold you to it."

#

Ian pressed another cup of caff into Helen's hands. "Anything else you need?"

"You out of the way," she smiled but took the cup. "I think I'm almost done." She glanced around Ian. "Salla has grown up."

"It happens, squirt," he said. Helen's way of jumping from one subject to another no longer caught him off guard the way it once had. "One day, you'll be all grown up, and I'll have to vet your boyfriends."

Helen rolled her eyes. "Boyfriend? Yuck. Not going to happen. What would I do with a boyfriend? kissy face?" She shuddered and took a sip of the caff. "All smushed up against each other like you want to be with Salla."

"One day, you might enjoy the kissy-face situation." He reached out to ruffle her hair.

"Not a kid. Stop it." She ducked out of his reach.

"Sorry, guess I'm going to have to adapt to you getting older." Thirteen wasn't old, but she was growing faster than he'd given her credit for.

"No problem. One year, then the next, we all grow older." She peered into the mug, nose wrinkled. "No honey."

"Too many people about. Didn't want them to see where Mom stores it."

"Oh," she set the cup aside. "You like Salla, don't you? I mean, really like her. More than kissy face."

Ian didn't glance back into the family room. "Not the best place to talk about this. And you're supposed to be working."

"Yeah yeah, you want to kiss Salla." She screwed up her face, pursed her lips, and made kissing sounds. "And lots more. All the naked stuff."

"Helen..." he warned.

"Salla and Ian sitting in a tree -- we don't have trees out here, only in the dome. Would you sit on something else with her?" Her eyes narrowed. "I don't understand why they say sitting in a tree."

"Because there are trees on Earth."

"But we're on Pluto."

"And the rhyme comes from Earth."

"Oh, then it's old." Her eyes lit up, one finger tapping the cup. "Old. Mode. Code..." the last word drifted off.

It didn't often happen, but when Helen started stringing words together like this, it usually meant she'd fallen deep into her work. With her eyes half-closed, the tapping continuing until she set the cup aside, and dived back to her work, muttering to herself.

"Helen won't give up until she has everything working, son." His mother made her way out from the kitchen, her gaze sliding to the main body of the family room. "And these people need an answer, a glimmer of hope. We all do if even half of what they told us is true."

"I don't think they'd be out here if they didn't believe what they told us. Lawbook doesn't strike me as the type to lie, but Stone, he's another matter." Sure, with his trench coat and shaggy hair, Stone had the appeal of a rogue. As a straight guy, he wanted to crawl around in the man's mind, dig out all the exciting stories and save them up for when he was lying in bed, staring at the ceiling.

Not as if he'd tell me half the things he's done if I did ask him.

No, a man like Stone kept his secrets buried. Along with a body or two, no doubt.

"Keep away from Stone," said his mother. "You can't trust him, not unless he's taking orders from the Sergeant."

"Already figured that one out, mom."

"And I'm never going to stop worrying about you, just remember my words. Won't matter if you're forty, or four hundred, I'll still be checking in on you." She leaned in and pressed a kiss against his cheek before he could protest.

"Mom," he rubbed away the kiss.

"There will come a time when you miss my kisses, so let me steal them when I can," she pressed one hand over his cheek, capturing his attempt to clean away her kiss. "If we are facing aliens out there, then we don't know what's going to happen next. I could lose you, your sister, even your dad without knowing it until it was too late." Tears glistened in her eyes. "I'm frightened, yes I know a parent isn't supposed to tell their kids they're afraid, but there you have it."

He nodded, not sure what to say.

"Keep your sister safe. If anything happens to us, get her out of here, hide, I don't care for how long, but you don't let them get her."

Worry crept to the front of his thoughts. "Mom, you're serious, aren't you?"

She gave the half-hidden Helen a pointed glare before she met his gaze. "Deadly."

"It's working," Helen wriggled out from the guts of the comm. "Going to run a test." She hopped up on the stool and pressed their old-fashioned headpiece against one ear.

"I swear, there's nothing that girl couldn't fix if she had a mind to tinker with it." His mother shook her head, a look of wonderment across her face.

How long they stood there, watching Helen, he didn't know. He didn't need to. For now, his family remained safe, and Helen was at peace working with the machines which understood her far better than humans ever could. They didn't judge her odd moments, or lose patience with her, no more than she did with them.

"Not good, really not good," Helen muttered as she reached

out and adjusted the set before reaching for a pencil and scrap paper. Her hand moved, uncertain at first, as she scribbled her notes. "Bad. Very bad."

"Helen?"

"Need the Sergeant. She'll know what to do. Need her here, now."

#

"Sergeant?" A gentle hand touched her shoulder, the voice one she recognized but her sleep claimed mind refused to release the details. "Sergeant?" A pressure on her shoulder, enough to make her crack her eyes open.

"What?" Her mouth worked reluctantly, filled with cotton wool, sticking when she tried to form more than a single word, the tissue gummy. She closed her mouth and rolled her tongue around. It helped, a little, but there would be improvement once she grabbed a drink.

"You're needed up at the comm. Helen's got it working again, but something is going on."

Ian. The oldest kid. No, not a kid. An adult. She blinked, trying to force her eyes to work as she gave into automatic pilot and sat up. Her body protested, wanting to be back in the bundle of warmth and safety she had given herself to. How long had she been asleep? She rubbed one hand over her eyes, sleep parting beneath her touch as she wriggled her toes. "Minute."

"Understood," he patted her shoulder and stood, taking up space along the wall. "Hard to come too when you've been in a deep sleep. There's fresh caff waiting for you upstairs."

Did he have to talk when she was trying to get her mind out from the welcoming darkness she had given herself to? A yawn split her lips as she tried to cover her mouth. "How long?"

"Four hours."

She groaned, enough to get into a deep sleep, not enough to completely recharge her body. "Damn." A steady drumbeat behind her eyes, and she fought the pull to close her eyes and return to sleep.

"I'm sorry. I wouldn't have woken you unless there'd been another way, but Helen insists you hear this."

"Uh-huh," she shoved her feet into the boots, relieved she'd collapsed still dressed but her for her boots. Helen. She struggled to put the data into a usable form before she finally remembered who Ian was talking about. "I'll be out of it for a bit, need to wake up." Water, she had to wash her face, try to get her mind wrapped around whatever the teen wanted to show her. "Comm?"

"Working, but she picked up a broadcast, and she wants to share the information with you," said Ian, his voice gentle.

She glanced back over her shoulder. Stone was on a cot, awake, and moving slowly. Walker slept, deeply, for the first time since he'd been injured. If nothing else the Marine would have a chance to recover before they tried to find a way of repairing his shoulder.

Stone lifted a hand and pointed at the door.

Yawning she rose, grabbed her rifle, and stumbled toward the door. How she prevented herself from falling before she left the room, was beyond her ability to comprehend. Cora struggled to push the fog out of her mind, but her thoughts remained clogged with the remnants of sleep. She rubbed one hand over her face, then back through her cropped hair.

Gunny would have my head for not waking up quickly.

True, but the man would have also been there to answer the summons from Helen.

Helen waited at the top of the stairs, shifting her weight from one foot to the other, hair loose about her shoulders, eyes bright. She darted away the moment she realized Cora was up and moving.

"She's excited."

"Yes, but wouldn't fill us in until you were with us. Never seen her like this before," said Ian.

"Important then." At least she was managing two words now.

Not ideal, but it was an improvement. She grabbed the railings and hauled herself up the single flight of stairs, aware Stone was moving behind her. Had he managed any sleep? He hadn't been in the room when she'd collapsed into her much-needed semi-coma.

Helen peeked around the corner when Helen was half-way up the steps and vanished again.

Whatever had gotten into the young woman, it wasn't going to vanish anytime soon. The last few steps were the hardest as her body pleaded with her to return to the cot and surrender to sleep. Her legs heavy, eyes lidded, but she kept going and made it into the family room.

"News," Helen announced. "Big news. Bad and good." The teen sat on the stool in front of the comm, all but vibrating as she spoke. "Heard them. The aliens. Don't understand them, but there are others in the background. People. Human voices and words." The words short and choppy.

Cora blinked, trying to make sense of the words. She closed her eyes and tried to push away the last of the fog before she dared to speak. "You picked up transmissions?"

"Yes, broke through the block." She gave a rapid nod. "Easy once Jakob and Salla told me the idea. Explained everything. Took time to find the right channels, but once I did, it was easy." She glanced back over her shoulder and flashed a grin. "I don't think they believe we're very intelligent." The more Helen talked, the less her differences stood out until Cora couldn't hear the hesitations which had been there before. "Silly really, they underestimated us."

"What did you pick up?"

"Sit, sit. I'll play it back."

"Sounds like a plan." Stone's voice rumbled from behind her.

Cora forced herself not to tense. "Hopefully we can use whatever she's found." She settled down, still fighting the need to collapse in the nest of blankets. Grit clouded her eyes, and she blinked repeatedly to force the unwanted scratchy invaders away.

"If we can't, there's still enough of an improvement to make a difference for our survival." Stone pulled up a chair. "Don't think she'd want us woken up if it wasn't for a damn good reason."

She rolled out her shoulders and waited, letting her body relax but not to the point where she'd fall asleep on the chair. She blinked, rubbed her eyes again, and tried to focus.

Helen waited until they were all ready, then hit a button to trigger the playback.

Clicks, hisses, a gabble of unfamiliar noises carried through the air. Different tones. Accents? Suggested more than one speaker. She didn't know enough about languages to do more than make random guesses.

"Where's my daughter?" A cry, female, and human broke through the other sounds.

The first alien speaker responded, its vocalization harsh. Angry?

"I don't understand. Please, I need my daughter back. Why did you take her?" The same human. Desperate for her child. Other voices rose with the first. Human as hers had been.

Prisoners.

The aliens chided the humans. A crack of skin against skin, a woman's cry of pain, then a new voice.

"Please show respect to the honored ones. Your children have been chosen for service, be thankful, they will be raised above you, taught their place in the universe." Male, human, but not a colonist?

The aliens spoke again. Sharp tones, instructions, or orders.

"Yes, honored ones, I will endeavor to teach the new servants their place in life."

Slaves. They were taking slaves. Cora kept silent as she continued to listen. It wasn't much longer, another three minutes, but it was enough to confirm there were at least two humans in the group who understood the speech of the aliens and were in their service.

"Fuck," Stone sighed. "Not the best of news."

"They're taking the kids."

"For indoctrination," confirmed Stone. "Makes sense. Kids are easier to wipe clean without resorting to dangerous methods. The two traitors might have been kids like these, but no idea where they came across humans."

Where they traitors if this is all they'd ever known? She shook off the idea. Not her place to decide. "We can't help them if we don't know where the children are being kept." The knowledge twisted in her guts. Kids. Helpless. Torn away from their families, and for what? To have their world destroyed around them as they were broken down and trained to be willing servants ready to serve their captors.

"I know where they're taking the children," offered Helen. "At least, I think I do, another couple of transmissions and I'll be able to triangulate their exact position. It's in the dome, close to the military complex. I can dig deeper when I pick up another message."

"You figured that much out already?" Cora lifted her head, gaze fixed on Helen.

"Yes, was easy. Well, for me." A small acknowledgment, she was different. "Going to need lots of people, but I can contact the other settlers now. Will make it easier if we get more people."

"More people for what?" asked Stone.

"Kids. Need to get them," said Helen as she worked at the Comm.

"How many more?"

Helen closed her eyes, though they continued to move beneath closed lids.

"It's easier for her to track everything if she shuts the rest of us out," explained Ian, his voice barely audible.

"How did she manage to get past the blocks?" If Helen could bring enough people in from the other mining settlements, they had a chance. A slim one, but it was enough to build on.

"Took what Jakob and Salla told her, and extrapolated from there. She didn't need more than the opening comment before she was onto an idea, and now we have this," said Ian. "It's how she's always been, and she gets better with this each passing year." Pride filtered through his words.

"Fifty, maybe more," Helen declared.

Fifty more men and women who knew how to use a weapon. "We don't have fifty, we've got what we have here, and the majority are underage, like Jakob." Would she trust either Jakob or Salla to follow her orders, hell yes. The but didn't come from their age but from their lack of experience. It could cause them to hesitate at the wrong time.

Happens with fully trained Marines.

"We'll have more soon. I'm going to contact the other settlements, see how many are willing to help. Most will. They like me." She grinned and turned her attention back to the comm. "They won't like the aliens."

"Alright," she began. "If I'm going to make sense of all of this, I'm going to need at least another hour's sleep." She could manage on the four hours but would be crashing at the wrong point. If she could get an hour, maybe two, before she was forced to sit down and make a plan, she'd be able to think things through.

"No stim?"

"Don't want to drop at the wrong time," she said.

Stone inclined his head. "Same policy. Rarely use them."

Many did, especially in stressful situations, but this was different. She was the nearest thing any of them had to an officer. Except she knew how things worked. Either way, stim use would send the wrong message unless she grabbed it in the middle of a dangerous situation, aware it was the only means of getting her through a tension moment, or ten. "Don't want to ever be reliant on the blasted things."

He grunted, which was the only reply either of them needed as they made their way back to the cots. Her mind raced, throwing up ideas, suggestions, and problems, but she shoved them to the back of her mind. If she didn't sleep, didn't get enough rest to cope, she'd be more likely to make a mistake. This wasn't a situation where her adrenaline now raced through her body, giving her the extra kick needed to handle whatever was thrown their way, but then you eventually crashed, curled in a ball and either passed out or let the shakes take control of your body.

"We'll figure out a plan. Can't leave those kids. Not with what will happen to them."

Kids, they're taking our children for slaves.

No matter the odds, it was a situation she couldn't ignore.

#

Kids. Taken by the aliens to be trained, broken from old habits and returned as servants for the invaders. It was better than death, but he didn't like it. No matter what he'd done in the past, or would do so again in the future, he'd never agreed with kids being pulled into adult matters. And slavers? The lowest of the low.

Stone rolled on his back and stared at the ceiling.

Trafficking in misery, like dealing in drugs, was one of those things on his no way in hell, list. The few he'd met who kidnapped and sold people, often for a private harem, or underground brothel, disgusted him. Anyone who dealt in the trade needed to die. Slowly. Strangled by the chains, they kept on their trade goods.

The aliens obviously had different beliefs.

He moved to his side, closing his eyes as he tried to rest. Lawbook wouldn't be alone in this. Sure, he still wanted to get the hell out of Dodge, and would the first chance he got but didn't mean he'd sit back and watch a bunch of kids be turned into slaves, locked in service to their captors for the rest of their lives.

And what happened to the parents?

He forced himself to calm, visualizing a blank wall as he counted each breath in and out for ten. His muscles relaxed, the tension easing from his body. Sleep was the answer, then he'd face the harder questions with Lawbook when they were both with it enough to make sense of everything happening around them.

#

Cries filtered into his dreams. Human. Men, women, and children, screaming for their families. He groaned, rolling into a fetal position, shivering as the images refused to release him from their grip. Slaves. They were slaves. The children taken to be trained. The adults kept away from their kids.

Cruel.

Dangerous.

They're aliens. What do I expect?

Zac whimpered and tore himself free of the dream. Cold sweat coated his body, leaving him chilled to the core. This wasn't a dream. The noise, muffled but real, reached out to him from beyond the cell.

How many had been taken as prisoners, and now woke to find themselves wearing collars?

Too many.

And there was nothing he could do about it.

Interlude Four

Treizaek glanced up from the built-in station as data continued to scroll. Nothing from the planet to ease his concerns, though he was aware his mate had been planetside for several units. His jaw clenched, a tension rippling through his wings. She would not be allowed to let him down. He would not tolerate it. She'd been granted chances few others had access to, and now the mother of his potential children faced the hardest of tests.

A female walked past him, moving from one station to the next, her wings a delicate shade of blue. Not a warrior, not from the way she ducked her head rather than boldly meet his gaze. A shy glance his way indicated her interest, but she took it no further. As one of lower standing, she could express her interest but nothing more, any move would be his and his alone to make.

His body responded to the elegant line of her wings; the sensual colors of her scales, the subtle twitch of her wings as she walked past. The small parting of them offering him a glimpse of her back. Something a male was seldom shown unless they were behind the female in a flight, or more likely, with the barely seen movement this female had displayed, an invitation to explore her back, to cover her and mate.

He wasn't dead, the idea of meeting with the female when they had finished their duty, appealed to him. But for now, he had a mate, a strong warrior female at his side, and she would either return with her mistakes washed away or would die in the line of duty. Either worked for him.

"Our forces have met with a small pocket of resistance within the colony, but they were subdued and collected." The comms operator announced. "The first of the young will be transported once the holding ships have arrived."

"ETA for the Holding ships?"

"Seventy-Nine units."

"Keep me informed if there are any changes." He rose, casting

one last look around the bridge. "Second, you have command."
Food, rest, then he would be ready to deal with the arrival of the
ships destined to collect the first of the human young. They would
be loud, weeping for their families as they were collected and
trained. Not all would survive, but young flesh was a treat he and
others would enjoy.

Humans. They didn't go to waste, no matter if they failed
or succeeded in their training. Their bodies were processed into
various materials, those who had the tenderest flesh were fed up,
cleansed of the toxins which might taint their bodies before they
were slaughtered and hung where required.

His stomach rumbled. Yes, a meal of tender young flesh would
be suitable for a celebration when the time came. Newborns were
the best, fresh from birth. Still warm.

Living.

He shuddered in delight at the memory.

Soon.

It would be his again, with a mate at his side, and the plan to
raise his own young with the female he found to be worthy.

Chapter Ten

"Rest break," said Jones.

Leigh groaned, and half sat, half dropped on the floor, and leaned against the wall. Her legs ached, head pounded, the need to close her eyes and sleep for days, continued to throb through her weary body. Mags settled down near her, and rested his head on her leg, tempting her to reach out and stroke his head. But she hurt too much to move and closed her eyes. At least she no longer feared running short on oxygen, thanks to the extra cylinders the survivors had brought with them.

"We need more than a few minutes," said Jackson. "It's going to be a push, but we've got this. Won't let you drop."

"Yeah, I know. Shit, I thought we'd be there by now." How long had it been since she'd had a real sleep? Before the ships were attacked? Since then, she'd been running on fear, determination, and adrenaline since waking in the pod.

"We took a wrong turn. It's easy enough to get lost down here, but we're on the right path now. Should be able to get to the ground cars before much longer, but none of us are in the state where we could drive the damn things without causing an accident. Wouldn't kill us to have an hour here."

"Two," Leigh mumbled the word. "Three would be better. If I'm exhausted, I can't imagine how the civilians are holding up."

"They caught a rest break in the safe room before we had to leave," said Jones. "I know, we're all tired. But we won't be safe here."

"Safer here than up there," she gestured up. "I don't want to think about what it's like under the dome."

"I've had to. The sergeant was up there, I think they all got out, but not something I want to think about until we have no other choice." He reached out and touched Mags. "Thirty minutes rest, and we make the final push to the ground cars, it won't be too bad. We can rest in the cars, where we're out of sight, can open the suits, and sleep in the chairs." Jones continued.

A chair, not a solid piece of ground under her nearly numb backside. Alright, she could live with the idea. Getting there was another matter. I can do it. How she'd made it through training, now she had a chance to look back on the situation, was beyond Leigh. But she had, and it was the only reason she hadn't collapsed several hours ago. She wanted to rub her thighs and calves, to feel anything other than the deep-rooted ache which had infested her limbs, but it would only draw attention to her current weakened state.

One of the men in the group, a civilian with a scowl carved across his features, stared at her. He hadn't stopped since she'd joined the group. Yet he'd not spoken with her, nor had anyone introduced him. Either way, her skin crawled any time he glanced her way.

"You holding up?" Jackson settled down next to her, his voice pitched low as he offered one glove covered hand to the waiting dog.

Mags nudged the offered hand, then returned to rest his head on Leigh's leg. "Worn out, but I guess we're already to collapse," she shrugged and leaned against the wall. "Not like we're trained for this stuff."

"You really are just out of training, aren't you?" asked Jackson.

"Yeah, and I know it shows. I don't know how the rest of you have managed this long, but I'm ready to curl into a ball for the next three days and spend two in a hot shower."

"Good luck with that."

Rest, she needed it, but would it help?

"Close your eyes, you're safe. And yes, I know Steven is watching you, but you'll be fine. Marines stick together."

"Oorah," she murmured as she allowed her eyes to close.

Jackson wouldn't let her down. He wasn't the type of man to say one thing and do another.

"Count backward, it can help."

She smiled. "Thanks, worth a try."

She let her body relax as she started at one hundred and began the slow count backward. Even if all this gave her was fifteen minutes of sleep, she'd take it, hope it recharged her enough to get on her feet, then handle whatever the universe threw their way.

#

Stone yawned and fought the need to get up, check on everyone around him. The low background noise informed him both Walker and Lawbook were still in the room. Either asleep or resting, it didn't matter as neither moved more than the slow inhale and exhale of breath and the odd creak of the cot beneath their bodies.

Had there been news from the other settlements?

His mind clawed through the details he'd learned in the last few hours. All the information he'd been exposed to. Helen's ability with technology continued to surprise him, and he doubted she'd taken a rest when he'd sought out his cot. Whatever information had spread beyond the Hunter's place, would wait until he had the desire to get up and find out for himself. It wasn't as if there was anything to do before decisions had been made.

Kids.

He scowled but didn't move out of the bed.

Lawbook wouldn't allow the kids to remain at risk. She'd go after them no matter if she did, or didn't have the manpower to deal with the aliens who were holding the kids. That was the type of woman she was, and he couldn't find fault with her need to get them to safety. He tried not to remember the faces of the children he'd met when they'd found the survivors. He didn't want to see their faces, to look into their eyes and explain why they were safe, and the others from the colony weren't kept from harm.

He sat up and glared in the direction of the door.

He had to get moving, get himself in a better headspace before he faced the rest of the day, night, whatever.

"Giving up?"

It didn't surprise him that he'd been wrong about Lawbook. "Need to get myself moving. Joints are stiff." He rolled his shoulders. "You?"

"Been hard to rest, but I grabbed at least three hours, which puts me in a better position than I was when we returned to the cots." She rose, rifle slung over her shoulder as she did a slow sweep of the room. "Might as well get myself up there, see if there's any news or at least information I can use." She paused by the side of Walker's cot, checking on the man. A curt nod and she headed for the door.

"Be there shortly."

"Expect you will."

Lawbook continued to grate on his nerves, but he wasn't going to tell her. Not this time. She'd seen enough of his behavior to understand they weren't ever going to be friends, and she didn't make an attempt to smooth things over between them. Still, he could admire her strength, follow her for now, and tell her when she was jumping ship with her ideas. The Marine had, with his help, kept them all alive. Not an easy feat with everything going on.

He rolled out of bed and stifled a yawn. He had slept, more would be better, but the idea of laying in the cot and trying to grab another hour or two didn't appeal to him.

"You'll keep an eye on her, won't you?" Walker's voice reached out of the darkness.

"Yes, don't see a point not to." He wandered over to the injured Marine. "Holding up?"

"Yeah, made a fool of myself with Amber Dreams," said Walker. He shifted on the cot, winced, and settled again. "Won't make the same mistake again. Not if I have a choice."

"Maybe, but you've pulled through, and in a place where you have a cot, people watching over you, and they've strapped up your shoulder." He would have reached out to pat the younger man's arm, but with the damage done, he didn't want to add to Walker's discomfort. "Using Amber dreams wasn't your first choice, and I wouldn't stress the situation. You were injured, and you're still in recovery mode."

"I feel better," he shifted his arm and winced. "The strapping helped. Don't get me wrong, I still don't want to move my arm much."

"Wouldn't advise you try. Give yourself time. Your body is still healing. It's going to be a long road to recovery."

"Will be healing for a long time unless they find a doctor with a handheld regen."

Not likely but Walker knew the truth. "Baby steps, we'll do what we can, when we can." He indicated the door. "I'll see if there's anyone else who can sit with you, and check-in with Mrs. Hunter, she might have a few ideas we haven't explored." Mrs. Hunter had been the one behind the strapping, and she'd mentioned a few options she needed to check into.

Leaving Walker on his own opened up other potential problems.

Nyssa.

Wouldn't be long before the woman tried to find her way back to Walker's side. A dealer didn't like to lose their hold on a new customer.

By the time he climbed the stairs, he could hear a conversation in the family room. Mostly calm, with the occasional raised voice. Nothing he needed to be worried about, nor would he be in a position to get into the middle of any discussion. Just as well, he wasn't in the mood to be dragged into a fight.

"Stone, did you get enough sleep?" Virgil asked.

"Enough to cope with. Have a few knots in my back screaming at me, but it's part of the life I live. Getting old before my time."

He shifted his shoulders, refusing to wince at the strain it put on his protesting body.

"Should get that seen to before you put any more strain on it."

"I know, I'm battered and bruised."

"Aren't we all?" Virgil gestured to the rest of the group. "Half the kids are still asleep, which makes it easier, we're running out of space."

"So I see," he gestured to the group. "Hope the Hunter's are coping with the influx of bodies."

"Seem to be. It's obvious they know the news, guessing you heard it as well. The kids?"

"Yeah, I did. I was with Lawbook when Helen filled us in. Shit. Kids. Don't like what's happening to them. What might happen with those who don't pass the training? Or the adults who don't comply." The missing dead and injured now nagged at him. If there were a use for the dead, it wasn't one he wanted to think about in-depth.

Food.

His stomach turned. They didn't know what the aliens ate, or the amount of food they would need in the days or weeks to come. Would they eat humans? He shuddered. There were other options, but it didn't mean he liked the idea, the thoughts of men and women strapped down for scientific research.

"Your ideas are headed in the same direction as mine."

"Yeah, they are. Not sure if we're right, or wrong, but damn, it makes sense when you look back at the situation." Nausea rolled through him, his body unwilling to accept the situation. It didn't matter whose children were caught up in the mess, he couldn't stand back and allow this to happen.

So much for being the cold businessman, only staying around long enough to find a safe way out. Grab my ship and escape. Not now, can't leave the kids to face life with aliens. Or end up on the dining table.

"We might be wrong. Could be the dead were taken for

research, even fuel. I mean, we don't know what they used to power the ships. Same with the injured, it could be they're handed over to scientists." Virgil mused. "Better than our original ideal. I mean, they're aliens, we don't know what they want, why they've come here, or what we've done to piss them off."

"Maybe we didn't do anything at all. As you said, they're aliens. They could have reasons which would make no sense to either of us." Stone continued as he glanced around the room. "We'll get to the bottom of it sooner later. A lot of small details we need before we finally understand what we're dealing with." And what if their original ideas were correct? If the beings who had attacked Pluto had done it with several goals in mind, including slaves and food? He didn't want to think about the fates of those taken by the invaders, not when his mind was all too ready to throw graphic images at him.

"Stone, Virgil," said Lawbook as she made her way over to the two men. "Helen managed to get hold of a few of the other settlements, and they're sending representatives this way."

"Good news then?"

"For the most part. A couple of holdouts and one idiot announced he'd go and check the dome himself before he ever believed there were aliens on Pluto." A wry smile ghosted across her features. "Can't really blame him, wouldn't have believed it myself if I hadn't seen the situation first hand." She smoothed one hand back through her hair, brushing stray strands away from her eyes. "Shit, feel like death warmed over."

"We all do, but at least the sleep helped."

"No arguments there," she inclined her head in Virgil's direction. "How are you holding up?"

"Alive, ready to kick ass and take names, but I'd be happy enough to curl back up on a cot if I had the chance."

"If things work out, we'll be able to all get decent rest in the future. A lot depends on how things work out when the cavalry arrives." She frowned but continued on with her thoughts. "We can't leave the kids in their hands. If we can get them out, then it'll be worth the risk."

Information, they'd need more before they had a chance to organize their attack. "Any idea where the kids are being held?"

"Not good news, Stone."

He winced. "The main colony?"

"Yep, close to the base."

One of the hardest places to enter in the entire colony. Or it had been before the attack. "Wouldn't they have flattened the area?"

"I know I would if I'd been in charge of their attack, but from what Helen's been able to piece together, a few of the hangers are still intact, and there are holding cells -- no other way of describing it -- set up next to the hangers."

Hangers for the adults, or the kids? "Need to get eyes on the situation."

"Which we can't do until we inside the dome again. It's not going to be pretty." She glanced back at Helen, the teenager still at work with the comm, the occasional word filtering through the background noise of the gathering. "Not easy, but it's doable."

"Has to be if we're going to grab the kids." He followed Lawbook's gaze. "And I don't think Helen will accept it if we decide to focus on other plans and leave the kids to their fate."

Virgil hissed through clenched teeth.

"She wouldn't be the only one, Stone. I can't leave the survivors in their hands. If we can only get the kids out, so be it, but if we're going in there, we're coming back with as many survivors as possible."

Chapter Eleven

Cora sat down on the edge of a stool, pulled out her datapad and went through the current round of information. It didn't matter how she looked at the readout, the report continued to convince her she was doing the right thing. No matter what happened, she wouldn't change her plans. The kids couldn't be left in the hands of the aliens, not and allow her the option of sleeping in the near future. They'd haunted her dreams when she'd crashed for a time, now she could hear them, pleading for their parents, for help, for home, and a dozen other things.

"You're pale." Cora glanced up from the pad. Helen stood in front of her, hands behind her back. "Bad dreams?"

"Something like that." Dreams, she hadn't dealt with nightmares in years. Not since joining the Marines. "Any more news?"

"Two more settlements answered, one's sending people in, don't think I can get more to change their mind until we've spoken to the first set." Helen's tone matter of fact. "Think we have enough if they agree to bring people in. But not sure there's a clean tunnel route to the--" a beeping near the comms system cut off Helen's voice as she turned back to see to whatever the alert might be.

Cora watched as Helen returned to her work. Whatever the young woman was up to, Cora had learned enough to know when to trust and when not to. In Helen's case, there wasn't a mean bone in her body. She was intelligent, often wrapped up in her own world, but had learned to deal with, and interact with others when she had to.

"Never seen Helen this content before." Ian came up behind her. "I wouldn't doubt she's enjoying the challenges. She knows the kids are in danger, it has registered with her, but she's focused on what she can do, not what she has no power over."

"A skill we could all use, especially in situations like this." Was it wrong to be jealous, even momentarily, of Helen's ability to shield herself from the ongoing situation? "If she needs any help, let me know. She's working miracles, and I don't want your sister to think we're using her."

"She's in her element," said Ian.

Cora rubbed the back of her neck. "Think I'll grab a mug of caff if there's any going spare."

"Always, there should be a full pitcher on the counter."

"I'm never going to get this done," she murmured.

"Don't put yourself down. You've done more than most would have believed possible, considering the events of the past two days."

Two days? She glanced at the time on her datapad. Not even a full forty-eight hours. Too much had happened in a short period, which left her wondering what would happen the next time she turned around. Or answered a call. "Should still be in the GetAway, enjoying a pint, or two."

"No arguments there. Kinda wonder what happened to Jones and the others." Stone admitted as he reached for two mugs, filling them with caff. "I hope they made it out in one piece."

The single message, the only one they'd risked sending out the other survivors, had been brief but filled with the information needed. "You and me both, but there's no way of knowing unless they make their way out here." Which was a decent possibility. Jones would know which of the nearest settlements would be safe to approach. If they didn't make it to the Hunters, there was a chance there'd be news with one of the groups heading their way.

"Jones is decent people, if anyone can pull them through, it's Jones."

And Jackson was a capable Marine. He had a fondness for knives, using and collecting them, but no Marine she'd met didn't have a quirk or two in the mix. "Yeah, I know. They'll either be here or they won't, either way, it doesn't matter, and we can't do anything to change the outcome." Not and get everything worked out, planned, so they had a chance to--

"Here." Helen popped up from her work. "They're here. First group."

Cora swallowed her caff, shuddered and blinked the last of the sleep away. "Thanks, Helen."

"Good. Bad. Curious." Helen tipped her head, eyes narrowed. "It'll work out. We'll find a means of helping the trapped ones."

Trapped ones. The term fit, and she wasn't about to argue with Helen. "Yes, we will." Not a feat they could have done without Helen's assistance. "Alright, where are we meeting them?" Wouldn't make sense to bring them all into the house, not with the number of people already here.

"Figured it would be best to hold any meetings in the main storage, there's plenty of room in there. Most of our equipment is out, being used in the field, stored closer to where we need to use them." Mr. Hunter explained as he walked over. "The space in storage is clean, for the most part, and those who come asking questions aren't expecting anything fancy. I've sent out messages to head straight to the storage. The airlock is set up to allow people entry, two or three at a time. Smaller lock than for the house."

"Better get my ass over there."

Hunter nodded his mouth set in a grim line.

"We'll be with you," said Stone as he clapped one hand on her shoulder.

"Thanks." She reached back and touched his hand. What was she doing? The man was dangerous. And all she did was acknowledge the support. Stop double-checking everything you do, Lawbook. Easy enough to say, harder to get her mind to wrap around the idea. "Time to get this done."

#

"Ground cars ahead," Jones announced.

Leigh lifted her head, letting her gaze take in the wished-for transport. Ground cars, she wasn't seeing things; they existed. Her legs screamed in either pain or relief, either way, she didn't care. There wouldn't be anymore walking. At least for a time. Which meant she'd be able to rest. They all would, then what? Find out where they were supposed to go, if they had a safe location to travel to, if the Navy had shown up to help them out, or more Marines had arrived to save the day.

It's what Marines did. Or so the recruitment officer had told her. And if I had that blasted woman in front of me now, I'd shove all her lies down her throat and rip out her heart. The idea appealed to her, despite the fact she didn't know if she'd ever see the recruiter again. All safe in her sweet little office. Ug.

"You holding up?" Jackson paused at her side.

"Will be once I can sit down again," she said, not ashamed to admit it to her fellow Marine.

Jackson nodded and headed toward the cars. "Give me time to run checks, see if they're safe."

"Why wouldn't they be?" A civilian demanded.

"Steven, if I were the enemy, and I knew about these cars, I'd have used them to trap myself a couple of fat juicy humans to serve up for dinner." Jackson smacked his lips. "Long pig, nothing like it."

"Long pig?" Steven shoved his way through the group until he stood next to Leigh and Mags. "What's he talking about?"

"Human flesh," she explained.

Steven shuddered, a sickening gray-green flushing around his eyes. "Do you people do that?" He turned to meet her gaze, eyes widening. "Oh, you're -- well, I wouldn't have thought a woman like you would ever be a Marine."

Mags pressed against her leg, a low vibration playing through his body. "Not sure what you mean."

"You're attractive, not a butch female like the Sergeant. Not that you met her, she parted ways with us a while back." A small shrug, but he didn't turn away from her. "Left us to fend for ourselves."

Leigh's skin crawled. "No two women are the same."

"I can see your point," he stepped back, giving her a once over. "You'd look attractive in the right dress."

Her cheeks burned. "Thanks. I think."

"No, thank you. It's a relief to have decent company around for a time." He grinned, teeth flashing. "Instead of Jones' leftovers."

Shark. That's what he is. She forced herself to turn away from the man and followed Jackson into the cavern. The more distance she put between herself and Steven, the better it would be.

He followed her. "What are you up to?"

"Helping Jackson. It's what Marines do. Besides, Mags will be able to tell if the cars have been tampered with." Not a lie. Mags ability to tell when something was wrong had already saved her life on this trip.

"He's a dog."

"Yes, he is."

"Don't get me wrong, dogs can be cute, but you're telling me he's--"

"He's trained to detect problems," she said. It wasn't as simple as she made it out to the man, but she had no desire to spend any more time with Steven. "I have to work. I don't want to step into a car and have it blow up beneath me." She picked up her pace, leaving Steven behind. Damn man is creepy.

Mags uttered a soft woof.

"Need help?" She didn't touch the side of the cars as she watched Jackson perform routine checks of each of the vehicles.

"You up to this?"

"I'm a Marine." The words left her mouth before she had a chance to think. "Mags is also trained to check. He can activate a small filter to allow the scents to enter his suit without losing his oxygen supply. It's not as accurate as when he's out of a suit and allowed to feel his way around." She smiled down at Mags. "Kept me alive out there. Knew where the trapdoor was, I wouldn't have found it without him."

Jackson vanished behind the fourth car, then appeared again. "Sure, I'll take all the help I can get with this. And bonus, it keeps you away from Steven."

"Yeah, what is it with him?" She double-checked to make sure her comm was set to private. "He was hitting on me back there."

"I wouldn't doubt it."

"Don't know if I should be relieved or creeped out."

"I'd go for creeped out. But at least he's on his own now."

"Do I want to know?" She let her gaze focus on the cars, taking the time to do a visual inspection before giving the signal for Mags to inspect the vehicles. A small click rang out through the comm, letting her know he'd begun his investigation.

"He had a friend back in the bar. It wasn't good. Tried to take over the group, turn everything to his advantage."

"Where is he?"

"Not here, and it the only thing which now matters."

Ohhkay...

"You're safe. I may be warped, but I don't kill those I work with. Can't say Carl ever did anything but cause problems, including firing on some damned alien space bats. Kid you not, those things looked like big ass bats, with long claws and fangs. Dripped venom or gunk, didn't get the chance to find out what. Though if it was venom, it wasn't fast-acting."

"Alright, don't let the space bats bite me. Got it." Was he serious about the description? She hadn't seen anything which fitted his description. It wasn't as if she was ready to dive into the entire belief of alien invasion, but she sure as hell was leaning that way.

"You'll do fine with us. And yes, it wasn't easy to get everyone on the same track. An alienÂ invasion isn›t a situation we were set up to believe, to handle first hand. I didn't believe it, not fully until I saw those damned bats." He shrugged, then gestured at Mags.

"How's he doing?"

She followed the movement, a smile touching her lips. "He'll tell us if there's a problem. Honestly, without the filter, he wouldn't be able to do this, and I'm not sure how it works. Only that it does."

"The tech types aren't going to explain the ins and outs of everything to a bunch of Jarheads."

Where had the term come from? "I guess not. Still, it would be a change to at least pretend to understand how it works."

"I'll stick to weapons. Knives. They're my favorites. But I like a decent rifle." He petted the rifle he carried. "This one isn't bad, but it's not military issue. Jones had a few stored away, damn glad he did, it's come in handy."

She tried not to smile at the gleam in his eye. She'd seen it often enough before now. "Nice piece."

"Want to see my knife?" He leaned in, wriggling his eyebrows.

She laughed, she couldn't help it. "Are you hitting on me, Jackson?"

"Who? Me?"

Mags barked, the sound sharp, a warning she couldn't ignore. "Mags?" Leigh was moving before she realized it, covering the distance between herself and the canine. "What is it."

Mags sat by the side of one of the cars, tail wagging, nose close to the front landing gear. He barked again, urging her on.

"I checked there, didn't see anything."

"He wouldn't alert unless there was a problem." She crouched, then lowered **to** her belly to crawl close to the gear. "Might take a minute, but I'll find whatever it is."

"And if there's nothing there, what do I get?"

"A swift kick up the ass," she laughed then settled into the job. Mags had never been wrong, not in the years they'd been together, and she wasn't about to believe he'd made a mistake now. Leigh switched on a small light, tipping the beam up into the landing gear. *What am I searching for?* Anything which felt out of place.

"Why is she under there?"

Steven. What the hell did he want?

"None of your business," drawled Jackson.

"If anyone should be crawling under the cars, it's you, not a woman."

She tried to shut out the conversation as she continued to search, tipping the flashlight, tracing it over cables, and metal. Had Mags made a mistake? No, it wasn't possible.

Doubt built, forming pressure in her throat as she twisted, ready to call it done and a dud, when the beam illuminated a piece of metal. A small, jagged, device, and not a human design. "Got it." What it was, she had no clue, but there was no denying it didn't belong on the car.

"Describe it."

"Round, but jagged. Black. Appears metallic, but no real way of knowing from here. Seems to be stuck to the gear, no lines coming out from it."

"Any readings?"

She shifted her left arm, bringing it close enough to try to get a full read on the piece. "Magnetic energy? Could be nothing more than how it's attached, but something's off here." She chewed on the inside of her bottom lip. "I wouldn't want to remove it unless I knew what I was doing."

"How big is it?" Steven asked.

Damn civilian. Still, it was information Jackson needed. "Can't tell for certain with the angle involved. Best guess, five, maybe six centimeters."

"Huh? Why isn't she using inches?"

"Because military uses metric. Has done since the UTG formed, dumbass."

"Enough with the insults," growled Steven. "I'm not Carl. I haven't tried to turn the others against you."

No, he'd merely eyed her up as if she were a rare piece of

steak.

Light flickered. Blue, red, blue again. "Something's going on under here."

"What?"

"Lights. Red and blue, over and over again, picking up speed." Mags whined.

"Shit!" Leigh scrambled out from beneath the car. "Get back. Now!" She ran Mags at her side, not waiting to see what the other two men would do.

BOOM!

Pressure struck her back, lifting her up into the air, thrusting her forward toward the scant safety of the tunnel. Mags howled in distress, and she had a brief flash of her dog trying to claw his way through the air as the blast lifted and tossed them both on the floor, and darkness swallowed Leigh whole.

#

Stone kept pace with Lawbook as the Marine made her way through the connecting, flexible tunnels, and into the storage building. Under normal circumstances, he'd have paused to test the tunneling, checking for weaknesses he might be able to use at a later date. But the past two days had been anything but ordinary.

Lawbook spoke over her shoulder. "Thank you, Stone. I could have done this on my own, but I appreciate the back-up."

Not military back-up she meant. Miners and military seldom went hand in hand. The occasional riot on other colonies, problems with taxes, miners ignoring the laws laid down by the UTG, and a few dozen other reasons often meant the military and claim holders ended up on opposite sides of a fight.

"Figured there should be one person present with a level head," he replied.

She snorted and turned her attention back to the connecting airlock as she stopped in front of it. It didn't take long for the two of them to pass through into the storage building.

Twenty men and women, perhaps more, watched them. All conversation ceased, drifting off mid-sentence, but no one made a move to greet them. Stone watched the other airlock cycle to allow more people entry. Eyes narrowed, jaws firmed, smiles turned into a dark line of compressed lips.

No, there was no love toward the military here, which meant she had a tough crowd.

"May I have your--"

"Marines," a man snorted. "Doubt we'll hear anything worthwhile from her. Why are we all here, anyway? Not as if they've ever helped us."

"Now, Dave Owens, you give the girl a chance." A middle-aged woman pulled on Dave's arm. "Besides, it was Helen who got the message out to us. And the young 'un wouldn't go wasting our time. She's not like that."

"Could have been pressured into it," grumbled Dave. "Who knows what her lot will have done to the girl?"

"And you really think the Hunter's would allow their daughter to be pressured, you know them. Do they strike you as the people who'd allow harm to come to their kids? You know better. Give the Marine a chance, if it's important, we'll need to know. If it's a waste of time, then we'll deal with it, but until then, let the Marine speak."

Dave muttered under his breath, but the words remained too low-pitched for Stone to hear.

"Thank you," Lawbook inclined her head. "I appreciate you all coming here. Especially considering the well-known dislike miners generally have toward the military."

A few mutters were the only reply, but the majority of the group appeared to pay attention.

"I know this will be hard to believe, but the main colony has been attacked. Pluto is under the control of an alien force, and we have no idea what brought them to us. Or what they want at this time."

A dozen voices rose in protest, anger, disbelief, yells back and forth, but Stone didn't interfere. He watched, listened, taking in which of the newcomers might be a problem, which ones leaned toward helping them if the request was made.

"We have survivors with us, men, women, and children from the dome. I only have a handful of fighters, mostly Marines with a couple of civilians, and I had no plan on taking a force back to the colony until Helen provided us with the information I can't -- we can't -- ignore." She paused long enough to silence the group. "They're taking the children. Any kids they find, the little ones that is, and training them. They have at least one adult human working with them, we've heard his voice, which suggests this training is to prepare the kids as slaves. I don't know what they plan on doing with the adults captured, but we know at least a few of them are still alive."

"Training kids? Slaves? But why? It doesn't make sense."

Questions rose, most audible, others consumed in the wealth of noise created by the miners.

"We don't know why," said Stone. "It's happening, and we don't want to leave the kids behind. If they're being trained as slaves, the sooner we get them out of there, the better it will be for us. I don't like the idea of heading back into the dome, not after I've been in one fight with those bastards."

"You've seen them?" Dave approached them, his wife lingering by his side.

"Yes, we both have. Not pleasant. We've run into four different types to date, at least two use weapons on par, if not better, than ours. Beam tech, powerful, dangerous. Two of the breeds are winged. One has six limbs, including the wings, the other is smaller. Like a bat back on Earth, only bigger. Fangs and claws. Followed us through the tunnel, but we managed to kill it." Stone focused on the couple in front of him. "One of the Sergeant's men was seriously injured in getting the civilians out. Shoulders shattered, and we don't have a doc in our group. If anyone has medical training, I know she'd appreciate a doctor or med-tech taking a look at him."

"Kevin Turner, you back there?" Dave's wife called out.

"I am ma'am. I am." Younger than the couple, Kevin made his way out from the rest of the civilians.

"Kevin went to medical school back on Earth. Did his residency from what his parents have said. Only came home three or four weeks ago," the woman explained.

Tension eased from Lawbook, but Stone doubted anyone else would have seen it. "Doctor Turner, if you'd be kind enough to check on Walker, I'd be grateful. We've done everything we can, including strapping his shoulder up, but it's about as far as my medical knowledge goes."

"Will do, and I'll help in any other way I can. No way I'd want any kids in the hands of whatever we're dealing without there." Kevin offered his hand to Lawbook.

"Thank you." She shook his hand. "You know how to get into the house?"

"Yeah, I do. Been here a time or two." Kevin grinned before he headed toward the airlock.

One problem down, but still a dozen more to deal with.

"I know the idea of an alien invasion is more than most of you were ready to deal with. And I'll be honest if I hadn't seen them for myself, I would have a problem believing it. But I have seen them, as has Stone. The kids back in the house, the adults with them, they've all at least caught a glimpse of these things. And what they saw wasn't a joke or an illusion. These things fight back, they have no fear toward humans, and they outnumber us. If you can't believe me, believe them. Believe what Helen has said, the danger to us all, and understand if you can't offer help, then you'll still be facing these things eventually." Lawbook continued. "I'm going back to the dome to collect as many of the kids as I can. I have no intention of leaving them behind. Allowing them to be turned into slaves who no longer remember what it's like to be free."

She was on the right path. Her words passionate enough to rile up the miners, without directing any anger at her or the Marines in general.

"Don't know about you lot, but I'm with her. Don't get me wrong, a few of you might know me, or have had dealings with either myself or Duncan back in the colony. His daughter, Salla, is one of the survivors by the way. She witnessed her father being snatched, she's one tough kid." He let the information sink in. "I don't like the military, they interfere in my business too often for comfort, and they aren't easily bribed. But I'm going back in with Lawbook here." Sure, a part of it was so he could find out if it were safe to break away from the planet's surface, if the alien ships were still there and check in on his own ship. But hey, they didn't need to know everything.

"You're that smuggler, one who brings in the decent whiskey from time to time." A dark-haired man spoke up.

"Yes." Or it could have been one of several other smugglers, but why muddy the waters?

"Alright, I'm in. Same with my boys. Don't want my girl caught up in this, might bring her here to be with the other kids." The man glanced at Lawbook. "No offense meant, Sergeant. I don't believe this is any place for a woman."

"None taken, you're entitled to your opinions," said Lawbook. "But I'll be leading this attack, and it's a fact you'll have to accept if you wish to help."

"Sergeant, you're a Marine. I wouldn't expect anything else."

Stone grinned. Apparently, Marine trumped gender.

"Alright, then those who want to stay and help, if you already have your weapons with you, let me know. If you have any combat experience, tell me. And those who want to coordinate with the Hunters, to have people kept here, best you talk with Mrs. Hunter."

A ragtag squad. Better than nothing at all, but how many

would make it back in one piece?
It was a question he didn't want to ask.

Interlude Five

Sheila paced.

It had been hours since the message had been sent out for a health check on Popcorn, how long did it take for people to get back to her? She glared at the cot, the narrow piece of canvas covered by an old, scratchy blanket, and a thin pillow. How the hell was she supposed to sleep on the blasted thing?

I managed it during basic training.

Fine, she had, but that had been six years ago.

"You're going to put a hole in the floor." A familiar male voice drew her attention, and she stiffened. Grant.

"I doubt it, sir." She turned toward him, schooling her features into a mask of calm. "But thank you for your concern." Adding the polite touch didn't cost her anything, but the man would jump on any weakness, or error in how she spoke with him.

"You didn't have to bring in the admiral, it wasn't the act of a friend," he stepped into the barrack, his gaze lingering on the empty cots before returning to her face.

"We're not friends, sir." Her body screamed at her to step back, to keep as much distance between them as possible. But if she moved it would be seen as weakness, a mistake she couldn't afford to make. "I believe this is the women's dorm, sir. Men aren't permitted unless it's a medical emergency, and you have medical staff with you."

"You hurt my feelings, sweetheart." He smiled, darkness entering his eyes. "You have to make things up to me, Sheila."

"Sir, I was doing my job, and the duty sergeant agreed, the information needed to be passed up the chain."

"It wasn't your decision to make."

She hadn't made it, not exactly. "I followed SOP, sir." What the hell was he doing? He was already in trouble if he was found here. He doesn't care. Realization struck hard and fast. Her stomach clenched, but she still refused to move.

"Stupid move and you're an intelligent woman. I believe you should have known better. The sergeant wouldn't have done a damn thing unless you'd pointed it out. You had to know that. I know you did." He closed the gap between them. "But you'll make it all up to me soon enough. We've got a lot of work to handle between us. On. Your. Knees."

It wasn't happening. Things like this were almost unheard-of these days. Sure, it might have been common practice centuries ago, but here and now? "Not going to happen, sir. I believe you're suffering a mental breakdown and should report to the medical wing immediately." This wasn't working, he wouldn't back down, not with how things had worked out. The man was insane, risking what was left of his military career by entering the dorm.

Her hands trembled, but she didn't move, didn't back down, mind racing as she tried to come up with a means of dealing with the man. Or at least get away from him before he struck.

"You were always a tease, giving me those come and kiss me eyes, the way you'd nibble your bottom lip when you knew I was watching at you." He reached out with one hand, tracing her jaw with the tip of his finger. "I know what you want. What you need. And you don't have to pretend here." He eased his hand up into her hair, combing through it before he fisted his grip.

Her mind raced. Fighting Grant, when he was expecting it, wouldn't work.

She swallowed down her fear.

"Fearless and eager for my touch. I know you are. I can see it." He tugged on her hair.

A weapon, anything, she couldn't allow this to go any further.

He leaned in, lips close to hers, ready to claim her.

Whooowheeee Whooowheeee.

The siren was all she needed. She stepped into his body, jerking her knee up into his groin.

He groaned, buckling, fingers loosening from her hair. She

struck again, lashing out with a clenched fist, hitting his chin. His head snapped back, eyes dazed, following up with a second strike. She didn't step away, didn't stop. Feet and hands, she lashed out with both, kicking, punching, forcing him back toward the open door as the siren continued to blare.

"What's going on?"

She didn't stop, yes there was someone else there, another woman, but she refused to take her eyes off Grant. Her knuckles ached, skin split as she continued to fight, to push Grant out of the dorm. "Get security."

"Fuck is that -- shit, Grant isn't allowed in here."

"No shit, Sherlock." She lashed out again, fist connecting with his face, blood mingling with sweat across her hands. "Get him the fuck out of here." One last punch sent Grant stumbling backward out of the dorm and into the corridor.

Whatever the man wanted, it was too late. She had a witness.

A witness to me beating the crap out of him.

Which could be enough to end her career, except for the fact Grant wasn't allowed in the women's dorm.

"You alright?" Tammy Swenson offered a hand. "You look like shit."

"Feel like it," she rolled out her shoulders. "Bugger wanted me to -- it doesn't matter. It'll be in the report." She hadn't lost control, hadn't tried to kill him. If she had anything to take from this, it was never let her guard down. Nor matter where she was her bed, her dorm, a shower.

"He's finished after this."

She could only hope Tammy was right.

Chapter Twelve

Leigh groaned, dust filling her eyes, or was it grit? She blinked, trying to clear her vision, aware of a pressure over her legs, weight on her chest, her body aching from bruises she'd yet to see. Her eyes watered. Her mind tried to crawl out from the depths, a sluggish attempt which collapsed as soon as it had begun.

The mask. It should have kept pieces from hitting her eyes. Not grit? Sleep? It didn't make sense.

"Jackson? Leigh?"

A man. Jones? She closed her eyes, unable to put the pieces into place. It didn't matter who was calling for her. She wasn't alone, others had survived the...

What had happened?

Explosion. One of the ground cars. A device she'd seen.

Mags!

She tried to move to reach out. Where was Mags? He'd been at her side when the explosion had lifted her up and slammed her down in one painful move.

A wriggle. Something moved at her left. Or was it the right? She groaned, unable to know where she was, what kept her pinned, or what she was supposed to do.

"I see the dog. She has to be close. The dog would be close to her."

She wasn't alone. Would never be alone as long as Mags remained in her life. He wouldn't leave her.

"Mags?" Her voice weak, barely recognizable, but it was hers. She felt the word, tasted it as she spoke. Yet her body still refused to move.

"We'll get you out. Don't struggle, you'll bring the entire pile down on you."

She closed her eyes, lacking the ability to move even if she wanted to. Tired. So damn tired. All she wanted to do was sleep with Mags pressed against her side, the way he always did.

#

"Jakob, they want to leave us behind." Salla hurried across the room. "We can't let them do this. We've got friends, maybe family out there. Prisoners of those things." Her gaze shifted, jaw tight, anger flashing in her eyes. "I'm not going to sit back and let them tell me we're kids and need to remain out of the way."

Jakob waited until Salla had finished before replying. "How are we going to stop them? Not as if they're going to take any notice of us." Jakob forced his voice to remain calm. "I don't like it either, why would I? I mean, we've been in this, together, from the beginning. It's not right to push us aside."

Salla sat down. "We can talk to the Sergeant. I mean, you and I know the colony better than she does. I've still got access to my father's data. They'd be idiots to leave me behind, and I'm not going anywhere without you." She crossed one leg over the other, her foot tapping against the air. "I know the tunnels they won't have access to."

He wasn't going to argue with her, she was right, but persuading the Sergeant wouldn't be easy. "I know, and they're going to need any edge they can grab. Those things are dangerous, and they've outnumbered us from the beginning."

Salla ducked her head, eyes half-closed. "Sorry, I shouldn't have marched in."

"No, you had every right. Nothing to be sorry about is there." His arms ached with the need to wrap her in a hug, but Salla wasn't the type of girl -- no, woman -- you did that too. Not without asking first. "No one would think twice if you'd been a guy."

A small smile flickered across her lips. "No, they wouldn't. Especially not my dad. Same with the Sergeant, if she stalked in, most would accept it."

Being a woman had to suck at times. "Maybe, depends on who was there when it happened. If they see the uniform first and not the woman, sure. But if they're one of those who see the woman before the uniform, I'm not certain they'd accept it from her. Not without putting her down."

Salla rolled her eyes. "Dad warned me when he was training me, that I'd have a double battle to face through life. He did tell me, according to the stories, it used to be a lot worse for women. There's always going to be room for improvement, on both sides."

"Remember something like that from the history chips." He didn't know enough to do more than give a vague comment.

"Thought you might." She leaned back, hair half in her eyes. "Doesn't mean I like how things still are. We're kids to them, though I'm a legal adult. I'm a woman, and will always a child or worse in the eyes of many."

"So, use it against them. Whoever they maybe."

"Believe me, I've tried. I've had to, through the years. It's the only way I've made it out of Pop's training in one piece. Damn man is mean when it comes to tests, training, and forcing me to reach for the next goal. Should be thankful, I guess." She rubbed one hand across her brow.

"Hello?" A male voice spoke from the entrance into the bedroom. "I'm looking for a man called Walker."

Jakob glanced past Salla to the newcomer. "He's in the bedroom at the end of the corridor. What did you want with him? He's injured, isn't really up to company." Not from friends or from a man he didn't know. Or did this newcomer -- no, of course, he didn't. Otherwise, he wouldn't have said a man called Walker. "You've never met him before, have you?"

"No, I haven't. I'm Kevin Turner, Doctor Turner." He held out his hand as he approached them. "Sergeant Bloodlaw asked me to check in on him, see if there's anything I can do to help him. Speed up his recovery."

"You're fully qualified?" asked Salla.

"Yes, finished medical school, and my internship before shipping back to Pluto. Aren't enough doctors out here. I figured

I'd be better off being where I can be useful."

Jakob took the offered hand. "And you think you can help Walker?"

"Won't know until I get the chance to do an exam, and work out the extent of his injuries," Turner admitted. "I'm hoping I'll be able to at least make him comfortable. From what Sergeant Bloodlaw mentioned, his shoulder is in a terrible state, pieces, shattered from an alien weapon?"

"Yes. I saw the scan briefly. Nasty. Even to my uneducated eyes."

"Then I'd best get down there and see what I can find out." He nodded a greeting to Salla. "Unless you'd like to join me, both of you?"

Salla tensed, sitting up straighter. "Why would you want us there, aren't we kids?" Bitterness touched the last word.

"Kids? Doubtful. Salla, you're only a couple of years younger than me, if you're Duncan's daughter."

"I am." She grinned and stood. "Alright, let's do this. Might be better if we were around anyway. Walker at least will recognize us, better than being left in the hands of a stranger with no one around to explain what's going on."

Jakob wasn't going to disagree. "I know I wouldn't want to wake up to a stranger treating me, and no one I know to answer questions." He followed Salla, his fingers itching still with the need to touch her, offer her help, comfort, and anything else she might need. "Think Walker might want something to eat?"

"Water more likely, but not until I have a chance to examine him," Turner explained as he headed for the door. "And any help you can give me will be greatly appreciated. He's going to be my first patient on Pluto, and I don't want to be in a position where I lose him or cause him unwanted pain."

Salla glanced back at Jakob, a glimmer of a smile shining in her eyes. "Then I think we'll get on well enough. We haven't known Walker for long, but he'll at least recognize us."

And we know who to look for if anything goes wrong.

#

"How many men are you taking with you?" asked Stone.

"As many as I can take with me, and still sneak into the dome. We're going to be outnumbered regardless, but no point in getting killed in the first few minutes." Cora didn't need to add, and women, to the statement. If they could fight, take orders, and not panic, then they were welcome regardless of gender. "Not going to be easy, and some of my choices will upset the civilians, but I need people at my side who I can trust." Her thoughts shifted to those who'd come with them, made it out of the dome.

"You're thinking about the kids." A statement, not a question.

"The ones I'm taking aren't kids anymore."

"Salla and Jakob?"

"They proved their worth when we left the colony. Salla has her father's training, which will be useful in trying to get back in." She turned enough to meet his gaze. "Whatever their age, they don't act like kids, they think things through, and they've shown they can remain calm under pressure."

Stone didn't reply.

"Something you want to say about my decision?"

"No. It's your skin, and theirs."

"Yours as well, if you plan on coming with me." Would he back out? "We might have enough people to do a small, tactical strike, but I'd like to have a few more people with who know how to handle a weapon. More likely to be able to manage that with the miners than I'd have found in the main colony." Fighters, men, and women willing to take a chance and listen to orders weren't going to be easy to find, no matter what she tried to tell herself.

"I do, doesn't mean I like what you've got in mind, but leaving those kids behind." He shuddered. "Not even I can do that. Enslaved to aliens, wiped of their ability to fight, break free, to find their own path. Not happening."

"So, you aren't all about the profit."

He grinned, one eyebrow arched. "Of course, I am. If there's alien tech to be snatched up and sold, I'll be on it. And there's no trading going on when we're dealing with invaders. Not as if I can jump into my ship, skip off from Pluto, and find the next load to bring in."

Cora struggled not to react, not to jump him with a dozen points she could use to argue for or against his declaration. "Ever the businessman. I can work with it. As long as you follow orders when we're out there."

"Of course, wouldn't want to be on the business end of your fist again." He glanced down at her hands before he continued. "You've got a mean right hook."

"I try." For now, she needed him, but once they had Pluto cleared of their invaders, perhaps before, he'd be gone. "Try not to get yourself killed. I still have use for you."

"Bad business to die before getting paid. And there will be a pay off for me."

"Sergeant?"

Cora turned, smoothing her features into a mask of calm. "Yes, Mrs. Owens?"

"No formality needed, it's Pauline or Paula, we're all friends or family out here. Have to be when you don't live beneath the protection of the dome." She paled at the mention of the colony. "Not that it's offering much in the way of protection these days. Those poor people, I can't imagine how frightening it was for them, being forced to pull on suits, and race for cover." Her eyes misted.

Cora watched emotions flashing across the older woman's face. "What we're about to do won't be safe, or easy. But I'm not going out there without a workable plan. No point in getting everyone killed."

"I didn't think you would. Not as a Marine. Don't mind my Dave, he's never liked the military. Many of the miners out here have poor experiences with your kind, but we listened, and we want to help," said Paula.

Cora gave the leading group of settlers a pointed glance before she spoke again. "They asked you to speak with me because you don't have an ax to grind."

"And because I'm a woman. A few of them are a touch on the old-fashioned side. They may say they're fine with a woman leading the charge, as it were, but they're not comfortable with it."

It didn't surprise her. "What are we about to negotiate?"

"Oh, just getting them there and back in one piece. Or as much as is humanly possible." She gestured to a scattering of sturdy boxes. "Shall we sit, it will give them the impression we're going over your plan?"

"Instead of?" Cora led the way to the nearest box and offered it to Paula.

"Whatever we discuss instead." She sat down. "I'm no fool. It won't matter how detailed your plan of attack maybe, I'm aware no plan survives first contact with the enemy."

Cora pulled one of the boxes closer before she sat, aware that Stone didn't sit, but took up position close to her back. "Sounds like you have experience with military situations."

"Both my parents served in the UTG. Navy for my mom, Marine for my dad. Long story, but not one I'll go into here. Not relevant to what we're discussing." Light highlighted strands of silver in her hair. "Not everyone will come back in one piece, if at all." Her brow furrowed. "It's part of going into the fight. You learn it as a military brat. Even if your own parents make it back, they've seen friends injured or killed. They aren't the same people anymore, never will be again." Paula's eyes glistened with unshed tears. "I didn't think I'd be faced with the same situation again. Not out here. Pluto's been a peaceful home for a decade, for us at least. Now. Well, you understand what I'm saying."

She did.

Cora didn't respond instantly, giving herself time to form her words. She was right, death changed you, maybe not immediately, but it was a scar you learned to live with. Gunny. Her throat tightened, and she swallowed down the lump before it had a chance to fully form. "I'll do my best to bring them all back."

"It's all I ask. All anyone could ask of you."

Chapter Thirteen

Stone waited until they returned to the family room before he pulled Lawbook to one side. "How many are you taking out there?"

Her eyes lidded as lines furrowed across her brow. "Hoped for fifty, but I'm realistically looking at half that."

"Twenty-five to take on God alone knows how many aliens. Not the best numbers." Fifty wouldn't have been much better. "Shit, we're going to die out there."

"Not if I have anything to say about the matter."

"When do we head out?" How much longer did he have before the world crashed down on him? If he had any sense, he'd find his way out of this mess before the shit hit the fan, but it was no longer an option. Not unless he wanted to be labeled a coward. Better a coward and alive, than a dead hero.

Lawbook didn't respond, her gaze moving past him to rest on the others in the room. No one was close enough to hear each word, but his shoulders itched, a spot between them informing him they were being watched.

"I want to talk with Helen, see if she's picked up any more information, but as it stands, we'll be heading out in four hours."

"That long? The kids might have been moved by then." Why not sooner.

"I have to give the rest of the group time to prepare. Some of the men and women coming with us haven't had enough sleep to be safe. Four hours isn't much, but it will help revitalize the half dozen coming with us."

He didn't like it, but arguing with the Marine would be a waste of energy. "Are you going to grab a nap?"

"If I can, but not before I check in with Helen, Walker, and a few others." Her gaze slid away from him again. "It's going to be hard work out there. I don't know if we're doing the right thing. Shit, for all we know it could be a trap. I don't believe it is, but there's always a chance." She leaned back against a wall, eyes narrowed as she continued. "I can't leave those children to be raised as slaves. It goes against everything I believe, and if you want to pull out now, I'd understand."

At least she was being honest. "You need more people, not me dropping out at the last minute." He shrugged, not wanting to draw attention to their conversation, at least, not any more than they already dealt with. "I'm coming with you, as I said."

A small, barely there, a smile flashed into life, only to vanish a heartbeat later. "Appreciated. We didn't get off to the best start, but you've shown you're willing to stand your ground in a fight. A skill I'm going to rely on."

"I won't let you down." He deliberately paused. "At least, not unless there's profit in it for me."

He didn't object when she slugged his shoulder.

#

"Winter? Open your eyes, Winter. We need you awake for this."

"Tired," she mumbled. "Ten more minutes." Her limbs were heavy, the pressure holding her in place both warm and dangerous. Why wasn't she moving? "Need more sleep."

"You're hurt and running out of oxygen. It's why you want to sleep."

"Oh," she blinked and tried to focus.

"We have to get you back to the ground cars. Hook you up to fresh supplies."

The words made sense, it explained why she wasn't eager to move, why she was tired. "Mags?" The voice. Not Jones, but Jackson. At least he was safe. Had to be if he was helping to get her free of this mess.

"He's right by your side. He isn't going to move until you're safe again."

Leigh ran her tongue over her bottom lip, trying to wet it. Her mouth dry, eyes unwilling to open, but she wasn't ready to give up. She wouldn't leave Mags. Her dog, companion, and friend. "Mags."

He wriggled closer, a nudge enough to touch if she could move if she were in a position to reach him, but it didn't matter. He was here, she wasn't alone. But why was she running out of oxygen? She'd had enough in her suit to last for hours. "How long?"

"We've been digging you out for over five hours. You've been in and out of it for most of this. We're nearly there now. Shouldn't be much longer, but I need you to stay awake if we're going to get you out of here alive and in one piece."

Five hours? Why so long? Leigh closed her eyes, not to sleep, but to rummage through the information stored away. "No equipment."

"We've been doing this by hand. We had to shift a lot of rubble before we got this far, but we need you to help yourself now." Jackson continued. "Can you hear me?"

"Yes." What did they need her to do? It wasn't as if she could dig herself out.

"I need you to focus. We've got to get this done before you pass out on us. Can you feel your legs?"

She frowned and wriggled her toes. Sensation, not pins and needles, but a normal feeling. "Yes. What has me trapped?" Her heart raced, the need to understand what was going thrust to the surface.

"Pinned down by a large piece of rock, but it doesn't appear as if your legs are damaged. Can you feel pain anywhere?"

Her eyes still closed she tried to move, a twitch here, a shift there. Pain danced across her ribs in liquid flame, a hiss of pain torn into life. "Ribs."

"Alright. Not going to hide what's going on, but this is going to hurt."

"When?" And why would it hurt? She wasn't moving. Hadn't moved except to test her body the way Jackson had wanted.

"We're going to lift this piece, and Jones is going to grab your shoulders. I need you to push with your feet. Find a way to help us get you out of there, but whatever you do, don't sit up. Don't fight when you're grabbed. Can you do that for me?"

Her shoulders. Why would he reach for her shoulders and not her hands? She twisted her left hand, it moved without a problem. A small space around her wrist and hand. How far did it go? She tried to move her entire arm, not enough to twist free, but she wasn't hurt except her ribs. She tried the same with her right hand.

It didn't move. She tried again, twisting her arm. Nothing. No sensation, no wriggling of her fingers. It didn't make sense. "Why can't I move my right hand?"

"I'll explain when we get you out, Winter."

Mags whined, and her hand ached to touch him. "I'll be alright, buddy. Be free of all this mess soon." She had to be, wouldn't give up, not as long as Mags needed her.

A fuzzy warmth touched her mind, familiar, and different at the same time. Not her own thoughts, more emotions than anything else, then it was gone. She needed it back, wanted the touch, craved the way it felt.

"Going to count down from five. Don't fight us, no matter what happens. Push with your feet, the faster we get you out, the easier it will be."

Hand. She couldn't feel the one hand. "Alright." A part of her mind hammered at the rest. She was missing a piece of the puzzle which she needed to make sense of everything going on.

Sharp, painful, something snagged at her shoulders.

"Five."

What were they doing?

"Four."

Leigh tensed, not wanting to fight, but the uncertainty grew with each beat of her heart.

"Three."

This wasn't right.

"Two."

She eased her feet into position, heels pressed against the ground. Or whatever she was trapped against. *What's wrong with my hand?*

"One."

She pushed as they pulled, her body unwilling to remain trapped. Her heels dug in, muscles tensed as she tried to help them, one side of her body, her right, refused to move. A woman screamed, the sound echoing around her, vibrating through her as they pulled.

A heartbeat before she passed out, Leigh realized the one screaming was her.

#

Cries. Children's voices. The noises merged, forcing Zac awake. When had he fallen asleep? He had no idea how long he'd lain on the sleeping mat.

"You hear them too?" Matthew asked.

"Yes, I'm not sure what's going on with the kids, but they're not happy." Zan scrubbed a hand over his face and stood.

"They are being prepared for transportation, it's a great honor." Edward smiled as he came into sight. "It won't be long before they begin their new life. In time they'll forget there was ever another way, and accept their new lives."

Zac's throat tightened. "You're wrong. They'll never forget."

Edward tipped his head to the left. "I wish you would accept your fate, it will make it easier for you all. But I was warned uneducated adults fail to understand the beauty of the offer before them."

What had happened to the man to turn him this far away from life as a free human being. He frowned as he approached the front of the cell. "What happened to your family?"

"They were raised on the servant's colony, and are still alive, to the best of my knowledge," Edward explained, his smile peaceful lacking any sign of the stress Zac expected to see from a man bound in servitude. "If the Blessed Ones are pleased with my service, I will see them upon our return to the Nest."

Nest? Is that what they called their home? No, not Edward, but the aliens. "Tell me about them? The Nest?"

"Ah, you are willing to learn. This is a good sign." Edward beamed. "When I return I'll tell you about the Nest, and the wonderful things the Blessed Ones have introduced our kind to. There have been many advances, but for now, they need me to help with the young. Their fear will ease, then they will accept their place in the universe." The man gestured in the direction of the exit. "I will return. I promise you this will be wonderful, all the delightful treats waiting for you. I would almost want to be in your place for the chance to see this with new eyes."

#

Ian listened to the conversations in the family room as he moved through, searching for his parents, or Helen. He frowned, pausing to check by the comm set up. Still working, but no sign of Helen.

Odd.

She hadn't left her post, not since the first message had come in, except to use the bathroom, or quickly check in with their parents. The hair on the back of his neck rose as the comm crackled into life.

"Hunter settlement. Can you read me? Come in, Hunter claim."

Ian settled on Helen's stool. "This is Ian Hunter, who is this?" A male voice, one he knew, but couldn't put a name to.

"Jones. From the GetAway."

The bar owner. "Good to hear from you. The Sergeant let us know you had been seen, and went into hiding." How was the

154

man now close enough to contact them? "Where are you?"

"Five klicks out from you people, with an injured Marine."

Ian paled as he stared at the comm. Injured Marine? "Understood. How bad is it?"

"Pretty bad, we've got the bleeding under control, but she's going to need medical attention ASAP," replied Jones.

"Understood, we've got a doctor here. Long story, but I'll alert him you're incoming. Sending you the correct approach path. Don't stray from it unless you want to run into one of my sister's security measures." Booby traps, why not just call it what it is?

"Will do. Coming in fast and hard. Won't be slowing down until there's no other choice. Breaking out to the surface in three minutes."

"Got it. See you soon." Three minutes to the surface. Using the tunnels then, made sense. The less attention they drew on themselves, the better. How bad was the Marine? Wait, didn't Jones say she, not he? And Lawbook had spoken of a man called Jackson. Miscommunication, maybe?

"Anyone seen the Sergeant?" He twisted around on the stool, searching the room for any sign of her or Stone. His gaze touched on one of the other Marines. "Ready? You seen the Sergeant?"

"She's checking gear in the storage shed," said Lackey.

"Can you let her know she's got an injured Marine coming in with a man called Jones."

"Shit, Jones? Is Jackson hurt?" Ready turned, his full attention locked on Ian.

"Not sure, Jones said it was a woman who'd been hurt. Might have been a problem with the comm, but can't be certain." He made his way through the room. "I've got to let Turner know, in case he's still busy with Walker." Two injured Marines and the fight to get the kids hadn't even begun.

Breathless, he made it down the stairs, sprinting where he had space until he grabbed the edge of a door frame and swung into the room. "Turner?"

A man packing up a medical kit glanced up from his work. "Yes?"

"Appears as if you've got another patient coming in." He glanced around the room. Walker lay, breathing but otherwise silent, on his cot. Jakob leaned against the wall to the left, Salla sat on the edge of an otherwise empty bed. "A Marine, not certain of the details, but they're five klicks out."

"Appreciate the heads up."

"Be here soon, did you want to meet the ground cars." The newcomers had to be arriving via the ground cars; otherwise, it would take a lot longer for the survivors to arrive. "They're coming in as fast as safety will allow. Should be breaking the surface about now."

"Let me grab another kit. Salla, Jakob, you want to help me, or stay with Walker?"

"I'll stay with Walker," said Salla. "I know Lawbook didn't want him left alone."

Blonde, petite, with a gentle smile, the woman rested one hand on Ian's arm. "I can watch him."

"Nyssa, right?"

Her smile widened. "Yes, and I have enough medical training to let the doctor know if there's a problem."

Salla's brow furrowed as she shot a glance at Jakob, then back at Nyssa. "Erm, I don't think the Sergeant wanted Nyssa in here on her own."

"Oh, what nonsense. We sorted all that out. I'm not a fighter, not like you, Salla, wouldn't it be better if I was the one to stay with him?"

She might have been talking with Salla, but her attention remained on Ian. Her gaze taking him in, lingering in places long enough to trigger a mixture of discomfort and interest. He shifted his weight, one-foot scraping against the floor. "Better to be on the safe side. Salla, if you want to stay, you're welcome to."

"Oh, but isn't it up to the doctor?" Nyssa brushed her fingers alongIan's arm. "I mean, we need to take into account the doctor's orders, don't we?"

"Don't drag me into this, I'm only putting bodies back together. If the Sergeant has given orders about who is allowed to stay with him, I wouldn't know." Turner closed up the kit. "Jakob, time to get moving." He lifted the box. "I'm ready if you are."

Jakob fixed Nyssa with a hard glare, then glanced over to Salla. "Catch up with you later?"

"I'll be right here."

Salla. He'd known her the longest. If she said Nyssa wasn't allowed to be left on her own with Walker, then so be it. "I'll check in with Lawbook, but let me know if something changes." Whatever the woman had done, it obviously sat ill with Salla, and Ian wanted to know more.

"They'll be in the storage unit in five," Helen called down from the top of the stairs.

It was all Ian needed to get the rest of the group running, with Ian bringing up the rear. Another female Marine. He knew they were rare, at least, he'd been told they were and hadn't seen many in or around the colony.

Yeah, middle of an alien invasion, and I'm thinking about women. Fantastic.

#

"Another female marine?" Cora looked up from her work. "Yeah, there are a few around, but as far as I knew, I'm the only one on Pluto currently." She glanced over in the direction of the airlock. "But anything's possible out here, after all, we didn't expect to expect an alien invasion." All it would have taken is one arriving shortly before the initial attack, and they'd have slipped under the radar. "Glad to hear Jones is on his way in though, and Jackson will be useful." The man was a decent shot, sniper quality but had a fascination with knives and had never gone for the final testing.

The first hint of noise from the airlock drew her attention

as she walked away from the weapons she'd laid out. With each one she'd taken the time to strip, clean and reassemble them. Fortunately, she hadn't been working alone. Both Lackey and Stone had worked at her side, allowing them to check the gathered weapons, and prepare them for the fight to come.

The airlock opened, a stretcher slung between Jones and Jackson as they carried it into the open space. A four-legged creature in a suit, bounded alongside the two men, as she reached for her sidearm.

"What the fuck is that?"

"Her dog, Sergeant," Jones said.

"Dog? What the hell?" There were no dogs on Pluto. Sure, a few were working with the Marines back on Earth, Mars, but out here? What the hell was going on?

"Mags, that's the name. Works with Winter." Jones jerked his head back in the woman's direction. "Doesn't want to leave her, but he's friendly enough if you aren't trying to hurt his handler."

"What the hell happened to her arm?" Stone asked as he hurried toward the stretcher.

"Cave in. One of the ground cars was booby-trapped. Don't know why they did it, but the aliens planted a bomb on one of them. Took out three cars, injured a few of us, but she's the only serious injury, Sergeant." Jackson explained.

The airlock leading to the enclosed walkway to the main building, hissed as it cycled open. Three figures hurried in.

The doctor.

"Set her down here," said Turner as he indicated a set of three boxes. "Should be stable enough to use."

Jakob and Ready pushed the boxes closer together before the stretcher was placed on top of it.

Lawbook stayed out of the way as the doctor got to work, her gaze fixed on the remains of the woman's right arm. How they'd saved her life, she didn't know. Nothing remained of her arm from mix upper arm down. The suit was damaged, but if they'd been quick in getting her into a ground car, it might have been enough to save her life until they sealed the remains of the damaged protective clothing.

Jackson met her gaze as he joined her. "Sergeant."

"Who is she?"

"Leigh Winter. First posting out of training. She and the dog are part of an experiment to see if working pairs are useful out on the frontier."

"Shit," she muttered and scraped one hand through her short hair. Mars, the dog handler pairs had worked there, but she'd been told nothing about them being used beyond Earth and Mars. "Not my idea of a decent first posting."

"The dog is the one who told us where to dig. She was thrown through the air, several of us were when the car exploded. Lots of bruises. One of the servers has a cracked wrist. Steven, one of the civies, is complaining he's been badly treated, but she took the brunt of it, damn bad luck. Wrong place, wrong time, but she saved the rest of us. It was her dog which alerted to there being an issue. Something about collectors in the canine suit, allowing him to smell for problems in low oxygen situations like the tunnels."

"What did you say the dog's name was?"

"Mags, short for Magnum. Has barely moved from her side, except to let us work on her." Jackson shrugged, his tone calm, though he didn't turn away from the stretcher. "Her arm was trapped, but she didn't feel it. Not until we pulled her out. We knew the risk. The scanners let us know we'd have to work damn fast when we pulled her out. Cut the remains of the damaged limb when we were getting her out of it all. Pity, she'll have to wait until we've dealt with our unwanted guests before she can apply for a replacement arm."

"Crushed?"

"Completely. No way we could have saved it, not without a full medical team and stasis pod to hand. We didn't have either.

Figured it was better to save her life than lose her along with the arm."

"Alright, she's stable, let's get her into the house," Turner announced.

"Looks like you did a decent job back there, you and Jones." The airlock disgorged newcomers into the room, but she didn't turn away from the woman on the stretcher. Not until Turner, Ready, and Jakob carried her away. "Lose many?"

"Lose many?" A man's outraged voice cut through the background noise. "This man and the bartender murdered my friend back there. I want them both arrested. Do you hear me, I want them arrested." Thin faced, his features washed out as he pushed the hood back from his face. "They're sick bastards, cruel, and murdered an upstanding member of the colony. One with a powerful family on Earth. And they refused to help me when I was injured out there. Look at my face." He pointed to a small bruise beneath his right eye. "This can't be allowed to go unpunished."

Great, she didn't need this. Not with everything going on. "And you are?"

"Steven Landon."

"And the man you claim was murdered?"

"Carl Froman."

"Then I'll deal with this at a later date. Right now, I have other things to deal with."

"More important than rounding up a pair of murderers?" Carl stalked toward her.

"Alleged murderers." Jackson murmured. "I can honestly state I didn't take his life."

"No, you left him to the aliens. Those damn space bats. As if he were nothing more than an animal. Worse, you'd protect that mutt of hers, but you gave Carl up to the aliens."

Jackson shrugged his voice calm. "He'd tried to kill Jones. I'm no fool, you don't leave an enemy at your back. You get rid of him. He bought us time to get the rest of you to safety, and it was that or shoot him."

"See, he admits it. I demand you arrest him."

I don't need this. Cora arched an eyebrow. "I don't see you wearing a uniform."

"Why would I?" Steven took a step back, his brow furrowed.

"You're attempting to give me an order, but I don't see you wearing a uniform or any other sign of rank which would mean I have to not only listening to your whining but obey you. Am I missing something here? Are you, perhaps, a member of Pluto security, working undercover?" Ice seeped into her words.

"Pluto security? Are you insane, woman?"

"Then I take it you're nothing but a civilian, one who likely owes his life to Jackson," she continued.

"Of course, I'm a civilian." His eyes narrowed.

"Then what appears to be the problem here? You're a civilian, not military, therefore not in my chain of command." She took a step into his space. "I. Don't. Take. Orders. From. Civilians." Each word punctuated with a jab from her finger as she built stabbed him with it over his heart.

"I don't have to take this from you. Where's the Gunny. He'll put you back in your place."

"Dead."

"Where is he?" He turned, edging out of her reach as he searched through the survivors. "He has to be around here."

Had he ignored her answer, or misheard her? Her gaze narrowed on the man. "He's dead. He died before we found the kids."

Steven paused. "I see, then who's in charge?"

"I am if you're talking about the military. Until I find a Marine officer to dump this onto, then it's on my shoulders."

"What about the Navy pilot?"

She allowed herself a smile. "Harvard doesn't have the experience to run a bunch of Marines." She didn't have enough to claim it was a squad, not unless she counted several civilians. "He made it clear he wasn't going to step in and try to take control."

"But he is an officer."

"Yes." Where was he going with this? Reporting the situation to Harvard? He's welcome to try.

"Then I'll take it up with him. Where is he?"

"Go find him, I have better things to do." If she was right, Harvard had claimed one of the empty cots.

"More important than dealing with a murderer?"

"The alleged murderer who saved your life, if I understand the situation. And your friend tried to kill or at least injure the man who offered you shelter." She deliberately turned her back on Steven. "Jackson, go find yourself a cot. We're going to need you in a couple of hours." Pushing back the start of the mission would allow Jackson a chance to recharge.

"Yes, Sergeant." He snapped to attention before heading for the main house.

"He's going to get you lot killed," Steven muttered but made no attempt to hide either his words or distaste. "And it will serve you right. You should have listened to me."

"Some people need killing." Stone came up behind her. "I'd put him at the top of the list."

"Might want to leave room on your list."

"Ever the optimist."

"Someone has to be."

Chapter Fourteen

Jakob kept pace with the stretcher, his gaze shifting to the woman as they hurried through the house. "Where are we taking her? Walker's room?"

"Yes. The full kit is down there. Hunters provided a lot of equipment, and there's enough to keep her from bleeding out when I start working on her arm." Turner explained as they reached the top of the stairs. "Go ahead of me, I need one of the cots raised, stripped but for a clean sheet. Spray down. You know which bottle. Don't cut corners. We can't take the risk of infection."

"Will do." He darted down the stairs. The spray antiseptic. He'd seen Turner use it before working on Walker. He jumped the last three steps, caught the edge of the banister and swung himself around into the corridor, never missing a beat as he sprinted to the room. "Need a cot set up for incoming." He grabbed the spray.

Salla rose, but Nyssa remained on the cot she'd chosen to use as a seat. He glared at Nyssa but didn't waste his breath. Whatever the woman had in mind, she'd shown her worth, or lack of it by refusing to help.

"The Marine, is she a woman or was there a mistake?" Salla jacked up a cot and grabbed one of the sealed sheets as she stripped off the other bedding. "How bad is it?"

"Yes, a woman. Lost part of her arm." He lifted the spray. "Hands."

She held out hers long enough to be sprayed before ripping the sealed sheet open. As she tugged it into place, he sprayed it, the cot and both of them. It wasn't ideal, but it was all they had available.

"Incoming," Turner warned them.

Jakob stepped aside, spraying down the doctor and everyone else, including Nyssa.

"Hey, cut it out."

"If you're going to stay here, you needed to be sprayed. The woman's injured, he's going to have to open the seal they've placed on the stump. He isn't going to want to risk infection, so put up with it, or leave. It's your choice." Jakob used the antiseptic on the woman and the room in general. He'd done the same thing before Turner had opened any wrappings covering Walker's wounds. It hadn't been as needed with Walker, but the doctor had talked Jakob through it, and why it was necessary.

"You're doing this to be annoying." Nyssa's gaze flicked to the injured woman. "She's not going to make it. Not with the amount of blood loss involved."

"She will, and there are enough people here to arrange a blood transfusion if we need one," Turner instructed as he helped strap the woman to the cot. "Can't risk her moving at the wrong time and...shit, we need to get the dog out."

Jakob turned, his gaze now fixed on the canine, still in his suit. "I'll take care of him." Wasn't as if he could do anything else. Salla had proved she was a deft hand working with a doctor, and someone had to watch the dog.

"Alright." Turner sprayed down his hands and pulled a mask in place over his mouth and nose. "Grab a mask, Salla, going to need an extra set of hands here."

"I'm a nurse, at least, a workplace nurse," Nyssa explained.

Jakob approached the canine and crouched down, peering through the mask. "Hey, boy? I know you want to be in here with her, but it's not the best idea. Not with her injury." He kept his voice gentle as he offered a hand. "Do you want me to help take the mask off? It can't be comfortable for you. And they'll be stripping the rest of her suit off."

The dog sat down, tail wagging.

"I'll take it as a yes. So, no biting me, okay?" He reached for the dog's mask, unclipping it before he pushed it back from the canine's face. "There you go, now you can breathe real air." He indicated the corridor. "We need to move out here, alright, pup?"

The dog rose and backed up, never taking his gaze away from Jakob.

"Wasn't sure I'd ever see a dog in person again." He followed his new companion into the corridor. "Heel boy. That's the right command, isn't it?"

The dog rolled his eyes but kept pace with Jakob as the unusual pair headed for the stairs.

"Go easy on me, I was a toddler the last time I saw a dog on anything but a holoscreen." He reached out with a tentative hand to touch the top of the dog's head. Soft fur tickled his fingers, and a weight he'd had across his shoulders, one he hadn't been aware of, lifted. "Beautiful."

A warm canine tongue reached out as the dog turned enough to lick his hand.

"You're a friendly enough dog, aren't you?" Jakob led the way up the stairs. "Wonder what your name is? Suppose I could look it up."

The dog nudged his hand for a fresh scratch behind the ear.

"We'll get you out of the suit, not sure if yours is different, well other than the space for your tail and legs, than a human suit, but I'll guess we'll find out."

"His name is Mags, short for Magnum." The bar owner, Jones wasn't it? Explained.

"That right, Mags?"

Mags gave a soft woof.

"Alright, Mags it is." He glanced over at the man. "Jones?"

"Yes, you'd be Jakob. Lawbook mentioned you."

Had she? He glanced around, catching sight of the Sergeant in the kitchen, one hand wrapped around a mug of caff. The Sergeant didn't turn his way, but she didn't need to. If Jones knew his name, and Lawbook was in the same space, then the information had to come from the Sergeant. "Ah, makes sense. You know anything else about Mags or the woman?"

"Leigh Winter, according to Jackson. He had more chance to talk with her than I did."

"Turner should be able to help her." He frowned, had there been something in the man's tone to suggest he believed Winter wouldn't make it? "He's done a patch-up job on Walker."

"Walker? He was one of the Marines who left with Lawbook, right?"

"Yeah, got hurt when they were giving us covering fire. Whole heap of aliens came down on us, he took a shot to the shoulder." He hadn't seen it, but they all knew about it. "I don't know how well Turner has worked his magic, but he's already working on Winter." Her arm, what would they tell her when she woke up? Mags whined.

"She'll be alright, Mags. Turner won't let her die." He reached back to the dog, his fingers finding his head before he worked his fingers through the soft fur covering Mags' head. "He's gorgeous."

"Smart too." Jones crouched down. "Let's get him out of this suit, at least he'll be more comfortable. Doubt he's happy about being parted from Winter, but I wouldn't think the doc would want him around if he has to operate."

"No, he didn't. Had me take Mags out of the room." He scratched behind Mags' left ear. "Alright, let's get this thing off him."

#

Stone glanced over as the suit was stripped from the canine unit and carried out to be flushed and cleaned before restocked with the standard supplies. He wrinkled his nose at the idea of the chore. They'd have to be careful with the suit as they didn't have a replacement unit for the dog. Not as if there were things they could make from thin air, and even if they'd had enough spare suits, one they could rig for the dog, it wouldn't work in the way it was needed.

"A canine unit. On Pluto. Never believed I'd see the day." Mrs. Hunter mused. "It's been a long time since I touched a real dog. Couldn't have been more than a child the last time I came across one." Her voice softened. "But I wish it were under better circumstances."

What was it about dogs which drew attention, the gentling of voice and eyes, a tenderness seldom seen unless it was around a baby. "I imagine it was a shock. Seeing one here, I mean."

"Yes, it was. But the good type." He nodded at the dog. "It's going to be a long day ahead of us. Are you alright with how things panned out." Mrs. Hunter wouldn't be going with the rest assault group.

"I'm no fighter, never will be. And I can't stop Ian from going if he wants to. He's a grown man." Her words said one thing, eyes another. "Keep him safe if he goes with, please."

"Shouldn't you be having this conversation with Lawbook?"

"She'll do her best to bring them all back, but has made it clear they will lose people out there. I'd be a fool to believe otherwise, and she's smart enough not to lie. Not about the truth, at least. Maybe I should be grateful for that, it doesn't fill me with warmth, but I prefer the truth." She paused, her gaze moving over those in the family room. "Don't let him throw his life away doing something foolish. It's one thing to know he might die doing the right thing, another to find out he made a silly mistake or acted the hero when he should have waited, and that's why he isn't coming home."

Stone watched her, taking in the serious tone, the care, a mother's love. "I'll do my best."

"It's all I can ask for. And if he dies, I can't promise I won't blame you or the Sergeant, but I'll try not to." She wet her lips, aging before his eyes. "He's my son, he may be a legal adult, but he'll always be the little boy I brought into this world."

He understood, on a surface level. He'd been the only son of a loving mother, but she'd died long ago, far away from Pluto. "I understand."

Her eyes narrowed as she watched him. "No, you don't, and I pray you never do."

#

No time or place for sleep now, not with the newcomers brought in by Jackson and Jones. She'd sent the Marine to grab an hour and suggested the same to Jones, but the man had stubbornly refused to be ordered around.

She didn't blame him.

Cora Bloodlaw closed her eyes and tried to bring her thoughts into order. It didn't matter what she wanted, what she craved, all she had to do was calm her mind, allow the tension to ease from her body, and focus on her breathing for a few minutes. It wasn't as good as sleep, but she'd take what she could get, and be thankful for the real rest she'd already grabbed before Jones had arrived.

"Sergeant?" A small hand touched her arm.

"Yes, Helen?" There was only one person it could be. The other kids were busy or asleep. Not here.

"You will bring them back, won't you?"

"I'll do my best." She didn't need to know who Helen meant. "I can't promise anything more than I'll try, I don't want to leave them there." Who would? A heartless soldier. She had no desire to lose her heart. It gave her an edge. One she wasn't about to walk away from. "You're going to stay here, watch your parents."

"I will." A pause, the fingers tightening on her arm before they released. "I was working on an idea which might help narrow down their location. The other kids, I mean."

Helen opened her eyes. "Show me."

Helen smiled, joy claiming her features before she turned and led Cora through the room, then into a small workroom behind the kitchen. "Dad lets me tinker with things." She stopped by a small table and pulled a box out of the way. "I started this a few days ago before all this happened. Not sure why."

Cora's eyes narrowed as she stared at the creation. A curl of wires, cords, a small screen. If Helen had been an adult, then she'd have asked how much the woman had had to drink before working on the Frankenstein worthy creation. "Alright, what do you want to show me?"

Helen frowned, her gaze flicking from the machine to Cora and back again. "Oh, right. You don't get it." She nodded to herself. "All the kids are chipped."

"They are?" Cora rattled through her mind. Chips. Safety chips. "Yes, the safety measure. Sorry, been a long day."

"Yes, days on Pluto are longer." Helen settled down and booted up the contraption. "Not sure why it's relevant." Her bottom lip caught between her teeth. "Oh, but this. It's to track the chips."

"How is it possible? The chips, the locator signal aren't on the public bands, and the dampening field, the block, wouldn't tracking those be difficult?" Impossible, according to the techs, but Helen had already shown she had a way with these things.

"Yes, it should be. Not to me. Machines like me. They complain, but they do what I want." She stroked the side of her creation. "I've located most of the kids. I made certain to aim at the colony, in case they found a way to piggyback my system and use it to find the rest of us. Didn't think it would be a good idea."

"No, it wouldn't be," she urged Helen to continue.

"They're here, see?" Helen gestured to the screen. "All those small blips, those are the kids. The majority of them are here, close to the base. A few are scattered through the colony, the signal faint. I think they're in the tunnels. But there have to be at least fifty kids here, all young. Under ten."

Ten was young, to a thirteen-year-old. It was all a matter of perspective.

"You did good, Helen. Anyway, you can do a mobile version of this? Boost a datapad, so it works as a tracer, scanner, or whatever?" Tech science had never been her strong suit, nor had she needed it to be until recently. "Anyone ever tell you that you're amazing?"

Helen's face glowed under the praise. "No. I think I like it, though." She launched herself off the chair and wrapped her arms about Cora. "I like you. And yes, I can make a smaller version. It won't take long. Can have it for you in an hour, two at most. But likely an hour."

The kid was a miracle worker. Cora hugged Helen, releasing her grip on the teen only when the youngster tensed.

"You're an amazing young woman, and I'm damn glad I met you." Her mind raced. If they were to go after the kids, then they'd need a distraction. Something to pull the aliens off their trail when they tried to find their way back to the settlement. "Ever tried remote piloting?"

Helen tipped her head to the side, eyes narrowed. "Yes. Not supposed to, but yet." A glint played within her eyes. "Can hack anything." She ducked her head. "No, not hack. Hacking is wrong. Gets me in trouble."

"Oh, believe me, you're not going to get in trouble with me for hacking. Not as long as you clear it with me first."

Interlude Six

"There's been an explosion, one away from the dome."

Treizaek turned toward the door, eyes narrowed. "Who gave you permission to enter my chamber?"

The female, the same one he'd seen working the comm station, lifted her jaw, exposing her neck. "I believed this was important enough to use the emergency code, commander." She didn't move, her gaze shielded by lowered lids, the vulnerable portion of her throat ready for his retribution should he chose to act.

He rose, turning the full power of his gaze on the female. Her wings remained folded behind her back, hands with long, delicate claws, glinted in the ship's lights. "Present yourself, female. And pray your news spares your life."

"Verlianic, Commander," she formally introduced herself. "I've been assigned to your command since the beginning of this mission."

"Your first away from the nest?"

"Yes, Commander."

The admission wouldn't save her from punishment but might buy her a lesser sentence than death if her information proved to be lacking. "Speak and be quick about it." Sleek wings, beautiful delicate scales, she was young, never taken part in a mating flight. Too innocent for his usual tastes yet there was a glint in her eyes, the way she watched him when she believed he wasn't paying attention, which tempted his interest.

"I registered an explosion, but when I reported it to the bridge commander, he brushed it off."

"And you wouldn't let it go, is that it, child?" Would she offer her throat in a more intimate situation? Surrender without a fight? His blood warmed as he watched her.

"I'm no child, Commander. Forgive me for being forward. But

I am marked as an adult, ready to fight by your side, or die should you order it," said Verlianic.

He'd heard the words before, many a time from the males, females, and neuters who served aboard his ship. "We'll see. Now, speak. Tell me of this explosion. What have you learned?"

A light danced in her eyes. "Yes, Commander. May I show you the map?" She lifted the datapad she held. "It would be easier. Or I could bring the information on your private screen should you prefer."

He hissed a warning. "Don't be foolish. As if I would permit a nothing like you access to my personal screens."

She ducked her head, wings drooped. "My apologies, Commander. I allowed my excitement to get the better of me."

"A common error for those still new from their nest." He gestured to the pad. "Show me." If it were nothing, then he'd deal with the female, have her replaced at her station, and send her for correction.

The colors across her head, the delicate scales, shifted. A small touch of bronze, paling to silver. Fear; she hadn't learned to control as yet. Another mark of her lack of experience. "It is all here, commander."

Treizaek took the pad and turned it, letting the female enter the room enough to allow the door to close behind her. Had she understood the danger in approaching him? "What am I seeing?"

Verlianic's wings lifted and the tips touching the floor. "It's a tunnel set up, the type built by these humans. We assume they created them as a means of hiding away from the cold and lack of atmosphere. They are weak creatures, but I admit they have their uses."

"The tunnel, female."

"Your second sent scouts into the tunnel. The reports indicated the amount of time her scouts spent there, then they returned. The explosion matched with the location the scouts approached, but I can't say for certain they were connected with the explosion. At least I couldn't until I ran a full report." She tapped the datapad. "These readings indicate explosives known to our people, but not theirs, were used in this tunnel. A trap set up to deal with the rogue humans."

He scowled at the pad. "I see, this is news why?"

"Because I continued to scan the area, Commander. There were human life signs, the trap hadn't killed them. The signs were not easy to read, but I was able to narrow the scan, pinpoint the humans, and there was something else. A life sign I haven't seen before. It's not in our database either." She moved behind him, reaching past to touch the datapad. "This one, commander."

He shifted his weight, wings rustling against his back as he brought up the individual information for the small, flickering life sign. "I see." Unusual, small, operating on four limbs, but the rest of the information did nothing to answer his questions. "Interesting." He turned without warning and shoved the datapad back in the female's grasp. "You did the right thing, Verlianic. I don't know what this will mean to our assignments, but if nothing else the scientists will want to capture one of these creatures for testing."

Verlianic stumbled away from him, wings snapping out to correct her balance. "Thank you, Commander. Should I share this data with anyone else?"

"No."

She protested, then caught herself.

He watched, waiting for her to protest.

Nothing.

"You may leave, Verlianic."

"Yes, commander," she clutched the datapad close, hesitated as her gaze flicked around the room.

He dismissed her with a flick of a wing, watching as she withdrew from his sight. An interesting female, more compliant than his current mate. But females were a dangerous thing to underestimate. More than one male of his acquaintance had found his throat between the sharp teeth of the female they'd taken as a companion. Had their last thoughts been consumed by shock at the betrayal or a curse at their own foolishness?

A mistake he would never make.

"Ah, my Nyanaek. Would you be surprised to know I wish you nothing but success down there?" He mused as he replayed the information Verlianic had shared with him. Devious and yet oddly direct, his mate was a dangerous creature and had killed her way to his nest. But it wouldn't prevent him from passing the time with lesser females, should his mate be away long enough. A more passive female, like Verlianic, would fill the gap in his nest, and still, be low enough in ship and warrior status for Nyanaek not to be threatened.

It didn't mean his mate wouldn't kill the new female. Any more than he would dispatch any male she dared to take into her embrace while they were parted.

It was the nature of such things.

The strong did as they wished. The weak obeyed.

And only a pair of matched strength were allowed to bring new life into the nest.

Chapter Fifteen

Cora gathered the last pieces of information Helen had collected for her and turned her attention to the men and women waiting for her. Her gaze took in each face, assigning a name to it before she took a deep breath. "Thank you, all of you. Volunteering for this mission took a lot of courage, but I'm now giving you one last chance to pull out. I'll be blunt, the odds of all of us making it back in one piece if at all, are slim. We're outnumbered, outgunned, and have only limited intelligence."

"Sounds like a normal Marine mission, Sergeant," Lackey called out.

"Oorahh," the rest of the Marines added.

She smiled, how could she do anything else? "True enough, but in this case, we're taking civilians with us. Keep it in mind during this outing, and we're less likely to lose one or two before we get to the kids. Make no mistake, rescuing the children is the priority."

Nervous smiles touched the faces of several civilians, others shifted their weight, but none moved to leave the storage shed.

"You won't be thought less of if you decide not to join us on this joy ride. It won't be an easy trip, we'll use the ground cars for part of the trip, but there'll be a lot of running, and if you fall behind you'll put the rest of us in danger." How many would she lose? Civilians? Marines? Both? "If your families want you to stay, then stay. If you doubt your abilities to follow my orders, without question, under fire, then leave. There will be times when you can pass the word to me, make a suggestion, but if we're under radio silence and you break it, I'll break you." Her voice hardened. "Put us in danger and ignore my warnings, and I'll shoot you myself."

A nervous chuckle swept through the civilians. They believed her, she saw it in their eyes but didn't want to.

"Sergeant?" One of the three women who'd volunteered made her way through the group.

"Yes?"

"Do we have a chance?"

"Yes, but I won't say the odds are in our favor."

The civilian inclined her head. "Understood. I'm still in. I'd rather die trying than live knowing I left those kids in their hands. Claws. Whatever."

A rumble of agreement followed her words.

"Then if there's nothing else, take ten minutes to say goodbye to your family and friends, check your suits and gear, then report back. We head out in twenty."

"Sergeant, we're going to get those kids out of there," said Ready as he and the other Marines approached her. Only Walker and Winter would remain behind. "Hell, we escaped the horde back in the cavern, didn't we?"

"Yeah, blew the shit out of them." Lackey agreed.

"Dropped rocks on them would be closer to the truth," said Harvard.

"You weren't there, man," said Ready.

"No, but I was." Virgil slapped one hand down on Ready's shoulder. "We dropped rocks on them. Blew up the cavern first. Shit, it was your idea, dude."

"Sweet explosions. Gotta do that again." Ready's eyes glinted. "Wish I could have been close enough to see one of them flattened. Pancake batter."

"Purple pancake batter," said Lackey.

"Maybe he's had one too many hits to the head to remember where he was when the ceiling came in," suggested Liam.

"Of course he has, he's a Marine." Virgil high-fivedLiam.

She smiled. What other choice did she have? It didn't matter that two of her marines were civilians. The two men, Virgil and Liam, had proved their worth back in the cavern. They followed orders, they got on with the rest of her men, and now she had Jackson back in the mix, she had a decent core group.

Stone.

Yeah, there was Stone to take into account. He hadn't brought up payment since the cavern, but he would, sooner or later.

"Alright, alright, we have shit to do. Check your gear, replace anything you need to, and seal any stress points in your suits." She had enough time to go over her own gear for the fourth time. But she wasn't going to ignore the need to double, triple check every piece of her equipment. None of them were in full uniform, small parts had been replaced since they'd arrived at the Hunter's place.

Harvard had taken the worst of the damage to his clothing. He'd been in the GetAway wearing full civies except for his boots. A small blessing. Now he stayed at the back of the core group, his gaze calm. He didn't mingle easily with the Marines, nor they with him, but he wasn't excluded.

As an officer in the Navy, he wasn't expected to act like one of the guys. And the no fraternizing rule when shipboard, didn't help to form strong bonds between the various units.

"Harvard?"

He pushed away from the boxes he'd been leaning on. "Yes, Sergeant?"

"You up to this? Following my orders in a combat situation?" He had before, but who knew when it came to the Navy?

"Sure. Yes, I know, I'm an officer. But you're the one with ground combat experience. Looked you up earlier, you dealt with a smuggler hold out, couple of years ago."

A small shrug. "I wasn't in command."

"Not how the reports tell it."

"Officially, I wasn't in command." What was with the guy? Turning the conversation to her past missions wasn't what she'd expected. "Wrong place, wrong time type of thing. Beside the point."

"You're wrong, it's exactly the point. If the Gunny had made it, I'd happily follow his orders. Gunny trusted you. The reports make it clear you know what you're doing. Surprised you weren't bumped for officer training."

Cora shuddered. "Thanks, but no thanks. Not interested." Who would want to be an officer with their stiff uniforms, little fingers raised when they drank, or whatever else they did. Other than give people orders.

"You work for a living, right?" Harvard smirked. "Heard it before. And yeah, there are bad apples who make it through the academy, but shit, most of us didn't know what we were doing the first time we made it off-planet."

"No one does. Training only goes so far to prepare you for what it's like. Might be easier if you're from one of the colonies, but those of us born on Earth face a shock when we're first shoved out here." She shook her head. "Check your gear."

"Yes, Sergeant."

#

Jakob pulled on his suit. Salla. Why had the Sergeant agreed to allow Salla with them? It was one thing to tell her he wasn't going to let them head out within him, and agree with her at the time that Salla should be part of the group, but now...

The Marine, Winter, her arm, or what was left of it, replayed through his mind. The paleness, blood loss, the mangled limb. What if it happened to Salla? Would he be able to save her? His stomach turned, cold sweat beading across the back of his neck.

"Don't worry about her, if you do, you'll make a mistake and get both of you killed."

Stone's voice caught him off guard, and he struggled to maintain his balance, one foot caught in the leg of the suit. They'd all taken them off instead of stuffing them back into the pouches. To check for damage, according to Lawbook. Now he cursed the fact he couldn't slap the bag and trigger the suit so it would slide over his body, leaving only the seams to take care of.

"Easy kid, don't need you falling over." Stone grabbed his arm until Jakob regained his balance.

"Startled me."

"I see." He didn't turn toward Stone. "I'll be fine. And what did you mean anyway?"

"You want to deny you're worried about Salla?" Stone moved in front of Jakob, his trench coat parting as he walked before resettling around the man and his suit.

"Why do you wear that thing? Has to slow you down some."

Stone laughed. "Don't like the question, do you?"

"You answer mine, and I'll answer yours." Jakob regretted the words the minute he'd spoken them. "Shit, sorry, makes it sound like I'm a kid."

"You're not a kid, not anymore. Nor is Salla. Not after what you've both been through. I doubt there are many real children left on Pluto." Stone shifted his rifle, making a show of checking it. "It's lucky."

"Lucky?"

"The coat. Haven't been seriously hurt since I picked it off a man who tried to kill me."

"If he's dead, how can it be lucky? Couldn't it be a coincidence?"

"Never said it was lucky for him, did I?"

Jakob couldn't help but smile. He wasn't about to argue with the smuggler. He was strong, confident, and everything he wanted to be when the world no longer viewed as a child by the world in general. It didn't matter how long it took to get there, he'd make it. Maybe on his own, or with a woman like Salla in his life.

"You'll do fine, as long as you keep calm and follow orders. Salla will be doing the same thing, and she's smart. Her dad isn't the type to half train his daughter. You're going to have to accept it if you want to be in her life long term." Stone clapped one hand on Jakob's shoulder. "Don't make the mistake of trying to tell a woman like Salla what to do. Give her options, but don't assume she'll follow your orders."

Order Salla around? What would she do if he tried that?

Punch him out? She wasn't the type to stand there and take it, not from a man who wanted to be in her life.

And there it was, the admission he wanted her, not only as a friend but--

"Out in three minutes. Form up. We leave in threes. You know which of the ground cars have been assigned to you. Don't hesitate, get in, close the door, and maintain radio silence." Bloodlaw called out. "Time to get the kids and bring them home."

Home. Did they have access to a real home? He shook off the idea. The kids would be safer away from the colony. They'd find a way of hiding them from the aliens, keep them from being collected again. Then what?

Get rid of the invaders and reclaim Pluto, no matter how long it took.

Salla flashed a smile and took her place. He'd be with her, at her side, no matter what they faced. They'd do it together.

#

Ian sealed his suit and took his position in the line for the airlock. Not what he'd expected to deal with, or agree to, heading into the colony to bring the kids back. His mind drifted back to the two injured Marines. How many more would be hurt or killed during this mission? I knew the risks when I signed up for this.

Didn't mean he wasn't wary about the events ahead. It was one thing to agree to find the kids, another to be shot at.

He swallowed down the waves of fear, tried to settle his stomach. Whatever he had to do, he would. He had to. This wasn't the end, but a new beginning and he'd prove his worth to Salla. Then, maybe, she'd see him as more than a friend. It wasn't as if he'd ever done anything to suggest they could take things further. But he wasn't about to give up now.

He couldn't.

Wouldn't.

She'd want him. When he showed he was a man, not a boy.

Jakob.

Why had the Sergeant allowed Jakob to join them? He was little more than a child, never would be anything more if he wasn't careful. Sure, he was a friend to Salla, but what did she see in him? In this Jakob? Was he out of high school?

"Get your mind on the job, not the woman." Lackey leaned close, his voice pitched not to carry. "With a woman on your mind, you're more likely to die. And I've no intention of dying alongside you due to a stupid mistake."

He tensed. "I'm not going to get killed out there. Neither are you."

"Ah, bullshit, kid. If you don't remember death is waiting for you around every corner, not only are you dead, but anyone who tries to help you is dead."

He didn't like the idea. Ian scowled, refusing to turn to the Marine. How had he known what was going through his mind? Had he spoken? With people around, always close at hand, unless he was out at one of the claims, he'd learned to keep silent.

"You don't like the warning? Good, you might survive long enough to learn and make it back in one piece."

Oh, he'd more than survive. He'd show Salla precisely what he was made of. Duncan would never have approved of a man who couldn't take care of himself. He'd be able to handle whatever happened out there. It didn't matter what Lackey believed.

He could do this.

#

Leigh groaned as she fought to open her eyes. Stiffness locked her in position, her muscles unwilling to obey her and the desire to sink back into sleep tugged on the corner of her mind.

Where was she?

Sounds filtered past the thick, fluffy cloth which held her mind and body still. She tried to wriggle her fingers, but her body didn't respond. Sleep paralyzes, she'd been told it was a possible side effect of spending time on another planet, giving the body a

182

chance to adapt to the situation.

Planet?

Pluto, she'd landed. Crashed in a pod with Mags. The ship destroyed and-- the rest slipped from her grasp. She could see it, the boxes containing her life, memories, answers to what had happened to her.

A noise, a voice? Maybe, she couldn't be sure, not with the way she currently felt. Or didn't feel as the case may be. Heavyweights, like an old-fashioned weighted blanket, pressed against her body, holding her in place, on a bed.

When had she been moved to a bed?

She hadn't fallen asleep on one.

"Don't move. I don't want you to hurt yourself." A voice, one she didn't recognize. "I not long finished patching you up, don't want to have to repeat the work." A steady hand touched her shoulder.

"Who?" Her mouth didn't want to work, but the single word slipped past the cotton wool filling her mouth. She tried to swallow, but her mouth still refused to obey her. "Where?"

"You're at the Hunter's claim, and I'm Doctor Turner. I fear my bedside manner still needs work. You and Walker were my first real customers since returning to Pluto." He ran a small sensor over her forehead. "Small fever, to be expected after surgery." He tucked the instrument out of the way. "You'll feel it on and off for a few days. More common out on the frontier, something about the way the different gravity and artificial atmosphere affecting the human body. I'd go into detail, but I don't want to put you back to sleep. Not yet, at least."

How long had she slept?

"Can't -- move." Two words, an improvement as they were closer together than her first attempt. She wriggled her jaw but couldn't feel it. Not entirely.

"I had to inject you with a paralytic, to make certain you didn't move at the wrong time. It will ease, and you'll be able to move shortly, but I don't advise you attempt it before I tell you it's safe." He patted her shoulder, then stepped out of sight.

She tried to follow his path, the movement through the room, but though her eyes now obeyed her, her head didn't. She couldn't see beyond the small circle of focus above her head. "Surgery?"

"Yes, sorry about that. There was no way I could save the arm. Not with the facilities on hand. Perhaps not even if we'd been beneath the dome. It was a mess before they brought you to me."

Her hand? Gone? She tried to make sense of the words.

"It's a lot to take in." He returned to the side of the table, bench, or whatever she was resting on. "And I'll have to repeat the information to you every time you wake up until you're more like yourself."

She wanted to protest, to tell him she was fine, but the words refused to come. Her eyes closed, heavy, stealing her of sight as she sank deeper into the darkness. Odd, it was warm, not cold the way death would be. Or how she assumed it would be when her time came.

Was she dying?

"You're exhausted, will be for a few days. Don't push it. Don't fight it, you need to rest and give yourself a chance to recover." His voice lulled her, tempting her to give in. She didn't know him, had never met him before, but she trusted him.

Maybe there was a reason.

It couldn't be because of her injury, whatever it had been.

Hand.

Yes, he'd said her hand had been damaged. Why would he need to save it, and from what? Questions rolled through her mind, lingering long enough to make sense before they faded, replaced by a jumble of words.

"Sleep, you'll feel stronger next time you wake up."

Yes, more sleep. She'd be able to move around when she woke up. But she was forgetting something. A piece of her?

The arm? No, it was something else now. A companion, friend, member of her family. One who'd been there, at her side for years.

Mags.

Chapter Sixteen

No one spoke, not within the confines of her ground car. If they dared to talk in the other vehicles, she neither knew nor cared as she continued to check the data feed Helen had patched her into. Getting all the kids away in one piece wasn't going to be easy, and she had no idea if her plan would work or not.

What had Gunny said? A phrase repeated by one of the miner's wives. No plan survives first contact with the enemy. Which meant, no matter how carefully she planned, how thoroughly she explored every piece of information. Things would go wrong, and she'd be left relying on gut instinct.

Her gaze flicked to the main screen, then back to her datapad. Allowing Stone to be in her team, and drive, left her free to keep a close eye on the signals indicating the presence of the kids. The small, blinking markers no longer huddled in one group but had split into three large ones, and four lights kept in their own group.

Or in hiding?

She cursed silently. No way of finding out this far out, and once they were beneath the planet's surface, there would be no turning back. Not without leading the aliens back to the Hunter's settlement. A mistake she couldn't afford to make.

Which made the entire situation beyond dangerous. Whatever they did, be it run for another settlement, or return to the Hunter's, there remained the risk of being followed when they made it out with the kids. A fact which continued to plague her. There would be a way out of this, a means of keeping them all safe.

If Helen could do her part, they'd make it out of the dome.

"You don't have to continue," said Stone.

"If you're about to try to talk me out of this, it's not going to work." She didn't look at him, didn't need to. "I'm not going to leave those kids."

"You're acting from your heart, not your head."

"Using both." She shrugged. "You don't like it, you didn't need to come with me. Should have stayed behind with the others." What was the man's problem?

"You needed someone in the group who put their own skins above the need to get the kids." A small shrug. One she felt more than saw. "Don't get me wrong, I don't like the idea of anyone being trapped with those things. Trained as slaves. It's wrong, I'm never going to believe anything else about slavery."

"Unusual for a smuggler." She turned her focus to the area around the kids. The edge of the military section of the base, she knew the city, had been there more often than she cared to count. Why had the children been split into three groups?

"I don't deal with slavers."

"So most smugglers say, but experience tells me a fair percentage of you still enjoy the extra funds dealing with them provides you."

He growled, the sound low and dangerous, but if it was meant to frighten her, it didn't work. She bit back a laugh, shot him a sideways glance, and gave in. Laughter took over as she tried not to look at him. "Are you trying to intimidate me?"

"What the fuck?" He glared at her.

Despite everything, she couldn't stop laughing. Tears threatened to spill down her cheeks.

"You really don't take me seriously, do you?"

She shook her head, trying to get it back under control, but it didn't help. If she glanced at him at all, the laughter continued, gaining new life as it ripped through the ground car. Tears seeped from the corners of her eyes as the two others in the car, burst into laughter. She pressed one hand to her mouth and gulped for air.

A small, barely seen smile, touched his lips, only to vanish beneath a scowl.

Whatever the man believed, he couldn't hide the growing

need to smile, laugh, give in to the much-needed release of tension they all dealt with. The pressure which had built up since the first shakes had hit the GetAway back in the tunnels. At least they now knew Jones and the majority of the other survivors had made it in one piece.

"Whatever," he muttered.

"We're going to get them out of this, get them back into human hands." She announced once the last of the laughter was under control. "Do I think this is going to be easy? No, which is why I'm not taking any chances." Liar. The entire mission could only be described as taking chances. It wasn't going to be easy, nor would she give up. The kids had to be pulled free, there was no other choice in the matter.

"Right, so you have an escape route planned?"

"At least a distraction, enough to assist us in getting out in one piece." Helen, if the young woman came through with her end of the job, then they had a chance. And she had no doubt Helen would do everything possible to help bring her brother home in one piece.

"Care to run the idea past me?"

"Nope." She flashed him a grin.

"What if something happens to you?"

"It won't." Sure, fine, she couldn't prevent the aliens from trying to kill her. Or capture her. But she wasn't about to tell Stone, not when the man already knew what was going on. They all had the same chance of surviving, and the equal opportunity they'd be killed or captured.

"I don't deal with slavers."

"Sure," she increased the details around the captured kids.

"They're scum."

"People say the same thing about smugglers in general."

"Only when they don't want to pay the agreed prices."

She couldn't argue the point, not when she'd seen enough reports to know the real reason behind people turning smugglers in. Money not only talked, but occasionally persuaded brother to turn against brother. "What's your problem with slavers?'

"They're nothing like me. I don't deal in human misery."

#

Jakob leaned back in the chair, listening to the conversation between Stone and Lawbook. He wasn't sure what was going on between them, nor did he want to know as long as it didn't include him, or Salla. They didn't like each other, and if it meant listening to them banter back and forth, trying to work things out between them, he could put up with it.

If nothing else, it was better than being locked in his own thoughts.

"Think they've hurt the kids?" asked Salla.

"Hope not."

"They've been through more than enough. Seeing whatever happened to their families. Being dragged away from the people they know and love." Salla shook her head, her jaw set. "I saw them take my dad, so yeah, I've got a decent idea of how they feel right about now." She closed her eyes.

If she didn't want to talk about it, he wasn't going to push. "You get enough sleep?"

"Yeah, did you?" Sleep wasn't ideal, not with the dreams he'd dealt with.

"More than I expected." A shrug. "We'll get more once we're back."

"You could close your eyes now. It's what Ready said Marines do. Catch sleep whenever they can. Might be an idea."

Could he manage it? "Worth a try. Not like there's much else to do now. Not that's worth spending energy on."

"Shoot the shit, but yeah, nothing else. Joys of ground cars with their inbuilt entertainment package."

"You ever seen one of those?" He turned enough in his seat to be able to see her face. "In person, I mean?"

"Oh yeah, once or twice. I took a ride in one, least before Duncan caught me."

When had she gone from calling her father dad, and switched to his name? A means of distancing herself from what she'd been through?

The conversation between the two adults continued, but he no longer followed their every word, lost in what may never again be.

#

Stone kept his attention on the readings. Two more minutes, and they'd be in the tunnels. At least there they had a decent chance of not being seen. The tubes held dangers of their own, now he knew about the booby trap which had injured the Marine, Winter.

He'd avoided going down to see her, unable to bring himself to visit the injury which had kept the woman unconscious. The dog, however, was another matter. It had sought him out several times, and he hadn't pushed the animal away. Why would he? Not as if the dog meant him any harm, or would attack him.

Not unless he threatened the sleeping Marine.

"There it is."

"I see it," he replied, not needing to say anything more to Lawbook. The damn woman couldn't understand the difference between a smuggler and a slaver. His jaw clenched. Or maybe she did. Perhaps she was trying to keep his thoughts away from whatever she had in mind to get them out of this mess when the time came?

Warped and clever. Stone fought against the urge to grin. If that was her plan, and he wouldn't put it past her, it had worked for a time. Shit, it was the type of thing he might have pulled, if he'd been in her seat. Smart, an easy distraction, kept the conversation going until he was uncomfortable enough to put an end to their talk. Damn woman, she was sneaky.

The car dipped, a solid jerk raised complaints from the back seat, before they slipped into the enclosed darkness of the tunnels. Stealing the stars from their vision. His heart raced, tension returning the further they traveled into the tunnels.

It wouldn't be long before they were deep enough into the tunnels to make it pointless to turn around without a damn strong reason. He double-checked the map, going over the options. Yeah, she had it all worked out. Turning back once they were deeper in the passageways, was a choice most wouldn't want to take.

"Left hand-split coming up."

"I know."

The other cars followed behind, close enough to ensure they never lost sight of the one in front of them. Except for theirs. They were the lead car, and how had he ended up piloting the first car, the lead target? Why he'd done the one thing his father had always warned him not to do.

He'd bloody volunteered.

To get to my ship.

Good line, pity no one, including himself, bought it. Sure, he wanted to get to his ship, but it wasn't a part of the plan. Shit, he knew what they were facing down here, it wasn't as if they hadn't been through the tunnels before, facing the risks of aliens, and those blasted alien space bats, chasing them down. "We'll need to leave someone behind to guard the transport."

"Already figured that one out." Her gaze flicked back to the two younger members of the team.

He grinned as the pieces fell into place. "Makes sense to me. Wouldn't want to come back to the cars only to have one or more of them blow up on us. Jones was damn lucky the whole cavern didn't come down on them, or all the cars weren't taken out."

"They lost a few, but the others were easy enough to patch up. We won't have time to spare, not to search for booby traps, or repair any of the cars if they've been tampered with." He shrugged but didn't take his eyes off the route. Turns, a few here and there before they reached the split, and he took the left-hand tunnel.

#

No pain. No ability to move. Nothing she could control, yet it didn't matter. It should have done, but her ability to fight, to sit up, find out what was going on, refused to answer her demands, and she'd given up trying to force her body into action. Trapped, yet she wasn't afraid. Held in place by bonds she couldn't feel, but her heart rate never increased.

Her eyes remained closed as she listened. Her ears worked, a small blessing she was willing to cling to.

"Walker, all you have to do is open your eyes. We can talk. I can bring you something to ease the pain, like before."

A woman's voice. One she didn't know, couldn't put a name to.

Walker, she presumed it was him, groaned.

"Remember, I had the vial before. I still have one. She didn't take it all. I'm no fool, I'd never give up my only source. Not when I know I can help you and others like you."

Her skin crawled at the conversation. Or was it a tingle? Didn't matter, at least there was sensation. Nothing she could control, reach for, or use to her advantage, but it still existed. Her body wasn't dying beneath her, not yet.

Hand.

She couldn't feel one hand.

She tried to wriggle her fingers, but they refused to respond. She relaxed, despite the issue. There was nothing to worry about. It wasn't going to change until whatever the man had done to fix the problems, set in. The doctor? Yes, he'd been a doctor, and he'd want to continue to help her. It was the nature of their training. They tried to help, heal, cure, make everything the way it had been.

Mags.

She strained to listen for him. Searching for a small sign of the dog who'd been with her since the beginning. There'd been no life before Mags, or so the canine had convinced her.

"Open your eyes, Walker. I have a vial of dreams with me. It'll work. All you have to do is open your eyes."

Dreams?

What was she talking about? She tried to make sense of the conversation, but darkness, coated with cotton wool, wrapped her in its embrace, pulling her back to the lands of silent stillness.

Interlude Seven

"Cavanor report." The Admiral's voice called out from beyond the closed door.

She shot to attention, unable to do anything else, habit, training, it didn't matter, his voice commanded attention, and she pushed the door open, letting it close behind her once she was inside the office. Habit pulled her to the desk, head high, back straight, shoulders back. "Admiral."

"At ease," he flicked one finger in the direction of the waiting chair. "Sit. No point in being at attention for this. We'll get through this meeting, go over what you can tell me, then deal with the fallout."

Fall out. It was one way to put it. Grant wouldn't allow this to go past unanswered. He'd fight back. Find a way to reach out and strike. Sure, he would do anything it took to gain his revenge. Her heart raced as she sat on the edge of the chair. If he meant her to relax, it wasn't going to happen. "Yes, sir."

"Grant entered the female dorm?"

"Yes, sir. I didn't invite him in."

"I didn't assume you did." He leaned back in his chair. "He's been a problem for you before?"

"Yes, sir."

"Why is there nothing in the files about his behavior?" His gaze met and held hers.

"I didn't make a formal report," she lowered her gaze. Didn't the man understand how things worked? If you spoke up about a superior harassing you, odds were it meant you were punished for it. Oh, not officially sanctioned, but even if the officer was removed from the area, your career was hosed. "I know I broke protocol, but I believed it was for the best to try to handle the situation on my own."

"I see."

"With respect, sir. I don't believe you do."

"You know what I hear when one of my people says 'with respect, sir'?

"No, sir." She swore, repeatedly under her breath. What the hell had she gotten herself into now?

"You're an asshole, sir, and have no clue what the real world is like." He smiled, leaned forward, and steepled his fingers, elbows resting on the desk. "I'm not an idiot, Cavanor. I know how the fallout can hit the one doing the reporting. We like to think we're evolved, that we've moved past both sexual harassment and false claims. Truth is, we haven't, and I'm not sure we ever will."

She tried not to react, despite the desire to speak, to protest, to let herself be honest. But her training kicked in, silencing her where she would talk otherwise without caution. She wasn't enjoying a beer with a friend, she was in the Admiral's office, or the one he'd claimed for now. This was a meeting with a superior officer.

"Grant won't get away with this, he's already being held for a hearing. Â I doubt I'll be able to do much more than strip him of his rank. Unfortunately, he has contacts, rich and powerful people either in his family, or connected to his family."

"Sir?"

"You want to know why I'm sharing this information with you?"

"Yes, sir."

He leaned forward. "Because a man like Grant isn't going to let this go. Doesn't matter if he's moved away, stripped of his rank, he will find a way to pursue you."

Her heart sank, though she'd know the truth long before he'd given it life. "This isn't over, that's what you're telling me, isn't it?"

"Yes, I'm sorry, Cavanor. I wouldn't wish this on anyone."

It didn't make sense. No matter what he said, there had to be a way of keeping Grant from continuing this game of his. "Why me?"

"I don't have an answer for you. There will always be those men and women who want what they can't have. Whotry to take control of situations despite being told there were rules in place." The Admiral's voice gentled.

"He pushed for me to date him, despite regulations. I said no. Moved to another shift. But it didn't work out, he moved to the second shift with me." No way of escaping from the situation, he remained a part of the problem, following her, but even then there was nothing she could do to prevent it. Not without being transferred to another post.

"I know. I've seen it before. All of it."

She glanced down at her feet, her left leg trembling. Fear, adrenaline, uncertainty, all combined into a rolling stomach and a body locked by the shakes.

"Focus on the here and now, the work ahead, and your duty."

She lifted her gaze. "Sounds easier than it feels." This wasn't what she'd had planned. By now, she should be home and safe with Popcorn. Away from here. "I would have been home if this hadn't all gone to hell. Aliens. Shit. Who'd have thought this would be how we met them?"

A burst of rich male laughter filled the office.

She watched him, uncertain, eyes narrowing on the man on the other side of the desk.

"I doubt there are many who expected it to happen this way, Cavanor. Not since the Third War have we looked beyond our solar system in search of danger. We became weak. Once we reclaimed Earth from the darkness, the plagues and endless wars between countries."

She remembered the history lessons, the tales of the world sent into chaos. Triggered by a civil war which had spread out beyond the borders of the original country involved. "We've forgotten what it was like to always be waiting for the next attack, a bomb to drop, or a terrorist attack." She'd only half-believed the stories, despite the museums and formal lectures shared through lessons in school.

"Get some sleep, Cavanor. We'll all have work to face in the morning. But you don't need to worry about Grant anymore. He's in the lock-up, secure until we can convene a hearing. And yes, you'll be called to speak as a witness."

"Yes, sir." A hearing. In the middle of an alien invasion, when they had to hold a blasted hearing. Would they still handle it the same way if the aliens reached Earth? "Sir? Are we sending more help to Pluto?"

He rose as she did, though he didn't have to with the difference in their ranks. "Yes, we will. And we'll take Pluto back, it isn't out for negotiation as far as I'm concerned."

She didn't need to ask the rest. There would be others pushing for a peaceful solution. Men and women who wanted the government to be separated from the military in all ways. "I understand, sir. And thank you. For letting me know what's going on, I mean."

"We're going to need good people if this thing continues to grow. Can't afford to lose anyone of your caliber."

Chapter Seventeen

Stone watched as the two younglings joined Lawbook, it wouldn't go according to plan. Jakob and Salla wouldn't be pleased with the decision. He didn't blame them, but neither did he disagree with the decision. They needed people to watch the vehicles, especially after what had happened to Winter.

"I'll cut to the chase. You're going to remain with the cars." Lawbook indicated the small group. "It's not open for negotiation. I need people to watch the transport, and you're it."

Jakob turned but didn't speak as he shot a glare at Salla.

"You can't, you need us with you. I have access to the tunnel maps, the ones you're going to need to find the kids," Salla protested.

"And you're going to share them with me, Salla."

"Not unless you agree to take me with. I'm not about to stay back here. Not with everything going on."

"I see it's going exactly like expected," said Stone as he wandered over. "Salla, you're not going to fight handing over the maps. Not when it could put those kids at risk. And Jakob sees the sense of in this. You both heard what happened to Winter, she's lucky she's alive."

"I'm not Winter."

"No, but we all could be without leaving guards behind to watch this lot." Stone gestured to the cars.

She scowled, anger flaring in her eyes before she shook her head. "Fine. I don't like this, but here." She shoved the datapad into Lawbook's hands. "Don't make me regret this. Duncan would have my head for giving away intel without something decent in return."

"We'll figure out payment when we're back with the kids." Lawbook explained.

"Or you could forget the money I promised you, Stone." Salla turned toward him, lips pressed into a tight, thin line. "It would be fair, as you obviously knew what she had planned."

"Well, shit."

"She's got you there." Lawbook hefted the datapad.

"Might do, but we'll discuss it when we get back." Damn females. Always trying to find a way of doing him out of hard-earned money. Not like he could work for free. "Bills to pay and all that."

"Don't think anyone's going to be sending you final notices anytime soon, do you?" Salla smirked as she walked past him. "But sure, we'll talk later, when we're both in a better mood to negotiate."

"Sure, whatever." He cursed under his breath as the woman walked away.

"She's got you over a barrel, and you know it." Lawbook slapped him on the back. "But at least they'll be safe. And I've slaved the controls, with instructions laid out for Jakob. Should be easy to handle if they have to escape."

"If she does, it's your fault." Marines. Blasted Marines. He'd known they'd be a problem from the first time he'd spotted them in the bar.

"Alright people, we do this as we discussed. If I give you an order, you follow it. Not doing so could get the rest of us killed, including the kids."

#

"Waking up again, good." A hand brushed the side of her face. "Once you're able to move, and the risk of infection has been reduced, you'll be able to see your dog again."

"Mags." Had she spoken, or only thought the name. Her dog. She needed him, but he hadn't come to her. Hadn't been at her side when she'd clawed her way back out of the darkness.

"Yes, Mags. He's been asking for you. At least, that's what it appeared to be. I'm not sure what else it could be."

The same man as before. The doctor? Yes, had to be. She tried to open her eyes, but gunk kept them from obeying her mental commands.

"Don't try to open them yet, I'll get a cloth."

"I can do it for you, Doctor Turner."

"Thanks, Nyssa."

Nyssa. The woman from before. Offering Walker help with the pain.

"Walker?"

"Yes, he's here. And doing better than he was. It took a bit to put his shoulder back together. Not certain it'll hold as well as it would have done if I'd had a full medical unit at hand. But it'll hold until I can get hold of a regen tube. Ah, thank you, Nyssa." A cloth, cold and damp, touched her forehead before he moved it down over her eyes, patting the washcloth over her face. "Take it slowly, you're tired, and your body has a lot of recovering to do."

He kept using the other woman's name? Why? Nyssa would know her own name.

So I know who's here?

Odd, why had her eyes been gunk covered this time, but not earlier? She wanted to know, to ask what happened, why she still couldn't move. Her body didn't want to respond to her, but once the cloth was taken away, she opened her eyes, blinking against the light.

"Ah, there she is." Fuzzy, out of focus, the doctor smiled as he wiped the cloth down the side of her face. "You seem to be more with it. Your eyes will return to normal soon enough, but don't be afraid if you drift in and out of sleep for the next few days. Your body has been through a lot. The shutdown is a natural process."

"Wh-what happened to me?" Sweat beaded across her body, the focus needed to speak even two words, threatened to leave her drained.

"You were injured. One of the ground cars had been booby-trapped, and you were caught in the blast. There were a few other minor injuries in the group, nothing as bad as what you've been through."

She tried to move her fingers and toes. Her toes responded, but not her fingers. "Arm?" He'd said something about her arm being hurt.

"It took the brunt of it, along with a couple of cracked ribs. Fuser took care of the ribs, they were only cracked not broken. I didn't have to deal with any internal bleeding. The arm, though, as I said, I worked with what I had left. Which wasn't much." He rested a hand on her shoulder for a moment, then slid two pillows beneath her head, lifting her up enough to be able to see what was going on. "There's no easy way of saying this, so I'll stick to the blunt truth. I'm sorry, Winter. I couldn't save your arm."

Her arm?

She tried to move her fingers again, the left worked, the right, she could feel them, it took a bit, but they were there, numb, pins and needles following. "I-I don't understand." It couldn't be gone. She wouldn't feel her hand if he'd taken her arm. "It's there. I feel it."

"I can't explain how it works, except it's been a recorded reaction to limb loss for as long as the records go back. Phantom limb syndrome. I'll be able to treat you for the problem in the coming weeks, once we know if I need to go back in and operate again."

Operate.

No. He was wrong. Her arm was still there. Had to be. She tried to move, to lift her arm, sweat coating her flesh with the strain. "Need to see."

"I know, I was expecting you'd want to see for yourself." He moved down the side of the bed. "It's not going to be easy, but the sooner you accept what's happened, the better it will be for you. For your sanity. At least you've got your dog, he will help in your recovery. I doubt he's going to look at you any differently, and the cybernetic limbs are amazing these days." He touched her right arm and lifted it, except he touched her upper arm, not down by her wrist where she would have expected it. "I'm sorry, truly, I am. I don't like resorting to this type of butcher work, but it was for the best. It should prevent you from losing the rest of your arm, as long as infection doesn't set in."

Her gaze shifted to her hand.

No, not her hand, but the space where it should have been.

Her throat tightened as fear clawed a path through to her heart. It didn't make sense. Couldn't be. Not with what she could feel. They were still there. Had to be. This was a dream, a fever dream, she'd wake up soon enough and be able to understand what was going on with. She tried to wriggle her fingers, the ones her eyes told her were no longer there.

Tingles.

Sensation.

All the things which shouldn't have existed if she'd lost her hand. But her mind refused to surrender. "Hand. My hand." A whimper, but it hadn't come from her. She didn't want to believe any of it. "No. God, no. Please. Make it stop. I can feel them. I can feel them move." She wriggled the non-existent fingers, lost between the sensations, pain-filled tingled and the denial of what she was seeing.

"I'm sorry, Winter. It'll become easier in time."

Not happening. This wasn't happening to her. Tears streamed down her cheeks before she admitted to herself what she was feeling.

Why had she had to wake up?

A sob tore its way up from her chest. Pain. Loss. Sorrow. All mingled in the noise, only to be echoed by a howl she knew could only have come from Mags.

Chapter Eighteen

Lackey edged his way back through the tunnel. He didn't use the comm but pressed his face mask against hers to communicate. "Coming up on the first checkpoint. A Dozen winged ones, plus one of the other bipeds. Wings are different. Three different styles. Scales and colors vary from one to the other, but the styles, there's a pattern. Maybe a sub-race, gender, who knows."

"Armed?"

"Rifles, theirs, not ours."

She gestured for them to go back to the rest of the group. It wasn't much in the way of information, but enough to know they had to take a detour. They weren't close enough to the kids to risk a fight. It would draw the attention of others, and put the kids at risk along with the rest of her people.

Stone glanced up as they returned to the broader part of the tunnel where she'd left the rest of the group. She waited for the group to huddle before she spoke, using the touch of masks as a means of communicating without switching on the comm. They'd all agreed use of the comm had to remain as the last option, not to be taken unless there was no other way.

"Alright, we've got our first roadblock, and we're not in a position to take them head-on," Cora explained. "We're going to have to take the small passage here," she tapped the screen of her datapad. "Then go around them and come out here."

"Looks tight," Ready muttered.

"Thought you liked them tight," Lackey smirked.

"What would you know, doubt you've ever been with a woman," replied Ready.

Cora rolled her eyes but let the men continue with their banter. It wasn't personal, nothing more than a means of blowing off steam. Can't blame them for being nervous. She waited for the conversation to ease. "We take it slow and quiet, this passage will lead us around to the back of the base. We can take this exit here," she brought up the fine details on the pad. "We're going to be tested here, squashed, but we can make it through if we're careful." Belly crawling, no doubt about it from the readings. The bigger members of the team would find it uncomfortable, but their suits, between military and mining, were built to handle the potential of being caught on a rock and scraped without tearing.

"Won't be fun."

She shot a glare at Harvard. "Didn't know we'd signed up for a fun event. Here was me thinking this was a job."

"You know us Navy fly-boys. If we don't have our morning coffee, on a silver platter, we start complaining about hard times." He jerked his head in the direction they needed to travel. "And I'd say this counts as hard times, should be on improved pay for this mess."

"Put in your paperwork when we get back. See what brass tells you. Can't imagine they'd be happy about the claim. But have at. It's your skin." She lifted her gaze, taking in the group as a whole. It wasn't ideal, but the detour gave them a better chance of getting to the kids in one piece. "Time to get moving."

Silence settled over the group as she led the way past the guards. If the aliens had heard them, sensed them, they'd be caught. They'd be under attack. As long as they kept quiet enough, didn't allow the banter to take control, and didn't use the comms, they reduced the chances of being caught.

#

Stone brought up the rear of the group, his gaze shifting back and forth over the assortment of men and women. Only the Marines and Harvard had given into the banter he'd half expected from the rest of them. Maybe he'd been hanging around with the military too long, but the silence from the miners felt wrong.

Crazy bastards had never followed the crowd. Always searching for their independence. Still, if they fought at his side him, he could put up with the occasional problem. Didn't mean he trusted them. Come to think of it, he hadn't trusted anyone else in a long time.

Especially not the damned military.

Yet, here he was, ready to fight and die **with** a handful of Marines.

The walls closed in, narrowing the further they moved through the tunnels. He didn't complain, Lawbook had been upfront about the lack of space, and how far they'd have to travel. At least the kids were safe back at the ground cars, they wouldn't be in the middle of the mess when it all hit the fan.

And it would, sooner or later. No point in denying it, not when he knew the odds were not only against them but stacked up ready to fall on them just when things had turned for the worst. Sure, he might get one or two of the kids to safety first, but it wouldn't be enough.

I'm never going to get paid.

Oh hell no, he was going to get out of this mess, find Salla, get his hard-earned money, then get away from Pluto. If he never saw this planet again, it would be too soon.

Rock snagged at his left arm. He paused long enough to clear the snag and continued, scowling as he realized the men and women in front of him were dropping to their bellies. Tight pinch, but there was no going back now.

Cursing under his breath, he copied the others, easing down to his stomach. If it got much tighter than this ahead, he'd have to turn on his side to get through. They weren't going to come back this way, not if he had anything to say about it. If they got the kids, they'd have to get out fast. No slowing down to crawl. A fast run, sprint, joy, whatever.

#

"This. Sucks." Salla sat down on the front bumper and leaned against Jakob, heads touching. "I didn't come all this way to be left guarding the transport." She slapped one hand down on the grill. "We'd shown her we aren't kids, then she goes around and treats

205

us like we need to be protected. And yes, I know I'm whining. I have the right to after this bullshit."

"At least we were allowed to come this far, and I don't think we're here because she thinks we're kids. And I don't mind a bit of protection here and there. Besides, how else are they going to get out if anything happens to the cars?"

"That's where I don't buy this whole, watch the cars, thing."

Jakob approached the entrance of the tunnel, knowing she'd have to wait until he came back before she'd continue. He didn't want this fight, didn't need it, but she wasn't going to drop the subject. All he was doing was buying himself a few minutes of peace.

Unless she followed him.

He paused, tempted to glance back over his shoulder. A spot between his shoulders tightened. She was staring at him, and he couldn't blame her. She was in a foul mood, and he was the only possible target for her upset.

A movement, nothing more than a flicker, drew his attention to the upper, far left corner of the cavern. His eyes narrowed as he brought his datapad up, adjusted the settings, and focused the scan. His heart raced, fingers trembled as he watched the screen, then turned and walked as casually as he could manage it, back to the waiting ground cars and Salla.

She watched him, jaw tight, hands clenched at her sides.

Still pissed. He couldn't blame her. She'd earned her place with the Marines. Duncan had trained her, but to say he was relieved he wasn't on his own, would be an understatement.

Jakob gestured to the car and entered, settling into the driver's seat. It wasn't the first time he'd been behind the wheel, as his dad had called it, but he knew he wasn't as skilled with the car as Salla would be. Not with all the times, her father had taken her down into the tunnels for training.

The passenger door opened, then closed with a firm click as Salla took her seat. A small hiss confirmed the input of air, and both opened their masks.

"Fine, so talking in here, where we can both understand what we're saying without using the comm or connective communication, makes sense, but you could have at least let me know what your plans were."

Jakob turned to face her. "We're not alone."

Salla tensed her voice calm despite the flash of concern in her eyes. "I see."

"Space bat. Least, I think it's one of those things. I couldn't get a close enough look."

"Which means they know where we are."

Jakob gave a slight nod. "And they might be following Lawbook and the others." Or they might have only discovered the cars and was now debating what the next move should be. He shifted in the chair, watching the area where he'd spotted the space bat. "I don't know what we're supposed to do, but I know what I want to do. And that's get the hell out of here."

Salla didn't reply, not immediately. Her hands clenched as she leaned forward and took a look at the datapad he offered her. She didn't take the pad from his hands but continued to stare at the information. Her face drained of color before she settled back into the chair, jaw tight as she turned away from him. "This is why they left us here, isn't it. Not to guard the cars, but because of shit like this."

Jakob let out the breath he hadn't known he was holding. "Yes." He lowered his gaze, knowing the next piece wouldn't be a surprise to Salla, no more than it had been to him when he'd read the message Lawbook had left for him. "We're supposed to wait if we're spotted, wait for the signal, then get out of here. The rest of the cars have been programmed to follow us, which means we wouldn't be leaving them behind. Right now, if that thing can communicate the way we think it is, they'll be focused on us. Waiting for the others to return here. If things change, we leave. When we get the signal, we leave, it should confuse them enough to buy us time. But if more than three of those things show up, we head for safety."

Salla closed her eyes, the tension easing from her body. "I owe her an apology."

"Yeah, but you weren't to know. Your reaction to the orders, and how you spoke to Stone, helped sell the situation if we were being watched. Which we don't know, not for certain." He shrugged and sat up to look out of the front screen, his gaze returning time and again to the area where the single space bat still lingered.

"This still sucks."

"I guess."

"But at least we're here for a real reason this time, not the made-up protect the cars from sabotage."

Jakob glanced at her, then away. "I don't know. After what happened to Winter, having the cars watched made perfect sense to me."

#

Cora cursed under her breath as she continued to lead the way through the tunnels, turning on her side to make it through the tightest point. Her toes, protected by the combat boots she'd been lucky enough to still wear when they'd been in the bar, pressed against the mixture of ice and rock as she half pushed, half pulled her way through the tunnel.

If any of the group suffered from claustrophobia, this wasn't going to be easy for them. Fortunately, considering the work most of the civilians did, it was doubtful fear of enclosed spaces would be an issue.

Rock scraped at her left arm until she found the right place to grab and pull her through to the next section of the tunnel. The walls opened up, offering enough space to stand again. She hurried, wanting to allow those behind her to reach the part of the tube where they'd all be more comfortable.

With a twist of her shoulders, she was free of the tunnel.

Cora stood as soon and stepped away from the entrance to the smaller tunnel. Others followed behind her. The last section tight enough to slow them down. Now she caught her breath and took a better look at the rest of her group.

Faces pale with sweat, concern, and uncertainty, met her gaze as they exited the confines of the tight passageway one by one. Ready rested one hand on her shoulder and rolled his eyes. None of them spoke, not yet, but the occasional glances shot her way, the shudders more than a few experienced as she watched them, and the cold, dangerous glint in Stone's eyes told her all she needed to know.

They didn't want to go back the same way.

Joys of being the one in charge. I'm the one who will be blamed for each small thing they don't want, didn't enjoy, or see as the wrong choice. She smiled, remembering how Gunny had told her, only a fool wants to be the one in command unless it was at the end of the day when everything had fallen into place.

Stone moved through the rest of the group, touching helmets to talk. "Any more tight spaces like that ahead of us?"

"No, we're good. It's all easy going after this, comparatively speaking."

"Of course it is," he groaned but didn't break contact with her. "Should have taken a better look at the map before I agreed to this."

"Hard way, or the dead way. This was the hard way." She gestured back at the now-empty tunnel.

"Doesn't mean I have to like it." He shifted his shoulders, then smoothed one arm down the trench coat he insisted on wearing over his suit. A small tear in the arm drew his attention, and his scowl deepened. "Fuck. See what's happened. Torn. Damnit, I like this coat."

"Better the coat than the suit." She smiled and broke contact with him.

His lips moved, but without the contact, she didn't hear him.

#

Ian shifted his weight and rolled out his shoulders before he allowed himself the chance to look back at the tight space they'd wriggled their way through. His back and hips voiced their complaints. It hadn't been pleasant, but he'd made it out in one piece. They all had.

He shuddered, the idea of returningÂ through the tunnel wasn›t pleasant, but he›d been in tighter confines before. So why had he reacted to the tunnel this way? It made no sense. The chambers with streaks of precious metals, dotted with shimmering gems, those had been close, pressing in against his body.

Except they didn't shimmer.

No, but the imagery amused him. It was a small taste of the pleasures he might one day enjoy if he was lucky. He'd show Salla the gems, the minerals, everything he could use to provide for her. It didn't matter than the transportation of such materials would eat into the costs.

A small touch to his shoulder warned him it was time to move. He nodded, catching sight of the Sergeant and Stone, they knew what they were doing.

Right?

He was ready for whatever the universe decided to throw at him. He had to be if he wanted to return to Salla.

#

Jakob tried not to be obvious as he continued to watch the bat, the creature hadn't moved far, maybe a little left or right, but the type of movement he associated with trying to maintain position but work out the kinks in muscles. It wouldn't want its wings to feel stiff if it needed to move in a hurry.

"Think there'll be more joining it?" asked Salla.

"No idea, but if we're lucky, there won't be." Jakob checked the datapad for what felt like the hundredth time. "If not, we'll deal with it. We have the plan, we can handle whatever happens.

We're smart, right? I mean, we've dealt with everything else. The initial attack, getting out of the cavern. Making our way to the Hunter's place."

"True, but we don't know how many of those things are out there, waiting for us."

"Right now. One." He grinned, knowing he deserved anything she decided to throw at him for that one. "And if we continue to watch the bat, we won't be surprised by any others showing up without warning."

"Should smack you one. A good hard blow across the back of your head."

"Ah, but you won't."

"For now, but I'll get my own back, sooner or later."

"Look forward to it." He glanced at her, then back to the-- "it's gone." His heart sank, cold wrapped around his heart as he searched the cavern, trying to find the bat. "Where the hell did it go?" He half rose, hands on the console as he got as close to the clear plastisteel as possible. It couldn't have vanished this quickly, could it?

"What? Maybe it's picked another place to watch us from."

"You don't buy that any more than I do." Shit, if he didn't locate it soon, they'd have to leave. "Don't like this. Really don't like this." His heart raced as he sealed up his suit.

"What do you think you're doing?"

"I'm going to find the damn thing. See where it's gone. Once I locate it, it'll be fine." As long as it was on its own. If there were others, they'd leave. No other choice. He'd promised the Sergeant. Letting her down wasn't a part of his plans.

"Don't." Salla grabbed him by the shoulder and pulled him back. "It's not... safe out there." Her voice trembled.

Afraid? Since when had Salla been afraid? "Alright, I'll keep watching from here, for now." Until he had an answer.

"There." Salla pointed to the left. "It's there."

He turned, slowly, watching for the creature. A small

movement, but not where Salla pointed. "It's not on its own."

"That's what I was worried about," said Salla.

This wasn't how it was supposed to be. They should have been safe, but even as he continued to look around the cavern, searching every crevice the small nooks and crannies where the smaller bats could hide. This was different. They weren't hiding. Not anymore.

He didn't need to turn and look at the rest of the flock, if flock was even the right name, appeared. Filling the cavern, dozens, hundreds. More.

"Jakob." Salla whimpered, fear rolling through her words. "Jakob, we've got to get out of here. We can't stay. Not any longer."

He didn't speak, didn't say a word as he settled down into the driver's seat and hit the controls. "I know. Hold on, it's going to be a bumpy ride."

Interlude Eight

Treizaek let his gaze move over the members of his crew, males, females, and neuters who answered only to his word. Followed the laws laid down by his strength, as he followed the orders which came from the nest. One day there would be one who replaced him when he grew weak enough to be taken down, but it wasn't here, or now. His ship remained under his control. There was no one who could stand against him.

"Commander."

He didn't need to turn to know who'd spoken. The gentle, submissive female who'd brought the initial information to him. "Verlianic."

"You weren't due back on the bridge for two more periods." She **edged** in front of him. Her wings trembling, soft movements he'd noticed before in the female. How she hadn't attempted to hide her fear. "Is there something wrong?"

"This is my ship, I don't need to explain my movements to you, child." Ah, beta females. He'd never understood why they entered the service instead of seeking out a male to protect them. The same applied to beta males, and the neuters were a law unto themselves. They obeyed only those who were from the same greater nest.

He didn't turn to take in the rest of the crew. He didn't need to. They'd follow his orders, or die, either way, he remained in charge until such time when he either stepped aside from his position and returned to his home, or he died.

Killed in action, or by a crew member ready to take his place. As he had killed the female alpha, who had commanded before him.

"I understand, commander." She ducked her head, her voice

never lifting from the soft, gentle tones he'd heard the first time. "You are the one in charge here, and we live to serve. Not only you but the great mother and her consorts."

His top lip curled. The great mother. "There is no place for foolish religions and ancient superstitions here." He watched, waiting for her reaction. "If you wish to follow the crone, do so on your own time. They do not belong on my bridge." He raised one claw in her direction, "report if you must. If not, return to your duty." A pity, the female had been of interest until she'd begun her nonsense. Another reason why he preferred warrior females. Their young were strong, never weakened by the ancient beliefs those with sense had turned their back on generations ago.

Long before the human colony had been established, the servants given a chance to prove their worth in one way or another.

"Yes, commander." She inclined her head, gaze lowered.

"Is there any more information from Nyanaek and her scouts?" He turned away from her, addressing the question to the comm officer.

"Nyanaek's scouts are closing in on a small group of humans, commander. Sending the data to your console now." The male replied.

"I knew she would pull through. The rest of you should learn from Nyanaek's actions. She failed me. She disgraced herself. But instead of cowing, she moved to reclaim her position among my best warriors." He didn't look at the rest of his crew or those who remained on the bridge. Others worked elsewhere, tending their duties, they knew what was expected of them. Nor would they let him down. He'd made certain the crew understood what he would do if any of them failed him again.

One chance.

One lone chance to prove their worth after a mistake.

Nothing more.

Details trailed over his small screen. The scouts had done

their job, regained their honor, and he no longer felt the need to tear out Nyanaek's throat. "Good. Very good. We should have the last of these foolish creatures under our control within a matter of cycles." He closed the report down and smiled. "We will claim this world as our own, and then the rest of the system. Once we have their homeworld under control, we'll be able to bring the rest of our people here. The ones who no longer wish to remain in the nest."

The scales on the back of his neck itched. He tensed, dropped, and rolled away from the command chair, wings snapping out to balance him as he turned. "Fool. Who do you think you are, that you believe you can kill me on my own ship?" His eyes narrowed on the male.

"Y-you disrespected the great mother."

"Idiot. You'd die for religion? One any with sense have long since turned their back on?" He growled, the small claws on his wings curled, ready to strike. "You will pay for your mistake. A beta male who thinks he can kill an alpha warrior? Your petty beliefs will never be enough to protect you." Religions. The same thing which had sent the humans out beyond their system and into the void. They would never understand how weak it made them.

"Commander?" The female's voice trembled. "Do you wish us to remove the male?"

"No, I'll deal with the--" Pain. Bright, undeniable, it sliced through his side. "Wh-what." He turned, stumbling back before his wings flicked enough to keep him on his feet. He reached for his side, purple blood coating his claw as he lifted it away from his body.

The female. The beta female. It wasn't possible. They weren't supposed to be capable of attacking an alpha. Not from everything he'd read, been taught, had seen for himself. They weren't bloodthirsty, except in a group. Nest kin might work together to overthrow an alpha, but never alone.

"Not... possible." He coughed as the female slid the blade

from his side. "You're a beta. Submissive."

"In service to the Great Mother, Commander, many things are possible. I regret it came to this, but my brothers and sisters agree, we cannot serve beneath one who dismisses the guidance of the Great Mother. Not when it is she who sent us out into this system. When she is the one who sees the treasures this system will surrender to us."

He hissed, turning on the beta female, claws extended. "You will pay for this." He wasn't going to die, not at the hands of a submissive female, with others watching them. "I will strip your wings and pin them to my walls. There they will hang with the wings of all those who have decided to follow you." Life fluid dripped down his side, but he kept hold of the blade the traitor had slammed into his body.

"You are already dead, commander."

"Not." He yanked the dagger free, turned, pivoting on his left leg, his wings adding balance to the move before he slammed the ornate weapon into the female's neck. "Yet."

She screamed, mouth open, eyes wide, her wings snapping back and forth as she pressed one claw to the wound in her neck.

"Anyone else want to join her?" He indicated the dying female. "Step up now, and I will relieve you of your duties." Pain hammered away at his side, but he refused to fall. Nothing could be allowed to distract him from this mission. "You." He approached the male who had spoken out. "You are bound by the same beliefs, aren't you. A little beta male ready to serve the great mother? Idiot. Your death will be no loss, no more than hers." He flicked a wing in the direction of the female as she slumped to the floor.

The rich scent of her blood filled the air, tempting him to turn back to the dying female. If Nyanaek had been at his side, then they might have shared the feast, tasted of their enemies blood, and saved the heart for a private moment.

"Commander, I..." the male began.

"Words. Nothing but words. A warrior would have more to say to me, with blade, tooth, and claw. But you? Weak, like the female. And like her, you will die." His side ached, a small matter in the grand scheme of things, as long as he stopped the bleeding before it went on too long.

"Commander, if I may, you're injured." Another male voice, one he knew belonged to a crew member who had been with him from the start.

"And I'll deal with this small matter once the trouble here is under control." He didn't turn toward the speaker, he didn't need to know he would remain at risk if any of the others attempted to attack him. But there was still the male who'd spoken out, one who needed to be dealt with. "You, here, and bare your throat."

"Commander," the male in front of him bowed his head, trembling as he stood there. "I will not fail you again."

"No, you will not." Treizaek walked with a steady pace to the terrified male. It didn't matter what he said or did, the male had to die, or the rest would see it as a weakness. One which would only cause him more problems in the long run. "You betrayed me. This is unforgivable. You are either with me or against me. And you have made it clear, you are against me." He lashed out with wing and claw, slicing into the male's throat before he turned to look at the rest of the crew. "Clear the bridge of this mess. Their stench offends me."

"Yes, commander." They moved behind him, around him, obeying his orders before he walked off the bridge, head high, his wings in place against his back.

If others had given their loyalty to the religion, he'd deal with it, with those who froze when they were supposed to obey his commands. He didn't look back, didn't speak as he left the others behind him. They would never be able to see the weakness, the way he hurt. A warrior didn't show their injuries, the opening others would be able to use. He would remain the commander for as long as he had the strength to do so.

Hell's Children

It was the nature of life.
Their life.

Chapter Nineteen

"There're hundreds of them, we have to get moving," Salla insisted.

"Doing my best here. Operating all the cars at the same time isn't easy." Jakob didn't look at her, he didn't need to know she was afraid. "Help where you can. Be quicker if you double up on the controls."

"Sure, right. Sorry." She reached out, taking the secondary controls in hand. "I've got cars slaved together. You focus on this one."

He smiled, he didn't look at her, didn't suggest anything else. But they worked together. He glanced at the bats, the way they continued to move, darting close to the ceiling, brushing stone and ice with their wings. "Think they're going to follow us?"

"Betting on it."

He'd hoped the answer would be different this time, not that it mattered. They'd get out of here in one piece, with the rest of the ground cars following them, and buy the team what time they needed to get the kids to safety.

"Incoming!"

Jakob swore and yanked on the controls, forcing the car into obedience. He hit the power, increasing the speed of the vehicle. No giving up, no turning away from this. They'd not give up on him, on the prize hidden inside the ground cars. He didn't know if they'd follow all the way to the surface. It wasn't an idea he dared to spend much time thinking about not when there were other problems.

"Must go faster. Must go faster." He muttered under his breath. Odd, he could have sworn he'd heard the phrase before. The where and when escaped him.

"Shit, they're scraping the tops of the other cars, then moving on."

"Testing them." But for what?

"They don't know if there are others in the cars. I don't know what's going on, but I don't like it." Salla's fingers danced over the controls. "We've got this. I know we've got this. Won't take long to reach the surface this way."

Who was she trying to convince?

"Have to slow down. The curves coming up."

"No, don't. They'll be on us." Salla captured one wrist. "We'll fail if we don't keep up the pace." Her grip tightened. "We can't allow them to stop us. To get in here. They're testing to see which of the cars has passengers in it."

"Shit. What the hell for?" He swallowed. "No, don't answer that question. It's not as if they can get in past the--"

"They don't need to."

"What?"

"They don't need to get in the car, they can cause enough damage if they tip us, or trigger a cave-in," said Salla.

Oh no, he wasn't going to let it happen. "No slowing down."

"Agreed." She loosened her grip on his arm. "We've got this. Not going to let Lawbook down."

"Not going to let you down."

Wings scraped against the outside of the car. Plastisteel whined. A thousand taps of claws on the outside of the vehicle.

"Going to make it. We're going to make it." It didn't matter who he was talking to, himself, Salla, the ground car or the space bats. The words held power, and he wasn't going to let the Marines down.

Not going to let Salla down.

#

Stone edged in front of the rest of the group. He'd done his time bringing up the rear, and after the last tunnel, he was through. Lackey and Harvard took turns covering the group from behind, along with the sordid looks they shot each other.

Typical.

Navy vs. Marine. The power play between the two groups would never die. They wouldn't want it to. It was a part of who they were.

A light touch on his shoulder brought him to a halt.

Lawbook.

He edged close to the turn in the tunnel, lifted one hand, fingers parted, and counted down to indicate he was going to take a quick look. She tapped his shoulder twice, though he didn't look back at her. What the hell did the woman want this time? He shook his head.

Her fingers closed on his shoulder, the grip firm, and she used it to tug him back and put his back against the wall. Her eyes narrowed as she brought up her free hand. Pointed to herself, then her eyes, **and** the turn in the corridor.

Stone bit back the urge to tell her where to stick her orders and without lube, but he'd agreed to follow her commands. Same as everyone else in the group. Didn't mean he had to like it.

Stubborn woman.

Lawbook edged past him, steps silent, despite their close confines. How the woman was able to move without making a sound was beyond him. Sure, he was a smuggler, but his work was more hiding things in secret holds and bribing the right people than sneaking around dark tunnels and avoiding ambushes.

The Marine disappeared for a second, then returned. Her face grim. He mouthed the word, 'what'?

Bad. She mouthed back.

When a Marine said it was bad, did they mean bad for the civies working with them, or end of the world, we're all going to die bad?

He glanced at the way she'd come, **and** back at Lawbook. She gestured Stone to follow her, and gathered the rest of the Marines, along with several civilians into a huddle. Not speaking until they were all in a position to be able to hear her without turning on the comms.

"They've moved guards into place, closer than we first expected." She brought up the map, tracing where they had been to the point they now stood, **and** to the wider space around the corner. "Here and here, four in all. Equipment as well. No idea what it's for, but we're going to have to go in firing."

"Maybe," said Harvard. "Or we could..." his voice trailed off as he increased the zoom on the map. "Yeah, here. It's small. We'll get maybe one person through there, but it will bring them up here, high on the wall. Not watched because we don't have wings, so they wouldn't expect us to attack from this vantage point."

Not an attack as the Marines customarily used. But a sniper. "Whoever takes that spot is going to need to be a damn good shot, or we're all dead."

"You volunteering, Stone?"

"Hell, no. Harvard. I prefer side arms to rifles. And you're out, doubt you've put much time in on a range."

"I'll go," said Virgil. "It's my line of work. Let me take a better look at the map. Sergeant, where, exactly, are the four aliens located."

It wasn't much of a plan, but it was all they had.

"You sure about this?"

Virgil smiled, though it didn't touch his eyes. "You'd rather have someone else take position? Sergeant, I know what I'm doing. Might as well put those skills to use."

"I trust him, Sergeant. Besides, he's been with us since the bar. Hasn't let us down yet," said Lackey.

"Go for it. Rest of you, wait with me until we get the word. You watch me, watch for the signals, and no one else acts until I give the word. Virgil, one squelch from you to let us know you're in place. A twenty count, then open fire."

"Understood. Let's get this done."

Stone broke away from the group. Don't like this. What was there to like? They were underground, about to face aliens. Outnumbered, outgunned with little or no chance of pulling this off.

What in hells name was he doing here?

#

"They're never going to give up."

"I'm doing my best here, Salla. We'll shake them." Jakob pushed the ground car to its limit. He glanced at the map, the route he'd been told to take. A route best taken at a crawl.

"Be easier if we had weapons," said Salla.

He couldn't argue with that. Not with what he'd seen to date. "We do, just not built into these babies."

"Then what use are they?"

He didn't have an answer.

"Think I have an idea." Salla chewed her bottom lip. "Hit the brakes on a count of five."

"What?"

"Do it."

"Right, fine." Might as well try it her way, nothing else had worked.

"On five. Four. Three." Her left hand hovered over the slaved controls. "Two. One."

Jakob slammed on the breaks. If she were a fraction off, the ground cars would smash into the back of theirs, starting the mother of all pile-ups. His body jerked forward, kept from plowing into the clear plastisteel windows by the five-point harness both he and Salla had clipped into place. A habit which had saved their lives. His body protested, bruised flesh warning him there would be reminders of their trip through the tunnels. One he'd feel for days to come.

Small, winged, and dangerous, the space bats flew past them, twisting as they attempted to turn back to the cars. Several slammed into the rock, bodies crumpled, falling to the floor, as others found a way to avoid the same fate.

"Hit it, see how many of these bastards we can take out."

"Anyone ever tell you, you're brilliant?"

"Not recently, but I'll take the praise where I can get it. Floor it, Jakob."

#

Cora waited, knowing nothing could be done until Virgil was in position. She didn't move, her hands wrapped gently around her rifle. She didn't have to look behind her to know Stone and Lackey were close, the others in the group waited for the signal.

The kids. No matter what happened, they'd find a way to get the kids out of this.

Time dragged, though the reasonable part of her mind, reminded her time continued on as it always did. Small needles of doubt dug their way through her mind and into her stomach. She didn't move, didn't make a sound as she forced herself to keep breathing at a slow, steady pace. She wouldn't let them down, not the rest of her team, or the children whose freedom depended on what they did, how they performed, then escape in one piece.

The squelch startled her. Her breath hitching in the split-second after her mind had registered the noise. Cora Bloodlaw counted, a slow twenty, as she shifted her grip on the rifle, body tense. A ripple of energy passed through the rest of the group, tensing, prepared to attack, but unmoving until the first shot sliced through the scant air.

#

Jakob hit the controls. The ground car lurched forward, the slaved cars following behind them. Small, heavy bodies slapped into the front of the vehicle. Purple blood smeared the windscreens, but with the scanners, he didn't need to see out through the clear plastisteel. His jaw clenched. Small bodies smacked again and again into the car. He shuddered but didn't hold back. The more he destroyed, the better it would be.

"God, they're disgusting." Salla's delicate fingers continued to move over the controls.

"Tell me about it." He'd make it.

"Turn coming up."

"Got it." Would it never end? He peered at the purples smears as he controlled the car. "Hold on. I'm not slowing down."

"Wouldn't want you to."

"Salla, when we get out of this--"

"We don't talk about later. Bad luck."

He risked a glance at his companion. "Alright." There'd be time when this was done. He had to believe it. He'd ask Salla then. What would it be like to kiss her? He shook off the thought. First, they had to get out of this in one piece. Nothing else mattered until they were safe, away from the bats, the caves, and the danger they both presented.

#

Cora raised her rifle, leading the group around the corner, firing as she went. One winged creature lay, its body broken and sprawled on the ground. The others fired in the direction of the sniper, not reacting to the presence of the Marine until it was too late.

One staggered back, wings outspread, as it tumbled to the floor, its mouth opening and closing, claws curled as its life bled out before her. She'd already moved to the next target, only to find there wasn't one. Each of the four-winged aliens lay sprawled in front of her.

She gestured to the others, grabbed one of the creatures and dragged it out of sight, taking care not to leave a sign of their deaths as she indicated to the others to clear up any blood. Virgil made his way down to join the rest of them, his rifle slung over his back. She gave a thumbs-up, not wanting to risk a conversation.

Almost there. Whatever happened now, they at least had made it this far. Cora rolled out her shoulders, checked her suit, all buying time to go over the next stage. No alarms had rung out, that her datapad alerted to. It wasn't a certainty, but it was a hope she was willing to cling to.

With Virgil, Lackey and Stone close behind her, she edged toward the entrance. The last one standing in between themselves

and the children.
    Or their death.

Chapter Twenty

"She's healing slowly, but it's to be expected after a shock to the system. She wasn't aware of the loss of her arm until she woke. To be honest, I doubt she recalls much about being trapped. It's common for the human mind to put shields in place, and lockout memories of trauma." Taylor's words pulled Leigh from her sleep.

Leigh didn't move, didn't open her eyes. As long as the doctor believed she was asleep, he'd continue to speak.

"Thought I had it bad, but damn. Her arm. It's going to take some getting over."

"Easy enough to replace with a decent synthetic when this mess is dealt with," Taylor explained. "She has to be open to the idea, and there are rare occasions when the patient rejects a synthetic."

Walker. The voice and words combined to confirm the speakers' identity. Had he recovered from his injury? No, he couldn't have. Not with the way Nyssa had offered him a means to fight the pain.

"Not easy, Doc. We don't know how long it will be before the Sergeant can arrange transportation off-world for her. Not like there's a chance to find a replacement limb here. We don't have those kind of supplies on Pluto. Might be different if the Navy ships were accessible."

"Don't like it, but you're right. Bloody aliens. Screwing things up for us." Taylor's bitter laugh carried his words. "I should have been getting ready to open a clinic. And we don't know how many lives have been lost in the colony. Or what the aliens will do from this point."

"Sergeant will get the kids out of there. Bring them here where it's safe. Or better than the mess in the dome." Walker continued.

Kids. What children? She struggled to make sense of the

situation, shifting her weight on the cot before she had a chance to think about it. A moan of pain slipped into life, ending the conversation.

"Take it easy, Marine. You're still recovering." A warm damp cloth was swiped over her eyes and mouth. "I've got water here for you. Don't try to sit up, I've got a straw ready for you."

Leigh felt something brush her lips, parting them before she realized it was a straw. Her throat craved fluid, though she knew there'd been an IV set up at one point. It was gone now unless she'd grown used to its intrusion. Sweet, freshwater seeped into her mouth a small suckle at a time. She wanted more. Needed it. But didn't give in to the drive to drink it all down and demand a refill. Instead, she forced herself to slow down, not wanting to be sick.

Be just what she needed, throwing up when the doctor was trying to help her. He wouldn't appreciate it, and she wasn't a big fan of the idea.

"That's it, take it slow. You're doing fine."

She didn't try to open her eyes, focused on taking as much fluid as she could without triggering an unwanted reaction. How long had she slept? Not as if it mattered. Being awake wouldn't change what had happened to her arm.

The doctor withdrew the straw. "You can have more later, Winter. Your body has a lot to recover from."

Leigh nodded, the movement harder than she'd expected.

"Walker is here as well. You haven't met him, have you?"

"No," her voice a stranger to her ears. "Hadn't joined my assigned team when it happened."

"We'll get to know each other in the days to come, Winter. I heard you have a dog."

"Yes. Mags." Her dog. Where was he? "I need Mags. He'll be worried." Each time she took a breath, speaking became easier.

"You'll be able to see him shortly," Taylor assured her. "Need to double-check your wound is sealed, and there are no extra problems before we let him in here."

"Cute dog, from what I've been told," said Walker. "Looking forward to meeting him. Haven't seen a dog in a long time. There aren't any here on Pluto, or they weren't until you arrived."

She wanted to turn, to see man. But moving wasn't easy. Her arm didn't want to move, neither of them responded to her mental commands. She tried to wriggle her toes. They answered, and she didn't bother to hide her smile. The last thing she needed was to find out another limb had been damaged.

"You'll be up and moving in a day or two, once we've got back on your feet. But you need time to let your body recover. It's been through a lot, and we don't have the extra equipment or drugs here which would get you on your feet any sooner." Taylor's voice drew closer as she listened to him. "Open your eyes again, Leigh. I need to check your reflexes and your responses. Eyes first, then I'll check the reflex points."

Leigh reluctantly obeyed.

#

Cora crept forward, one eye on the datapad. Her heart raced, but she'd become used to the reactions through the years. As long as she continued forward, with the other men behind her, she'd remain in control of the situation. Not for the first time she wished the Gunny was with her. The man had more experience to call on than she and the rest of her Marines combined. But you couldn't bring back the dead, and whatever he might have done in her situation, it no longer mattered.

Not far now.

The twenty-plus signals from the implanted chips called to her. The kids. Not as many as there should have been, but it didn't take long to locate the others. Split into three groups in the short time since she'd checked last checked the pad. She cursed under her breath but didn't look back at the others. Whatever was going on, it didn't change the fact they were here, and she had a chance to grab the kids.

At least some of them.

The rest; she didn't want to leave them behind.

Cora raised her left hand, fingers spread for the count down.

No other options, they either got this done or died trying.

She wasn't fond of dying.

Two fingers curled down. A third. Fourth. Her muscles tightened, the need to move built within her.

It was time.

#

"They're still coming."

"I know, Salla. I know." He took a deep breath, forcing the ground car to take a sharp turn. His body rocked in the confines of the five-point harness. His breath burned in his lungs, muscles tight as he focused on controlling the car. "We've got this." He glanced at the screen. The bats, or whatever the hell they were, had been reduced by at least half. His jaw clenched. "Almost there. A little longer then we're out of this. We'll be safe."

"What do you mean, we're almost there?"

"Trust me." Six seconds. All he had to do was hold it for six--

"You're not. No. Oh, hell no. Jakob. Don't."

All he could do was smile as he forced the car to turn ninety degrees. It screeched under his handling, or Salla screamed. He couldn't be sure. His entire focus on the narrow spin-off tunnel and the drop off in front of them.

#

Stone moved, half crouched, behind Lawbook, mentally counting the creatures as they moved together. The other members of the team close on his heels. Forty. Easily forty of the beasts. More than they'd counted on.

Well fuck.

He dropped to one knee, firing. Moving from one target to the next, double-tapping the beast below the eyes. Wings moved. Claws extended. He couldn't get them all, not on his own.

But he wasn't alone.

Something moved. Not with the aliens, but behind them. His eyes narrowed, the need to understand what he was seeing. The images settled into a form he could understand. Children. The kids. Not all of them. Twenty, maybe, if they were lucky. In a clear cage. Confinement cells? Not like the ones he'd seen before, but he knew what they were dealing with. The children still wore their suits, with masks up. Oxygen. The cages had an air supply. Enough to keep them alive until he had the chance to get them out.

No. Not him.

They.

Ready moved past him, knees slightly bent, rifle firing, always firing.

Purple liquid spilled, droplets splattering, a few small enough to form perfect spheres which hovered in the air. Only the heavier ones hit the floor. His mind refused to make sense of everything he saw. No matter how real it was, how he couldn't deny the fact he was fighting against them, these creatures, the nightmares he could no longer deny existed.

Stone did the only thing he could. He kept firing. Picking a target and taking it out before he moved to the next one, and the next.

A body pushed past him. Two more. Each one doing the same thing.

Killing the damned aliens.

#

Ian dropped to one knee behind a small outcrop of stone, the rifle held against his shoulder. He knew how to do this. How to kill. It was simple, wasn't it? Pull the trigger and keep pulling it, until there were no other targets to deal with. His gaze flicked to the clear cage. He could do this.

His finger curled around the trigger, but it didn't work. Nothing happened. He couldn't get his finger to obey.

What use was he if he couldn't kill the damn creatures?

Fear clenched a claw-tipped grip around his heart. He wasn't a coward. He wouldn't have been able to volunteer if he counted himself as one locked by fear.

His finger refused to obey Ian, denying him the chance to help the rest of the team.

Useless.

He didn't deserve to be here.

His gaze shifted, taking in the chaos before it locked on the holding cell.

The kids. Someone had to get the kids out of here.

He waited, watching for a moment, a gap in the fight as the winged beasts opened up on the rescue party, no longer relying on their wings, claws, and fangs. With a silent curse he ran, keeping low to the ground, darting left, then right, right again, before he slid across the remaining gap, his boots hitting the clear cage.

Ian Hunter smiled at the kids, gesturing for them to put the hoods back in place, seal their suits and move back away from the front of the cage. He could do this. He had to be able to get them out. He skimmed his hands over the cage, searching for a seam, an opening, anything he could use to spring the kids free. He glanced back, watching the fight for a sign situation had swung in their favor.

A dozen more appeared, not the winged ones. Others, yes, the Sergeant had said there were other types. Four that she knew of. A part of him wanted to watch, try to understand precisely what he was seeing.

Another body thumped against the front of the cage. A small package in his hand. Lackey. The Marine pressed it into his hand. Gray. Pliable. He'd seen this before. Hadn't he?

His mind raced as he put the pieces together.

Explosives.

They had a way in. All they needed, after this, was a way out.

#

Where the hell were they coming from? Her fingers curled around her weapon, gaze skipping from one alien to the next. Too

233

many. Outnumbered didn't even begin to describe it. Her people, if she didn't find a way of getting them out there would be no chance for the kids.

Cora growled. She wasn't going to give up. Didn't matter how many more of the bastards showed up, she'd kill them all. If it took her last breath, she'd destroy every last one of the ugly creatures. Her gaze fixed on a shape. A biped. She'd seen this one before, hadn't she?

Not that it mattered. The creature would die along with the rest.

Movement near the cage caught in her peripheral vision, her mind filling in the blanks. Ian and Lackey. Good, Lackey would figure a way to get them out, if he hadn't already. It wasn't going to be easy, but she trusted her people. Always would.

Ian's knowledge of the tunnels, his experience as a miner, would be useful on the way out.

She shifted her focus, taking out two more aliens. Both winged. Others were here, she could sense them without turning, knew they were coming up behind her before she turned, picking off the first of the new attackers. Only when Cora felt safe, did she return to the enemy close to the cell and the frightened children.

Pain lanced across her back, but she didn't move, refused to allow it to knock her to her belly or knees. She was a Marine. A woman who'd done everything she could to honor the code, to keep her people safe during battle. If this was her last stand, so be it.

She'd go out with a smile on her lips, and the corpses of her enemies around her.

Precisely as it was meant to be.

Chapter Twenty-One

Stone shifted from rifle to sidearm, his shoulder demanding a break from the abuse provided by the rifle. He didn't wait for an opening, he made one. Firing at two of the winged ones before Stone ran, half crouched, toward Lawbook. She'd taken at least one hit, he'd seen her stumbled, but she was still fighting, still on her feet. She wouldn't allow them to kill her, too damn stubborn.

If she hadn't been prepared for combat, she'd have died during their exit from the dome.

Stubborn streaks had their uses.

Two figures, human, crouched by the front of the cage. He did a quick scan, taking in the shapes, the way they moved as they gestured to the children. Ian and Lackey? He couldn't be certain without taking more time to identify them than he was comfortable with. It didn't matter, they were both human, and nothing else mattered.

At least one of the men had something in his hand. Gray. Flexible.

Explosives. He smiled. That solved the problem of how they'd get the kids out. Miners knew explosives, and he had no doubt the Marine was familiar with the judicial application of the well-used tool.

A body fell to the left of him. Human. Male. Alive? Dead? The lack of knowledge didn't prevent him from approaching Lawbook. If the man was dead, there was nothing he could do about if injured, better to deal with the aliens first, and see to the other when the chance arose.

When the aliens were dead and not before.

#

Jakob's hands tightened on the controls. Sweat dripped into his eyes as he forced the ground car to obey him, no matter what else it wanted to do. It whined, complaining at how he handled it, and once this was done, the vehicle would need maintenance. He knew who would be able to fix anything which needed work when this was over.

Helen.

His wonderful, intelligent, genius sister.

Time slowed down, seconds passed like hours, at least for him. He didn't turn his attention to the woman at his side, and she was a woman, not a child. Not a teenager who had seen nothing of the system. She'd been places, done things with her father, and any man would be proud to have her in their lives.

His throat clenched, mouth dry.

The car squealed, plastisteel groaned, a scream of terror.

His own. Odd, he hadn't given himself permission to scream.

His side of the car slammed into the stone and ice wall. Something crunched, but he pushed the knowledge of what was happening to the back of his mind.

"Jakob."

"I've got this."

"We can't--"

"Yes, we can." It wasn't that easy. He knew it wouldn't be as easy as he wanted it to be, but this was the only chance he had.

"They're following."

"I know." He caught a glimpse of the woman out of the corner of his eye. Beautiful, strong, brilliant, courageous. There were other words he could use to describe Salla, but what was the point. Jakob knew what the woman meant to him. What he hoped he'd have the chance to tell her when this was over. "I expected them to." Planned on it. A little more, all he had to do was get around one more bend. One turning. "Seal your suit."

"What?"

"Seal. Your. Suit." He wouldn't have the time close his, but he'd be damned if he didn't warn Salla. Didn't do everything possible to protect her. "Now, Salla." Please. Don't argue. We don't have time.

"Fine." The single word both an acknowledgment and a warning. Her hands fluttered over her suit; the movement caught on the edge of his vision. She reached over, her slender fingers sliding over his suit, sealing it as she went. He tried to slap her away, but she growled a warning. "Cut it out. If I'm suited, you are."

"Facepiece." He warned. If he could hear her this clearly, she didn't have the final pieces in place.

She swore but obeyed him. The final words muffled by the sealed mask.

There wouldn't be enough time to put his own mask in place. Not enough to seal the remaining pieces. Not enough time to tell Salla what he felt.

#

Cora bit back a groan, her body on fire, the length of her back alight with new waves of pain. She blinked sweat out of her eyes as she continued to fight. Picking off one target after the other, then moving to the next. Never stopping. It didn't matter what she hurt, she couldn't stop. Wouldn't give up.

Aliens fell, others approached her and the remaining members of the team. She didn't know how long it would take to kill them all, nor did she care. She wasn't getting out of this alive.

Something trickled down her back, too thick to be sweat, too hot to be anything but blood.

Her blood.

Don't let them down, Sergeant.

Gunny's voice. Great, she was hearing things.

How much blood had she lost? Too much if she'd stumbled into the land of audio hallucinations. What was next, dancing elephants? Or did that only happen when you'd have too much to drink?

She rose, firing with each step. Driving the aliens back from the cage. A little more time, it was all she had to do, buy them more time. Ian had a plan. Lackey would help him. Stone and

Harvard would get the rest of them out if she didn't make it.

Large, coat flapping out, a figure slid into place beside her.

A coat?

Trench coat.

Stone.

At least she wouldn't let the rest of her people down.

An arm encircled her waist, tugging her to her feet. The initial urge to order Stone to let her go, faded before she had a chance to speak. Helping, he was here to help her, nothing more. She could accept his assistance. Cora leaned into him, allowing Stone to ease her toward a wall, a place where she had more than her own feet to keep her upright.

As long as she was breathing, she wouldn't give up.

#

Noise. Not alien, but human weapons? Zac turned toward the sound, searching for more information. He wasn't the only one searching for the source of the fight. The other two men in the clear cage rose, hands pressed against the confines of their cell.

Edward hurried into view, his eyes wide, fear flashing across his pale features. "Why are your people doing this? Don't they understand the damage they will do to the Blessed Ones?"

"I don't understand what you're talking about, Edward," said Zac.

"They're hurting our Masters. Shooting. Killing those who are far above them." Edward drew closer to the cage. "You could tell them to stop."

"How?" Was this a chance at escaping? "I can't talk to them from here. Why would they listen to me, when in their eyes I'd be a prisoner, forced to speak under duress." He kept his voice calm, his features free of stress. "They don't understand the dangers or the way they are putting others at risks. If they were given a chance to know the Blessed Ones, it would be different."

"Then tell them. Explain how our Masters are here to help us. They are brutes, like nothing I've ever seen before."

"How, Edward." He tapped the transparent material which kept both himself and the others locked away. "I can't hear them, not clearly, above the fight. They won't be able to hear me, and I can't get close enough to them to explain things to them." He forced himself to pause as if thinking things through. "But if you let me out of here, I can talk with them."

"I-I don't have the ability to let you out. Only our Masters can open or close the holding rooms."

"They're cells, Edward. Not holding rooms. If they were anything else, we wouldn't be locked in them. That's how humans see things."

Edward's eyes widened. "They believe the children are prisoners, at risk. Oh, I see."

"Yes, and there are many things which you might see as normal, acceptable, but the humans of Earth and its colonies don't. They haven't been educated, their minds are still focused on their ways and traditions." If Edward couldn't unlock the cage what was he supposed to do?

Low whines combined with the thud of projectiles. The fight drawing closer with each passing second.

"He's not going to let you out," said Mathew. "Might as well give it up."

"I'm trying to help him." Zac didn't turn toward the other man. "Are the kids safe out there? Edward, what will happen if they break the cages. I mean, containment rooms?"

Edward backed away from the see-through wall separating him from the three men. "They are wearing their suits, they should be protected."

"Should, but you're not certain?" If the walls were broken they'd be exposed to the lack of oxygen. "The area around the rooms, are they airtight?"

"No, but the Blessed Ones will keep them safe. They have to be able to protect them. The young are the most important of us."

Zac filed the information away. "I understand. You should

try to help the children." If Edward couldn't open the cells, then keeping him here wouldn't help. "Go, Edward. They will want you to protect the children."

Edward smiled, his innocent features lit by pure joy. "Yes, of course. I'll be able to serve them. Thank you. I will be back. I know you will continue to learn and grow within the confines our Master's set around us." The man backed away, speaking under his breath in an odd language.

No, not beneath his breath. He was communicating with the aliens. It was their language, a mix of whistles, clicks, and other sounds, he now used. The man knew how to speak their tongue. A skill Zac would need if he was to survive the days to come.

I don't know how many are out there, but my thoughts are with you. Get them out. As many of them as you can. Get them away from this mess and keep them safe.

As if sendingthe human fighters his thoughts would do any good, but it was all he had to give.

#

Ian manipulated the gray material in his hands, working it into a long thin sausage. He pressed his head against Lackey's, enough to keep their conversation private without turning the comm on. "Think we have enough."

"Yes."

"Ready to get them out of here?"

"Leave it to me," said Lackey, holding out one hand for the explosives. "I know where's it's going to be the most effective. You deal with the kids. They need to move away from the blast point. As far as they can."

Ian broke contact. With rapid hand movements, he gestured to the far side of the cell. For a moment no one moved, until the youngest of the children nodded and hurried away from the corner where Lackey now worked to set up the explosives. One by one, the rest of the children did as they were told, sealing their suits as Ian gestured for them to protect themselves.

Claws, long and dangerous, grabbed Ian by the back of the neck. He lashed out with both hands, fighting against the hold. No, this wasn't happening to him. Not when they were this close. He growled, one hand clenched around the rifle he still carried, the strap wrapped around his upper arm.

He didn't think, he reacted.

The butt of the rifle slammed back into the creature holding him. He didn't stop with the one blow. But lashed back again and again. "Not going to let you keep them." He growled, sweat beading across his face, jaw tight as he hit the alien. His body shuddered from the force he used to attack the winged creature.

It stumbled back, claws scraping at Ian's neck, though the suit protected him from damage.

"Counting down from five."

He didn't need to move to know Lackey meant the explosion. He slammed one open palm against the cage, fingers parted, hoping the kids would understand as he folded the first finger down.

Chapter Twenty-Two

Jakob didn't turn away from his planned course. He had to do this, had to deal with the space bats before they found their way Lawbook and her people. *Hold tight, Salla. I've got this.*

He yanked on the controls, sending the side of the ground car into the side of the tunnel, taking out dozens of the small creatures at the same time. With a curse he hit the power, sending the vehicle away from the wall, letting the remaining aliens mill around them before he sent the car into the middle of the wheeling attackers.

Plastisteel crunched and split around him, the five-point harness the only thing keeping him in his seat. A scream, a woman's voice, echoed through the comm and he didn't need to look to know who it was.

Salla.

Was she hurt? He didn't have time to check on her. Not when it took every ounce of strength he laid claim to keep the vehicle upright. Jakob struggled with the controls, knowing it was a long shot, but he wouldn't back down. The car bounced from one side of the tunnel to the other, each new jolt rattled his bones, but he didn't let go.

He swallowed down his fear, refusing to change course. If it cost him his last breath, he'd follow through.

"Jakob!"

He reached out, one hand closing on Salla's arm as the car spun a second and third time before it crunched to a halt. Jakob tried to focus, to see what was happening, but his body no longer wanted to obey him, the last, hard crunch of vehicle, stone, and bones. The door on his side of the car, buckled in. The large, clear window, made to withstand a cave-in, cracked.

They weren't going to make it.

Failed. He'd failed, and now Salla would pay the price with

him.

"I'm sorry," he tried to swallow down the pain as something warm and salty filled his mouth. "Salla. I'm sorry."

#

Cora leaned against the wall, pain sweeping up and down the length of her spine. Oxygen. She was losing air with the damage to the suit. Her fingers moved before she had a chance to realize what she was doing, activating the repair system to her suit. Foam hissed into the gap, sealing it, but she still struggled against the shock, lack of air, pain. All of it combined into a wave of sensation she couldn't ignore. Her vision wavered, images swam in and out of focus. She couldn't allow this to get the better of her, not when the lives of the children depended on her team.

"You're hurt." The comm crackled into life.

"I know." Cora closed her eyes for a count of five before she opened them again. "Nothing we can do about it for now." Taylor, the doctor back at the settlement, he'd be able to patch her up. *If I get out of this.* Gray tubing outlined a door shape in the clear holding room. "They're going to blow the cell."

"Understood." Stone pressed against her, shielding her.

He didn't have to do it. She wanted to order him away, but it would be a waste of energy.

She felt rather than heard the explosion. Waves of energy buffeted her body. Pain spiked. Her eyes watered, and she forced herself to remain silent. Pain was a weakness leaving the body. Yeah, it was bullshit, but under circumstances like this, she could cling to the lie long enough to get through the worst of it.

"Stop, you all need to stop. You're going to hurt the children." A new voice, male, the accent strange, not one she knew. One which spoke through a comm channel she didn't recognize. One which broke through the private channel, allowing her to hear him.

"Who are you?"

"Edward, my name is Edward. I serve the Blessed Ones, our

Masters. Please, don't hurt the children."

Cora waited for Stone to ease up on his hold before she moved, her gaze hazy before she focused on the newcomer. Behind him, the shattered plastisteel of the containment cells split and dropped away. Two familiar shapes gathered the children together, but the newcomer, his suit similar to the ones used by the aliens, didn't look her way.

A human traitor. Like the man Helen's captured transmission had picked up on.

A man she might be able to use to their advantage.

If she made it out in one piece.

#

"Get them out of here," Lackey ordered. "You know what to do."

Ian didn't respond, he didn't need to. Tremors ran through his body, no doubt from being close to the source of the explosion, but the kids were no longer in a position to wait. He darted toward the small figures, reaching out to pull them into a small group, checking the seals on their suits.

"No, you can't take them. You don't understand what you're doing to them."

Edward, he knew the name, understood the man's position in this new reality.

"You're wrong, I understand exactly what I'm doing. What we're doing." Lackey replied his presence a welcome one behind Ian's back. "These children will never be slaves to those things. They are human beings, not slaves."

"How can you believe your words? They are our saviors."

One of the children grabbed Ian's hand, her wide brown eyes peering up at him. It didn't matter if he wanted to stay, to listen to the man, find out more of what was going on. He had to get the kids out of here. Away from the danger offered by the aliens and their pet human.

"Come on, I've got you. Believe me, I'll get you away from

this." He reached for the youngest, pulling her up on his hip. He could do this, it didn't matter if he missed out on the rest of the action, he wasn't a killer. Wasn't able to pull the trigger, but he wasn't about to leave the children behind. Without another thought, he half walked, half ran toward the tunnel, the one which led to freedom.

Or at least the hope of it.

And hope was all they had.

#

Stone snarled, his hand finding his sidearm. Traitor. The man had betrayed his race, not only in thought but deed. Humanity had to come first, not service to a bunch of weird aliens seeking to take over the planet. Shit, he didn't know if they would stop at Pluto or move on other colonies before striking Earth.

"Step away from the kids, Edward," he said, focusing on the man.

"I have to get them to safety. You're hurting the children by taking them away. They're better off with the rest of the servants. They will know true joy." Edward took a step toward him. "The others understand. The man I spoke to wanted to learn more about our Masters. You could come into the light, understand the true worth of being protected by them. Like the ones I've spoken to."

"You're either a fool, or you've been brainwashed."

Lawbook reached out for his shoulder, her lips moving but nothing carried through the comm. He frowned, trying to make sense of her words, the pieces falling into place as he watched her speak again.

Take him prisoner.

Sneaky woman. If they hadn't been in the middle of a firefight against the weirdest looking creatures he'd ever come across, he might risk hugging her.

He inclined his head, a small movement but enough to let her know he agreed.

She turned, firing again. She'd keep his ass covered, and he'd see to the rest.

"You want us to serve them, right?" He didn't lower his weapon, uncertain why he'd shifted to the pistol, but it felt right. "These aliens? The very creatures who killed who knows how many? Men, women, and children killed when they attacked the dome. People scattered into the depths of space when they took out the two ships assigned to Pluto. Was it fair to them? Did they understand the lives lost when they attacked our home?" He walked, slowly, toward Edward.

"They are kind, loving, gracious beings. We live to serve them. It's how we were meant to be." Edward's brow furrowed. "They would never kill without reason. They're higher beings. Not like us. We're base creatures, we don't understand our place in the universe, or didn't before they blessed us with their presence."

Sick. Or programmed to believe in the lies the aliens told him. "You're blind to the truth."

"Am I? No, it's those like you, those bred and raised outside of the colony, you are the ones who are blind to the reality of our universe." Edward smiled, a beatific expression claiming his features. He spread out his hands as he approached Stone. "Come with me, I'll teach you. Show you how things can be. You will come to understand what they offer, how they love us and need us."

Shots, he didn't ignore the fighting behind him. The presence of the Sergeant and her weapons as she continued to protect him. There would be more aliens attackers, but the Marines wouldn't let him down.

He allowed his gaze to shift to the children. Lackey and Ian had them under control. A few more seconds, and he'd be able to grab the man, bundle him along with the kids. A little closer, that's all he needed, to get close to the man, and he'd be able to subdue him. "Tell me about them. What is it they need us for if they're so advanced what would they humans as slaves?"

"We are not slaves but treasured servants." Edward lifted his chin, pride glimmering in his eyes.

Stone launched himself, shoulder striking Edward's stomach, knocking him to the ground, bouncing the other man's head off the stone beneath him. "Yeah, and I know the key to eternal life."

\#

"Jakob? You have to wake up, Jakob. Please. You're trapped. I need you awake to get you out."

Words, nothing but words with no meaning or sense to them. He didn't open his eyes, unable to do what the woman wanted. He swallowed, his throat sore and tight as he tried to breathe. A weight pressed on his chest, his body unwilling to answer his demands.

"You can't leave me on my own, Jakob."

Who was the woman? He knew her, right? Her voice wasn't strange to him but welcoming. A part of his life.

Coughs racked his body, clearing his throat as he forced his eyes to open. Shadows swam in front of his eyes, clouding his vision before he closed them again.

"We have to move," she touched him. He could feel it. A brush of fingers against his face.

Mask. What had happened to his mask? His eyes snapped open. "Salla."

"I'm here. Oh, God, there's... Jakob, you're bleeding."

A shadow, her face masked by waves of darkness flooding his vision, but it didn't matter. She was there with him. "You need--" coughing stole his voice. Liquid, metallic and salty, filled his mouth. He tried to spit it out but lacked the strength. "Go. Get out."

"Not happening. You think I'm going to leave you here."

A light flickered around him, then shadows returned. "Can't feel my legs." A flicker of sensation in his arms, but no real pain. Only pressure. A weight on his chest, forcing him to struggle for each new breath. "Time. Running out." There was something he was supposed to do.

Important.

It had been important.

The Sergeant.

"Go. Other cars. Find one." Coughing struck again, stealing his hard-earned breath.

"The bats, they're gone. I can stay and help you."

"Sergeant needs you. Needs cars."

She pulled back, her face going in and out of focus. "I can't do this without you, Jakob. Please."

Why had she removed his face piece? She still wore hers. The touch, her touch, hadn't been bare fingers. Gloves, the thin, flexible gloves used with the suits.

"You. Can." His eyes closed. Opening them again wasn't going to happen. "Please." *Go. I can't speak anymore. Don't stay. Don't watch me...* His thoughts refused to follow through with the initial idea.

She didn't move. Didn't step away from him. Fighting with her was pointless. She was too damned stubborn for her own safety.

Love you.

The words echoed through his mind, forcing his lips to move. Better that she didn't know the truth. He was nothing more than a teenage boy with a crush. It's what she'd have told him if he'd been foolish enough to speak the words when he'd still had a voice.

"Jakob? What are you trying to say?"

Love you. Always have.

"Jakob? Please, look at me. Open your eyes. You can't leave me. Not like this."

Teenage crush, the last sane part of his mind knew it was a possibility, but it was all he'd ever have. *Love you, Salla. Love you. Lov...*

#

Zac paced the cell, unable to look at the other two men trapped with him. This wasn't how he'd envisioned it working out. Caught by aliens, trapped in a transparent cell, collars locked around not only his throat but those of his fellow prisoners. Edward, the man hadn't worn one, not where he could see it at least, but he didn't know for certain if the other man was trapped in the same way.

A muffled noise, louder than before.

Not the individual sounds of gunfire.

"What the fuck?" Mathew growled.

"Explosion. Has to be," said Charles. The older man had remained silent since Edwards first visit. Any attempt to draw him into conversation had proved pointless. "Marines. Or miners. Both have access to explosives."

"If we're lucky, they'll find us, and we can get out of here."

Mathew's features hardened. "Right. Then we'll all live happily ever after."

"But it could happen. They must have come back for a reason. For all we know there's a full team out there, which would mean the Navy is back, maybe from Triton." Zac's mind raced as he tried to put the pieces together. "It's not impossible."

"Just highly unlikely." Mathew clamped one hand on Zac's shoulder. "Shit, we don't know what these collars might do to us if we get out of this blasted cell without Edward or one of those things opening this thing." He nudged the invisible wall with his boot.

Zac touched his collar. "Hadn't thought of that. And unless Edward comes back, there's no one around to ask." Except for the aliens, who spoke a language, he didn't understand, had no means of translating, and left him without any means of escaping the cell.

"All we can do is wait and hope the next person who walks in is; one, a human being; and two, on our side," said Charles.

"No, there's one more thing we can hope for," said Zac as he turned to meet the older man's gaze. "We can hope whoever is out there gets the kids out before the aliens have a chance to retaliate."

Chapter Twenty-Three

Cora forced herself past the pain, knowing she would pay for it later. She relied on instinct, knowing her body wanted to curl up on itself and allow the blazing fire down her back to sweep her into a peaceful, welcoming darkness. Her hands trembled, little more than a small vibration, but she adjusted for it. Turning a double-tap into a triple or quad when needed. Her accuracy was affected, she knew without saying it. Her body was breaking down as the fight continued around them.

They were winning.

The numbers of aliens diminished, without replacements to boost them back up.

The odds had shifted in their favor.

She activated the comm. "Retreat, you know what to do." Cora didn't have to turn to know Stone had the human traitor. A man who had turned against his own people, chosen to serve aliens instead of fighting for his freedom. She growled, picking off another alien, barely noticing the spread of purple blood. It was unimportant. They fell. They died. The color of their blood no longer mattered as long as it was spilled.

Figures moved, human, men, and women, those who'd come with her to free the children. She backed away, firing, knowing the path to the tunnels. A route she had imprinted in her mind, no longer needing to look at the datapad to make her next move.

"You're hurt, Sergeant." Ready fell into place at her side.

"Another scar."

"Chicks dig scars," Harvard settled in on her other side.

"That they do." She grinned. It didn't matter that, to many, she was a chick. Gender didn't matter in this. She was a Marine, doing her job, killing anything which got in their way, and if it meant joking with the men who served at her side, then she welcomed it. "On the left."

"Got it," said Harvard as he picked off the new arrivals.

"Sergeant, you first."

"What?"

"You're injured," insisted Ready. "You'd do the same for us. Injured first."

She wanted to complain, protest, tell him she wasn't hurt, but it would be a lie, and the man was right. Injured first, it was SOP. They'd trained for this, hundreds of times, not only during basic but during the months, years after they became a part of an active unit. "Right. On it."

Cora spared herself one last visual check. Two human bodies. Both civilians. She marked and counted the two, knowing she'd have to tell their family when this was over. She turned, pushing the pain to the back of her mind as she retreated.

Helen. She had to get the signal out. If they were to get out of this with the kids, it was now down to Helen. With one trembling hand, she reached for the transmitter on her waist and hit send.

The other kids, they'd find a way to rescue them. But for now, their focus had to be on getting this group to safety, and as far away from the aliens as possible.

#

Stone shifted the weight of the unconscious man over his shoulder as he kept pace with the others in the group. Children, odd, he'd have assumed they'd be crying, whimpering, screaming for their parents, but they kept quiet. Some held the hands of older children, others moved with the group, never quite looking up.

He didn't want to know what they'd been through.

"They're going to be ready for us, the aliens, I mean," Stone muttered, the words carried by the comm. No one cared now if the aliens overheard them. They knew of the attack, of the cell broken into, and the children freed from their hold.

"Yeah, but the Sergeant won't let us down." A civilian miner. He knew the name, it was buried deep in the back of his mind, but it refused to answer his call. "Shit, Drake, and Philon didn't make it. How the hell am I going to tell their wives?"

"You tell them they died doing the right thing and these kids wouldn't have made it out, without their help." The words found life before he realized he was speaking. "It won't ease the pain, nothing will. All we can do is tell the truth and hope, down the line, it eases the sting."

Words, nothing more than words, but it was better than nothing.

"Yeah, I guess."

"They're following us, you know that, right?"

Stone flashed a grin. "Counting on it." A lie, but hey, if he could kill a few more space bats or whatever else they were, he was all for it. As long as he could get out of this in one piece.

"Keep close, when I give the word, you know what to do," said Lawbook, her voice carrying through the comm. "We're going to get out of here."

"Damn good Marine," the civilian grunted.

He didn't argue. No matter what happened, Lawbook wouldn't let them down. Not if it cost her life. She'd get them all out of this. And when did I suddenly start believing in a blasted Marine? When it became the right thing to do unless he wanted to take over and lead the rest of the team out of here.

No. Not going to happen. His life would return to normal once he found his way off Pluto. The rest, well, it wasn't his concern. Nor would it ever be.

The man he held lifted his head, a low groan vibrating through him.

"Don't fight me, or you won't like the outcome." Killing him would be easier, but the man held answers, and knowledge was power.

"You don't understand what you're doing," whined Edward. "Please, let me go I need to help my Masters. And the children. Oh, darkness take me, I can't be away from the Masters. They need me."

"And I need you to shut the fuck up."

Edward fell silent and slumped over Stone's shoulder, a shudder running through the trapped man's body.

"Do you think there are others like him?"

Stone glanced at the civilian. "Yeah, where there's one snake, there'll be others. More we can find out from men like this one, the easier it will be for us. Information is power, and he's going to tell me everything he knows when we have a chance to sit down with him." No matter what it took to tear the information from Edward, he'd do it, reach into the bastard's head, and squeeze him for answers.

#

Ian shifted the child on his hip, his body aching with the weight. She'd been all but nothing to begin with. A few kilos, nothing he should worry about, yet now each step warned him of the strain his body endured. He wouldn't give up, couldn't give up, he'd get these kids away from the monsters.

All the monsters.

"Exit strategy." Lawbook's voice rang out through the comm. "You know the route. Take it."

He smiled, a new wave of energy rising from the depths of his being. The Sergeant, she wouldn't let them down. No more than she would give up.

"Hold on, sweetie, we'll get there. A little more and we'll be safe. I promise you, no more monsters." Helen. He knew the plan, knew what his sister was capable of, but even for her, the task would be difficult. He had to have faith in Helen. She'd never let him down before and wouldn't now. "My sister's going to help us, you know. Help us get out of here." He smoothed one hand over the child's head. "Trust me. Trust the Marines. We're all in this together."

All he had to do was keep running, moving, and not let the

kids down.

"Pick up the pace!"

He had no idea who snapped out the order. A man's voice, strong and confident, enough to get the group running, despite the ache in their bodies, the burn in their lungs, the pain from injuries, bruises, cuts. They'd make it out alive, they had to, if for no other reason than to get the children away from their would-be masters. Nothing was more important than their safety.

"Won't be long now, and there'll be food, safety, people to watch over you. Hold on. All you have to do is hold on."

#

Cora's lungs burned. She didn't want to admit to the pain, the stress hitting her body, but there was no ignoring it. Not now. She'd pay the price when they found a place to stop when Helen had played her part if she hadn't already. The girl wouldn't let them down, she was smart, resourceful, and they wouldn't have made it this far without her help. Her ability to make electronics do her bidding was bordering on miraculous.

Helen had one hell of a future ahead of her.

If they managed to get the aliens off this rock, they called their home.

A lot of damned ifs standing in the way, but she was a bloody Marine and wasn't about to give up now.

"Sergeant, the cars. Where the hell are the cars?" Lackey jogged back to her position, keeping pace with her. They'd avoided the narrow route. This one was faster and no longer offered the dangers of the aliens standing in their way.

"Coming, they'll be here soon." They had to be, but not until...

Her datapad beeped, and she tapped the controls on the back of her left arm, sending the information dancing across her face mask. Her eyes refocused, allowing her to read it, take in the information, the flight plan.

"Sergeant."

"She's done it. She's got them distracted." The first, distant tremor of explosions above them, trembled through the ice claimed rocks.

"Picking up on the ground cars," Ready announced. "Shit, we're going to get out of this. We're really going to get out of this."

"Of course we are, we're Marines." She flashed a grin, one she didn't feel, but knew the other man needed it to see it. They all needed the reassurance. "They'll be waiting for us, would be rude if we weren't there to meet them." Cora drew in a ragged breath, silently cursing the pressure on her ribs, bruises, cuts, the burn of the energy weapon across her back. They'd make it to the cars, she could collapse, at least for a short time.

Cora spared a glance at Stone. He still carried Edward over his shoulder, though she knew the man was awake from the brief conversation between Stone and his prisoner. Information, they needed it, and Edward had it. He'd share it with them one way or another.

A dozen twists and turns in the passages carried them through the tunnels. How Cora stayed on her feet, she didn't know, nor did she care. She'd keep moving, collapse when there was time, and get the rest of the team to safety. Cora shuddered, each step jarred the injury across her back. Sweat beaded with the strain her body now endured, but she didn't care, didn't know what pushing through was doing to the injury or her stress levels.

"Sergeant?"

"Yes?" She didn't need to turn to see to Ready to know he was at her side.

"You're going to collapse if you keep this up."

"Not until it's safe." They were close, she knew it wouldn't be much longer. Her vision swam, heart raced, both enough of a warning to tell her she was about to drop. One foot in front of the other, it's all she had to do, keep moving.

"The cars, they're here." Lackey rounded the corner ahead of her.

"Good," she swallowed down bile as her body warned her she was pushing too far.

"Not all of them, there's at least one missing."

Missing? Alright, then they'd deal with being in close confines with the children.

She stumbled, one hand reaching out for the wall, slapping it with an open palm. Her legs trembled as she gulped in a fresh lungful of air. It wasn't enough. Her body rejected what was happening, the desire to be on her feet. Her vision shimmered with darkness before it cleared again. No matter what happened, she wasn't about to collapse.

"Let me help you, Sergeant." Ready curled one arm around her waist.

Cora didn't fight the assistance. She knew if she did, it wouldn't work and would make her appear weak. Injured was one thing, weak was another. "Not going to end up face down, nose in the dirt." What had the Gunny told her? Don't be afraid to lean on them, the others in her team.

"Of course not, like I'd let my Sergeant face plant when I'm here to help her. Not like we're all drunk and you've been exploring the cheap drinks one after the other."

She could hear the grin in his voice. "Marines stick together."

"Hey, we're not all Marines in this group."

"Honorary Marine, Harvard. And don't try to argue. Don't want to have to beat you up for disrespecting the Sergeant."

"As if you could," replied Harvard. "Officer, remember. You hit me, and you face charges."

"Typical, hide behind your rank."

She didn't stop them, knowing it was their way of letting off steam. Her gaze clouded, stealing her sight for a heartbeat before the darkness stripped away, allowing her to focus on the ground cars. Battered, dented, but there.

Most of them.

A figure exited one of the cars. Young, female, head bowed.

One figure.

A distant rumble vibrated through the ground into her feet. Stronger this time. How many ships had the girl been able to slave together? Helen, she'd underestimated the youngster's skills, but damn, was she relieved to know how intelligent Helen had proved to be.

"Where's Jakob?" Her chest tightened, a band wrapped and locked itself around her heart. She didn't need Salla's answer to know the truth. To understand he wasn't going to appear. "We'll talk. Later." Grief. It had its place. Not here. Not now. Once they were removed from danger, away from this, then there'd be time. "Get in the cars, split the kids up between the cars."

"What about the aliens, they're going to track us." Stone paused long enough to shoot her a look.

"No, they're not. Helen's got that in hand." A new wave of shudders played through the surrounding rock. "She's going to keep them busy long enough to get the kids away."

Ready tightened his grip on Cora but didn't say a word as they hurried toward the cars. They'd make it out, check in with the kids, then plan the next step when they had the time.

She winced, pain blazing across her back as she settled into the seat. Her eyes watered, hands trembled, her body demanding she surrender to the darkness. Not going to happen.

"Rest, Sergeant. Don't make me knock you out myself," said Ready as he placed one hand on her shoulder. "We've got this."

Her body took over, spinning her into the welcoming embrace of numb silence.

Chapter Twenty-Four

Stone glared at the prisoner. Edward didn't speak, hadn't since he'd dumped the traitor into a chair and locked the five-point harness in place before binding Edward's wrists. "You're going to answer a lot of questions."

Edward didn't respond, his pale skin clammy as he lowered his gaze, a deep shiver running through his body.

Stone rolled his eyes and settled into his seat. "You ready?"

Harvard arched an eyebrow. "Driving one of these things is easy, compared to the birds I've flown." He slapped the controls. "Weren't there two kids left with the cars?"

"Yeah." Stone's jaw clenched.

"Shit, what the hell happened to the other?"

"Whatever it was, it couldn't be good." Stone didn't want to get into this. He knew Jakob or had grown to know the young man. "Shit. Salla wouldn't have left him behind unless there was no other choice." He pulled off the facepiece and ran one hand through his hair. "Punch it, sooner we get out of here, the better." Dead kids, no one wanted to deal with dead freaking children. Didn't matter what Jakob had believed about himself, the boy had been a teenager. Older teen, sure, but still too young to be caught in this mess.

"We've all lost people in this."

His hands clenched. How much trouble would he get into for punching the pilot?

He glanced at the man, then turned away. None of the children had been put in their vehicle, to spare them more trauma by dealing with a traitor. One who might have been responsible for separating them from family and friends.

"Moving will be picking up speed. Make sure your harness is secured."

He glanced at Harvard but didn't speak. He shifted the parts of the harness and slid his arms into place before securing the clasp. The car shuddered beneath him, not only the engines picking up the pace, but a rumble from beyond the vehicle. He smiled as he leaned back in his seat. The traitor would talk with them, fill in the blanks, enough to allow him a chance to build up the information they needed.

Stone pulled out his datapad, letting it focus on the man behind him. It didn't take long to find the signal and shut it down. A low key frequency, one most might have overlooked, depending on what they were dealing with. His fingers danced over the controls, narrowing in on the signal. Three quick taps and it was done. The signal squashed. He couldn't dig the chip, or whatever the hell the aliens used, out of Edward's body Not without killing him. But they wouldn't be able to breakthrough.

Maybe.

At least as far as he was aware of. Helen would help him. The young woman's skills were beyond anything he would be able to do, and he wasn't above taking assistance where he could find it.

"They will come for me."

"Your tracking chip has been disabled, Edward. Not certain you'll be in a position to reactive it."

Edward struggled in the harness. "Impossible. You're nothing but a human. You lack the skills, the intelligence, to disable their technology."

"Is that right? Here him, Harvard? We're too dumb to outthink the bugs."

"Bugs? I don't understand." Edward ceased his struggles. "They are a superior species, not insects."

"Fine, so one lot looks like alien space bats, but it's just another bug hunt as far as I'm concerned. All we have to do is find the right can of insect repellent, then they'll be out of the picture," said Harvard. "Don't think he understands what the human race is capable of doing, Stone."

"Nor would he, the man's only been around other

brainwashed slaves and those creatures. Never dealt with free-born humans." Stone glanced over his shoulder at Edward. "That's right, isn't it, Edward? You've had no real dealings with humanity unless they're like you."

"I was raised on the servant's colony, beneath the protective wings of the Masters, as it should be." He sat straighter, shoulders pushed back. "You will come to understand when you surrender to them. They are kind to their servants as long as we do not fail them."

"You've no idea what's going on outside of their grasp. The amount of work the human race has put into building their colonies, and rebuilding Earth after the darkness, centuries ago," said Harvard, his voice calm. "You'll understand, eventually."

"Or he won't. He's brainwashed. He's never known anything else. If he was raised with them, to serve them, then he's never known anything else and adapting to the changes might blow what's left of his mind." The pilot shrugged.

Stone turned away from the prisoner. "Fair point." He tried to focus on the route they were taking, ignoring Edward, the rumbles vibrating through the surrounding rock, the danger offered if the tunnels collapsed. They'd left too many people behind. Children in other cages they hadn't been able to get to, and his gut knotted at the failure.

Gone was the coldhearted smuggler, at least for now. He'd rebuild the shield, put the past behind him, and be able to return to his normal life once the aliens were no longer in the picture.

Right, and it's going to take how long?

The question echoed through his mind, tormenting him with the knowledge that nothing ever went back to normal after the world had been turned upside down. All he had to do was go back through history to see for himself.

"This isn't how I imagined life turning out," he closed his eyes.

"Oh, you never planned on becoming a hero?"

"Hero? Shit, the last thing I am is a fucking hero. I'm a

businessman. All about the money, nothing else."

"Uh-huh," said Harvard. "Keep telling yourself the same lines. Not going to change anything, but hey, it's your choice. I'm not going to rain on your parade." He shot Stone a glance. "Not yet, anyway."

#

Cora groaned, her eyes opening, then closing again. Pain shuddered through her body, and she bit back a groan, unwilling to allow the sound a means of escaping again.

"Sergeant, we're here. We'll be able to get you into the doc in a few minutes."

Ready? She cracked open her eyes enough to see the Marine. "The children?"

"All with us, Sergeant. Helen did a damn fine job out there, had three ships slaved together. Lost one in the initial attack, but the other two are apparently still functional, and buzzing the aliens. She keeps them close to the ground; it's difficult for them to take out the ships without hitting their ground troops."

She nodded and instantly regretted it. A pounding rolled through her head, nausea followed on its heel, all eager to turn her world upside down. She swallowed down a fresh wave of bile, refusing to throw up. If she were going to be ill, it would happen when she was alone, or in the hands of the doctor. What had been his name?

Taylor. The man who'd patched up Walker. The same one who'd worked on Winter. Odd. Both patients had the same letter. She didn't though, breaking the pattern. Best way to be. A giggle threatened to break free, and she forced herself to take a deep breath, hold it for a count of ten before she exhaled.

"Brace for it, Sergeant. It's going to hurt, and we have to seal your suit back up." Ready pulled the facepiece back in place, working on the rest of her suit before he scooped her up.

She should complain, order the man to set her down. Sergeants didn't get carried around.

Rely on your people, Lawbook.

The words echoed through her mind, a call she wanted to ignore but couldn't. The Gunny was right, he'd always been right, at least for as long as she'd known him. The men and women he'd taken under his wing, all bore his stamp in some way. He'd chide her for being stupid, for trying to walk when she was injured. He wouldn't want her to add to the damage, not when it would be nothing more than a show of pride, a stubborn streak which she'd pay for later.

A fool's game.

The jolt of each step watered her eyes, but she didn't fight it. Tears seeped, but there was no shame in crying, not when you hurt. If Ready witnessed her tears, he wouldn't say anything. It was time to trust her team during the good and the bad. If they had questions, they'd ask. Ready, Walker, Lackey, Harvard, and yeah, even Stone.

Fine, Mason Stone would cause problems. She expected nothing else of the man, though he'd come through in getting the kids out in one piece.

The airlock hissed open, closing behind them before the exchange took place and Ready shifted his grip, jolting her back. Voices filled her ears, and the man tugged off his facepiece. Cora reached for hers, wanting to breathe, to talk, see what was going on around her. Her fingers fumbled, refusing to work.

"Where's Taylor?" Ready stripped Cora's facepiece away. "Sergeant isn't doing too well here."

"Have a bed ready and waiting for her. Stone called ahead, let us know what was going on."

She frowned. Had to be the doctor. She tried to turn, then remembered she was being held. "Down."

"I don't think so, not from the information I'm picking up from the scanner." Taylor walked over, waving the datapad in their direction. "Sergeant Bloodlaw, I'm afraid I'm going to have to do quite a bit of work on your back."

#

Ian ushered the last of the children into his family home. Small, wary faces peered around. Young hands reached his, seeking solace, as he searched for two faces in particular.

"Your sister's still working, she'll be out once she's got the ships dealt with," said his mother as she wrapped one arm around him. "I'm proud of you, Ian. Damned proud. And relieved you made it out in one piece."

"Not all of us did," he leaned into the embrace.

"I know, love. I know." She took a deep breath, her hold tightening. "You need to find her, don't you?"

"Yes." Ian glanced down at the children. "Mom, can you-- I mean, I don't know what to do about the kids."

"I've got them." Her mother gestured for the youngsters to follow her. "Come on, time you all had a warm meal, blankets and something sweet." Her smile brightened the room; it was a tactic Ian had seen her use before, when he'd been younger, and more than a few times on Helen.

"Go find her. She's going to need you."

Ian didn't need the reminder but appreciated it nevertheless. It didn't take long to know she wasn't in the main room, or anywhere on the ground level. He frowned, racking his mind. Where would she hide? No, not hide, but claim for herself to deal with it? He slipped through the crowded room, his gaze continually moving, searching for the woman he'd only caught a glimpse of before he'd joined several children in one of the ground cars.

Mags, the dog, found him first. A cold nose nudged his left hand, followed by a gentle lick.

"Sorry, boy, I don't have time. Have to find Salla." Why was he telling the damned dog what he was doing?

Mags sat down, head tipped to the side, then gave a pointed stare to the top of the stairs.

Ian sighed and rubbed the back of his neck. "Don't give me

that look."

Mags huffed.

Downstairs? If Salla had tried to find a quiet place, where she might grab a moment to think, the rooms in the basement would be the place to start. He ruffled Mags head before he took the stairs two at a time, the gentle scuffing noise of Mags' paws behind him made it clear he wasn't alone.

Conversation from the large room faded into a muffled blend of old and young voices before he reached the last step. She wouldn't be in the place Taylor had taken over as a mini-hospital, but the rest of the doors were open except for his bedroom. Not those, she'd not want to be seen if she was struggling with Jakob's loss, and he never left his door open.

One of the joys of having a younger sibling meant you instilled in them the rules about entering your bedroom without permission. And a closed-door was a damn good reminder to knock or check first before walking in.

"Damn woman, where the hell is she?" He turned, torn between seeking out his bed, or continuing the search.

His room.

Ian hurried to his room, paused and listened, straining to hear if there was anyone behind the closed door. His brow furrowed. He wasn't going to find out from this side of a locked, or what should have been locked door. He turned away, pacing back and forth. She was there, she had to be, but would she want company.

It's not about what she wants, it's what she needs.

And if he were wrong, she'd have every right to put him in his place. But damnit, she was hurting. She had to be. No way in Hell was he going to leave her to suffer on her own. If he could do nothing more than sit by her, silently waiting for her to speak, then he'd do it.

Ian glanced over his shoulder before opening the door. Without a word, he slipped inside and tugged it closed behind him. "Salla?"

The young woman sat on his bed, knees pulled to her chest, chin down, head bowed. Small trembles played through her form, but she didn't lift her gaze, didn't make a sound save for the ragged intake of breath.

"Oh, God, I'm sorry, Salla. I know he was a friend." He sat down next to her, not quite touching. "You don't have to speak if you don't want to." Would pushing her to speak add to the pain, or give her an outlet? Shit, he didn't know how to handle grief. He'd never seen a dead man until today.

A strangled sob echoed through the room.

Ian gingerly rested one arm across her shoulder, watching for a sign it was the wrong thing to do. She didn't flinch but remained stiff beneath his embrace. There was nothing he could do, or say, to ease the pain she was in, or bring Jakob back, except be there for her.

Chapter Twenty-Five

Stone paced. It wasn't like him, but he couldn't sit still. Not while Bloodlaw remained in the care of the doctor. Anyone not needed for surgery, including the two other Marines he'd treated, had been ushered out of the space claimed by Taylor for his work. Now, Winter and Walker, odd how they both shared names beginning with W, sat close together with the silent dog laying at Winter's feet.

Ready hadn't joined them, but remained with Taylor, an extra set of hands should the Doc need it. One of the last words before Taylor had knocked the stubborn woman's ass out, had been to order Nyssa out of the room.

He couldn't blame Lawbook for wanting Nyssa gone. He didn't trust the drug dealer as far as he could throw her, with one arm tied behind his back.

Why had Nyssa offered to help?

Questions whispered in the back of his mind, demanding attention, not only about Nyssa, but their prisoner, the children, and the plans the aliens had when it came to Pluto. If they were here only for Pluto, then he had no doubt the Unified Terran Government would attempt to find a diplomatic solution to the situation. It wouldn't work, not long term, the way Edward had spoken about the invaders, the devotion in the other man's speech, the way he wanted to return to them, all combined to confirm Edward worshiped them.

How long had it been? He checked the time. Taylor had to be out soon as the doctor had been working on Lawbook for hours. With all the changes in tech, it shouldn't be like this, with people waiting for answers, unable to help. Shit, his guts hated him, the need to do something, anything which would give him an answer.

"Not designed for this," he muttered.

"No one is." Mr. Hunter rested a hand on his shoulder. "Settle, if you can. You won't do any good pacing."

"Tried to sit, it didn't work." He didn't shrug the other man's hand away. "Shit, I don't even like the woman."

"Really? If you didn't, you wouldn't be worried about her." The older man shook his head, fingers tightening on Stone's shoulder. "Settle, I'm not claiming you're in love with her, not the way Jakob had fallen for Salla." His voice thickened. "It's going to be difficult for her to come back from. She's strong, but she's going to believe she did something wrong, missed a warning, she acted in a manner which led to his death. It's not true, of course, but it will take time for her to be willing to hear it, and longer before she accepts it."

Jakob and Salla. "Not the same thing. The kid had a crush on her, and she didn't know."

"If you believe Salla didn't know, then you've got a lot to learn about women." Mr. Hunter stepped away, his voice calm once more. "I'm not claiming you love the Sergeant, far from it. You respect her. Admire her. And if she dies, then a part of your life, their lives, will never be the same again."

"Why?"

"Because she's strong, capable of handling difficult situations, and there are a hundred other things I could tell you, but I doubt you're in the right frame of mind to understand."

Stone listened, his brow furrowed. "Not long ago I'd have told you that you were full of it."

"The world has changed around us, and you'd have to be dead to not change with it."

Dead. Like Jakob. Like the two civilians, whose names he'd never bothered to learn. "Yeah, well, still doesn't mean I like the situation."

"I've never met a man, or woman, who enjoys having change thrust upon them and..." his words trailed off, gaze shifting to the top of the stairs.

The conversation drifted, fading as all eyes turned to the same location.

Silent with deep lines across his brow and around his mouth, Taylor stood there, wiping his hands on a cloth, his body radiating exhaustion, the doctor took a deep breath before he spoke. "She's going to recover. It won't be easy, she isn't going to bounce back immediately, but she will be back on her feet. How long it takes depends on how her body reacts to what she's been through."

Relief exploded in his chest. A tightness he hadn't been aware of, vanished, allowing him the chance to take a deep breath. "Can we see her?"

"Not yet, she needs time to sleep. As do I. Honestly, if she hadn't had this many friends waiting for news, I'd have stumbled into bed, and slept for the next day." Taylor rolled out his shoulders as he walked into the room, the lines deepening across his features. "Give her time. All of us deserve the luxury of time. We need to catch our breath, heal, and plan. For now, the aliens are focused on the dome, not the miners and other settlements, but it'll change, and when it does, we'll be ready."

"She'll be ready," said Walker. "I know the Sergeant. She'll be ready to face whatever they throw at us."

Stone scrubbed one hand over his face, wiping away stress, weariness, and anxiety in one movement. They'd needed the news, needed the information she'd pulled through, to plan the next step. What would she call it, rallying the troops?

He smiled, letting his gaze take in the rest of the group.

Someone was missing.

Stone tried to put a name to the face he no longer saw in the large family room, heart racing as his brain provided an answer.

Nyssa.

#

"Open your mouth, bitch. Go on, open it."

Cora didn't move, didn't respond. She knew the voice, understood who it was, but the why escaped her.

"You're going to take this, Sergeant," contempt dripped from the words. "Open your goddamn mouth, woman. I'm done with you getting in my way. Stopping me from conducting my business. I wasn't hurting anyone. Shit, I was making things better for Walker, but you had to stop me, didn't you." Fingers brushed Cora's face before they closed on either side of her mouth.

Cora twisted her head away, eyes half opening.

Nyssa.

She knew the voice though her vision remained blurred.

"Ah, there you are," Nyssa smirked. "Still in there, well you won't be for long. Once you're too sick to take part in the planning, you'll be forgotten. I'll be your devoted nurse, ready to forgive and forget your cruelty." She traced one finger over Cora's lips.

She fought to move her hands, fingers twitching. An operation, there'd been a doctor. Taylor. He'd worked on her. Fixed her back, hadn't he? She closed her eyes and fought for control over her body. She had to find a way past the drugs Taylor used to keep her under when he'd put her back together. A matter of safety. Now she cursed, trapped in a body which refused to respond to her orders.

Her head snapped to one side, a sharp slap enough to jar her bones. Pain blossomed but muted, not the burning pain she should have experienced. Her face would pay the price later, bruises unless Taylor used a speed healing drug to push her through the operation.

"Stupid bitch. You can't defend yourself now, can you?" Another crack rang out, snapping Cora's head the other way. "I'm going to enjoy this." A hand cupped her jaw fingers pressing into the joints. "Open. Your. Mouth."

Cora's fingers curled, hand fisting. She focused, keeping her mouth closed, despite the pressure, Nyssa inflicted on the hinge of her jaw. It should have hurt, but the remains of the drug in her system helped keep the pain at bay.

"Stubborn. You're making this harder on you when it doesn't have to be. But hey, I'm not going to complain. Gives me more of a reason to teach you a lesson." Nyssa released her grip on Cora's face. "I'm going to addict you, leave you as nothing more than a quivering wreck."

No, it wasn't going to happen. The woman was insane.

Cora focused on her hand, trying to move it beyond the clenching of fingers. Sweat beaded across her body as she struggled.

"You could have turned a blind eye, let me ease his pain, but no, you had to get in the way."

"Fu-uck you," she spat the words. If this was going to happen, she'd fight all the way down, then claw her way back out of the pits.

"Ah, there it is. The fire and spirit, the defiance. Enjoy it while you can." Nyssa's form wavered in front of her. A blur of movement with the shape of a woman in the middle of the uncertain haze. "Once you've had the first hit, you won't be able to fight the need for the second, or third." She pressed a small container to Cora's lips. "Stop fighting, it'll make it easier in the long term. Not that you'll care about the long, short, or any term after today. You won't give a flying fuck about anything but your next hit."

Weak. Too damned weak to defend herself. Cora locked gazes with the hateful female. "Not. Happening." Sweat beaded across her brow, the strain of spitting two words at Nyssa more than she'd expected.

"And how are you going to stop me?"

A strong arm wrapped itself around Nyssa's neck, hauling her away from Cora.

A scramble of steps, bodies pressed into the room. A man swore, and a woman screamed her defiance. A table tipped, spilling a tray of instruments to the floor. The chaos of movement and sound swamped Cora's senses, then it was done, with only the threats from the now captured Nyssa to destroy the silence.

"Sergeant Bloodlaw, did she give you anything?" Taylor pushed his way past the struggling Nyssa.

Cora licked her lips, needing the moisture before she spoke. "No."

"That's something at least." Taylor passed a scanner over her body. "Get Nyssa out of here. I've no patience for those dealing in drugs."

"I'll deal with her," growled Stone.

"Secure her. The Sergeant will want to have words with Nyssa when she's more like herself," said Lackey.

"She can't. She's the target here," Harvard explained. "I'll handle the dealer."

Cora closed her eyes, "thank you." Her throat raw, exhaustion threatening to consume her.

"Rest up, Sergeant. I'll be here to keep an eye on you." Taylor traced a hand over her shoulder, a small comforting gesture. Enough to settle her nerves and give her a chance to heal.

She'd need all her strength if they were to band together. They had two choices, push the aliens off Pluto, or find a means of breaking free without being having their ship shot down. They'd pull their way out of this mess, one way or the other, but for now they'd hit the enemy where it hurt, and they'd do so again once she was back on her feet.

When they were ready to deal with the creatures determined to take over the colony and all who called it their home.

Epilogue

Treizaek stalked across the bridge, his wings flicking before settling into their folded position on his back. This shouldn't have happened. Humans, they were foolish beings, they could not fight back. Yet the young ones had been stolen by a band of the creatures. "How many did they take?"

"Seventeen, Commander."

"Seventeen human young. Out of the sixty, we had gathered." He turned away from the male, claws curled. His mate had failed him again. She'd been on the planet when this had happened. Sent by him. "She will pay for her foolishness. Send word to Nyanaek, she is to report back immediately and present herself for judgment." They'd destroyed his plans, his hopes for the future with the female he would have named as his mate.

A nest of his own, a power base to build from.

"Commander, Nyanaek has already reported in. She claims she has the rest of the young in hand and is unable to return to the ship at this time."

He turned, fixing the male with a glare. "She dares to defy me?"

"Yes, Commander. I apologize for her failure," He lowered his gaze, his fear leaving a bitter taste in the air. "I have told her what is expected, but she refused made it clear, she will not return until her duty is completed."

Betrayer. His people were supposed to obey him, bow down to his will. It was why he'd become the commander, the one with the strength to control them. "I will suffer no disobedience, not from the female, or any other." First, the loyalty to the Great Mothers, now his would-be mate refused to present herself for his judgment. "My shuttle, have it prepared." His most loyal warriors would be required for this. Nyanaek had her own people, males and females would do anything she commanded them to do unless he was present to overrule her.

"Yes, Commander. Is there anything else you require of us?"

He turned, wing slashing out, the tip tracing a line of purple blood across the male's neck. Thin, nothing which would leave long term damage. "Obedience. Now and always."

The male dropped to his knees, head bowed, wings quivering. "Always. I pledge unto you my life and loyalty. My blood and hearts are yours, should you demand them. Both I give unto you of my own free will from this day until the end of my days."

Treizaek let his wings fold across his back. "All of you remember this male's loyalty. Mark it and know I will require the rest of you to do the same when I return. Should any of you betray me, or fail me, I will tear your hearts from your chest and eat them before you take your last breath." He let his gaze take in the rest of the bridge crew, the males, females, and neutrals. Alphas and betas, but no omegas.

There'd never be an omega on his ship or any he commanded. They couldn't be trusted, would never be a part of the military, not if he had anything to do about it. He needed warriors, not those who believed in the old stories, the so-called mysteries of life, and when he returned home, he would arrive as one victorious. A male raised in station, and able to create his own greater nest.

Unstoppable.

No matter how many lives he had to end in the process.

The End

System Wars is currently in development as a D20 Table Top RPG. To learn more about the game, upcoming releases, and sneak peeks of artwork, behind the scenes research, snippets from new books, please feel free to join
https://www.facebook.com/groups/TSWeaverSystemWars/

Current Release Schedule.
Hell's Own – now on sale.
Jones: A Hell's Own Novella – now on sale.
Hell's Children – Thank you for Reading Hell's Children
Helen: A Hell's Children's Novella due September 30th 2019

Author's Bio

Originally from England T.S. Weaver now lives in Minnesota with her husband and family. She also shares her life with not only her service dog, but her pack sister's service dog. Between the two canines laughter is often a part of her life, and there was no life before the dogs, just ask the dogs.

She can sometimes be found, if she's escaped the chains connecting her to the laptop, at science fiction and fantasy conventions, still puzzling out why people are buying her scribbles.

T.S. Weaver also writes romance and smexy books under the name Terri Pray where this time the chains go on the characters.